DAYDREAMER

BREA BROWN

WAYZGOOSE PRESS

To my husband, family, and friends, who have given me unlimited support and encouragement. Thank you all.

REAL LIFE SUCKS. IT'S TOO... REAL. AND BOUND BY THINGS LIKE physics and economics, two subjects that have always boggled my mind. And mortality, which always seems to be getting in my way. That's why I lead a relatively active fantasy life. I think it comes from having a more-than-relatively boring real life. But who needs real life when you can have fantasies, which are, frankly, much better?

In my fantasies, I have a glamorous job that challenges my mind and fetches me a nice salary but doesn't require me to ever really work. I live in a London maisonette with gleaming surfaces. I drive a tiny, fast car that costs twice as much as it should just because it has a recognizable emblem on its hood. But I don't care, because I can afford it. I date (and let's be honest, screw) a lot of famous, wealthy, and interesting men (Colin Firth and Robert Pattinson are regular boy-toys of mine on either end of the age spectrum), who think I'm oh-so-cool and irresistible. I travel to exotic locales with my money and men. We eat fancy foods and drink expensive wines. I never have to work out or iron clothes or pay bills or eat alone. I have a fabulous fantasy life.

Who needs real life?

Today, however, in my real life, a little bit of fascinating has walked through the glass and metal doors on the tenth floor, right past the cubicle I inhabit 40 hours a week.

Lisa, one of the other administrative assistants in the mid-sized architectural firm where I work, sidles up to my desk.

"Who's the new guy? I hear he's not from around here..."

"He's from England," I try to say casually, keeping my eyes on my computer monitor, where I'm supposedly filling out a PDF permit application. "Name's Jude Something-or-Other."

Weatherington. I know his last name, of course. But how dorky would it be to admit that?

"Jude, as in 'Jude Law,' sexy Brit?" She growls and paws at the air like a cat in heat.

"He looks nothing like Jude Law," I object quickly. "He's more like... well... I don't know. I can't think of anyone right now. He's kind of unique-looking. In a good way."

She studies me until I feel the urge to run away. "Wait a minute... Does someone have a little crush already?"

"Don't be a moron."

"You do!" She leans around me and hisses into the cubicle across the aisle, "Zoe, get over here. Libby seems to have found a guy who finally meets her high standards."

Zoe scurries to my desk and looks around nervously to make sure none of the higher-ups are around to see us goofing off. "Who? What's his name? What's he like?"

"I don't even know him, much less have a 'crush' on him." I glare at Lisa and adjust the blouse that's been hanging awkwardly on me all day, making a mental note to toss it in the back of the closet when I get home, ostensibly to give away to charity, but more likely for it to sit there for months until I see it and think, *Oh, I haven't worn that in a while,* and wear it again for another torturous day of tugging and yanking.

I'm imagining a smarter version of me pinning a note to it so that doesn't happen, when Lisa says, "Stop daydreaming about the new guy for a second and help us decide where to go to lunch."

"Shhh!" I slap her arm. "Shut up!" I poke my head up like a clerical prairie dog and scan the area for him.

There he is, in his office with the door closed, blinds wide open on the windows. His back's to me as he stands in the middle of the room, seemingly doing nothing. Except looking beautiful in his tailored suit and shiny shoes. He shrugs off his jacket, revealing the silky back of one of those vests that I thought could only look good on Simon Baker or David Beckham. Oh, was I wrong! It looks really good on him. Really good. After running his hand through his hair, he seems to regret it and spends a few seconds trying to resettle the tousled dark-honey-colored strands. Then he spins so suddenly, I don't have time to duck out of his sight, so I simply turn slightly and pretend I'm inspecting the leaves on the potted plant on my bookshelf.

"You're so immature," I accuse Lisa (and myself).

Zoe disappears for a second and reappears with an armful of office supplies: a stapler, staples, tape dispenser, pens, two grease pencils, paper clips, a staple remover, a bottle of correction fluid, and a letter opener. "Here. Take these into his office for him. Strike up a conversation."

I stare at the items, then up at her. "Zoe, he doesn't need half of that shit. That's what we're here for."

Reassessing her stash, she unloads everything onto my desk except the grease pencils, pens, and tape dispenser. "Okay, just take these then."

Lisa says, "Yeah. It doesn't matter if he needs them; it's just an in to get him to talk to you."

"Whatcha guys doin'?"

The three of us flinch guiltily.

Lisa recovers first. "Nunya, Leslie."

Leslie narrows her eyes and smirks. "Very funny, Lisa. As in 'nunya business'?"

"Exactly. See ya."

Leslie isn't shaken that easily. "I don't know about you guys, but I'm swamped." She looks at the random office supplies on my desk and in Zoe's hands. "Swap meet?" She grabs the stuff from Zoe and says, "Hey, you know who probably needs this? The new guy. Have you seen him? He is delicious with a capital 'Come to mama.' And wait until you hear him talk... I'd be okay with him just reading the building directory to me."

"Good," Lisa snipes, "since that's about all he'd probably be willing to read to you."

"We'll see about that," Leslie replies with a smirk. "I think I'll go welcome him to the company and let him know I'm available... for all his *administrative* needs." She licks her bright red lips suggestively and strides away, an extra wiggle in her hips.

"Guh-ross," Lisa says when she's gone. "What a tart."

It's just as well. There's no way I'd want to introduce myself to him wearing this shirt, anyway.

I try to think of the perfect thing to wear when I do meet him. Black's always good. I have a black pencil skirt that makes me look twenty pounds lighter. And I look great in purple. I have a purple, fitted satin wrap-around number that I always feel sexy in. I mean, professional. I feel *professional* in it, which is how I want to look. Since this is a professional setting.

"And who is this?" he'll say, appraising me.

"Libby Fletcher," I'll answer confidently, offering him my firm hand to shake.

"Indeed. Libby Fletcher, it's very nice to meet you. But I have to warn you, I'm high maintenance." He'll raise his thick eyebrows provocatively.

"Well, you'll get over that quickly here," I'll flirt back, "Unless you're in the habit of bringing presents to the admins. Then you can be as high-maintenance as you want."

He'll laugh at my wittiness and predict, "I think I'm going to like you, Libby Fletcher."

THAT WAS THREE WEEKS AGO. OUR ACTUAL FIRST MEETING went like this:

"Oh, hey, Libby, I want you to meet Jude Weatherington," Gary, Vice President of Commercial Accounts, said as he passed me while I was on the way to my desk after visiting the break room.

I was dabbing at a mustard stain on the left breast of my hideous aforementioned blouse. My attention to the stain was making it worse; my attention to the breast was making my nipple stick out through my shirt. At the mention of my name, closely followed by Jude's, I pulled the shirt away from my chest and stood at an odd angle to him, hoping he couldn't see the stain. Or my nipple, when I had to let go of my shirt to shake his hand.

I'm sure he was too distracted by my flaming face to notice anything below my neck anyway.

"Libby, was it?" Jude asked pleasantly.

Sometimes the simplest questions are the trickiest ones. "Uh... yes. Yep. I'm Libby."

He looked at me and smiled slowly. "Are you sure?"

awkward introduction. "He works with Leslie most of the time."

"How does that make you feel?"

I wrinkled my nose at him and snorted. "I don't care! He's just another one of the people who mills around the office all day."

"Do you imagine romantic relationships with any of the other 'people who mill around the office all day'?"

I blushed and crossed my arms over my chest. "No! Ick! No one else is good-looking." Or has an English accent. Or eyes the color of Lake Michigan in winter.

"Oh. So this is purely superficial, based solely on the guy's looks?"

"When you say that, it makes me sound so shallow."

He laughed. "Sorry. Just trying to understand your ultimate goal when it comes to this guy."

"Goal? I don't have any *goals.*" *He should know me better than that by now,* I thought. "This is just another one of my fantasies. Period. And you're kind of ruining it for me, by the way."

He held up a hand. "I apologize. The reason I'm pressing you so hard about this is that I don't want you to start confusing fantasy with reality. And to warn you that you may be disappointed if you have a real romantic interest in him. He might not live up to the fantasy. That's all."

It was my turn to laugh. "Are you kidding me? We'd have to talk to each other to become romantically involved. So you don't have to worry about that."

I focused on a picture on one of his bookshelves. It's a photo I often stare at during our sessions. He's wearing a cap and gown (judging by his age in the picture, it's his college graduation), and he's standing next to an older, shorter version of himself (I've always assumed it's his father). The picture's so familiar to me after so many sessions that I don't even really see it anymore. But my eyes always go there.

"He's kind of a hermit, anyway," I continued, talking about Real Jude, staring at the photo. "He works late a lot. At least, I think he does. He's always still there when I leave for the day, no matter how late it is. Not that I stay late often. Or notice his comings and goings." I tore my eyes from the photo and impatiently said, "Can we get back to Fantasy Jude now? He's so much more interesting."

"Hey, it's your dime," he conceded. "Dream away."

❧ 3 ❧

"YOUR SHOULDERS ARE SO TIGHT," I SAY, STANDING BEHIND HIM AND *rubbing them.*

"*I'm really wound up at work. All I seem to do is sit hunched over that drafting table all day.*"

"*I've noticed that. But let's not talk about work. I know! Let's go to a spa together this weekend and get massages!*"

"*That sounds wonderful. You always have the best ideas, Libby.*"

"*I have another idea.*" *I lean down as he looks up at me, and we kiss. He swivels in his chair so he's facing me. Then I slide my skirt up around my hips, straddle him, and—*

"Yello! Libby!"

I use every ounce of equilibrium to stay in my chair as Lisa laughs at the struggle.

"What the heck?" she asks, when I finally come to a stop with both feet on the floor. She follows my earlier line of sight straight through Jude's office window. He's standing at his drafting table with his back to us, his arms spread and his head hanging, his weight on one foot more than the other. Then he runs one hand through his hair and rubs his neck.

"Oh." After taking a minute to watch for a while, she says,

"Yeah. I get it." Then she drops a stapled sheaf of papers in my lap. "Can you pretty up this proposal by the end of the day?"

"Sure," I answer, moving my chair closer to my computer. I blink my eyes hard a few times and roll my head on my neck.

As I get to work, she goes back to looking at Jude. "He has a terrific ass. Makes me wish I wasn't married to one of the sweetest guys in the world. You know, I always thought it was nice that we worked in an office with no eye candy. No distractions. But I'm getting really used to taking in the scenery over there."

Clicking and typing, I say, "Yeah, Leslie's enjoying it, too."

"So are you and every other person in this place who doesn't prefer women."

"No, I mean, Leslie's doing more than just looking."

"What a whore," Lisa mutters supportively, patting my shoulder on her way out of my cubicle. "Just give me a shout if you need help with that. Gary wants it to go out tonight."

Great. At least it'll keep me busy, though. I have to admit, my mind is starting to run away with me. I've imagined everything from his favorite color (red) to his favorite sexual position (um... some things are private!). I've decided I have too much time on my hands. I need to get a life. A real life. Despite the fact that real lives are overrated. Or maybe Dr. Marsh is right, and I need to get a fantasy life that doesn't include Jude. But... I don't want to.

I find myself looking forward to my downtime so I can daydream about him. Or not even making it to my downtime, as witnessed by Lisa. Some of my dreams are ridiculous, featuring me sitting on his drafting table, fanning him and feeding him grapes. Others are more disturbingly realistic, including conversations that I have to remind myself never happened. But most fall somewhere in between, like the mental mini-porno in his office, complete with hokey dialogue and steamy sex act. Fantasy Jude is a great… kisser.

I don't even have to be consciously imagining these scenarios anymore. Most nights he's in my dreams. The other day, I had a dream in my sleep that was so raunchy I couldn't look him in the eye at the vending machine the next day. As it turned out, I abandoned my craving for a Kit Kat and high-tailed it back to my desk before he was finished making his selection. And I was sweating when I finally made it there. When he walked past on the way to his office, I shuffled papers around on my desk so I'd look busy and unapproachable.

Not that he ever approaches me anyway. Not when he has Leslie at his beck and call. He's been working here for three months, and Leslie's been in his office several times a day, every day. I've started eavesdropping on her reasons for going in there. They're almost as entertaining as my own fantasies. Here are a few of my favorites:

1. "Coffee's fresh!"
2. "Do you have a fire extinguisher in here?"
3. "Wanda needs your t-shirt size. I told her you were probably a large—I'm a pretty good judge of these things—but she wanted me to ask you to make sure."
4. "Can I get your John Han*cock* on this letter?"
5. "I need a tall guy to help me reach something in the supply closet. Do you mind?"

And she ends just about everything she says to him with this annoying giggle: "Ah-huh-huh!" Like little girl hiccups. Once, involuntarily, I loudly mock-giggled along with her at the end of her sentence as she was leaving Jude's office. She shot me a dirty look on her way past, but when I peeked through his window a few seconds later, I caught him grinning at me. He looked down as soon as he saw me glance over.

I'm not going to lie; that made my day.

Of course, I reverted to my awkward self a couple of hours later, when I called him "Babe" before hanging up with him on a routine phone call about reserving the videoconference room for a client meeting. Yeah. That happened. In my defense, I was distracted (about work, for once, not one of my daydreams), and I meant to say, "See you later. Bye." But I somehow got tongue-tied and started to combine the words "later" and "bye," so it would have come out, "See you bater," which almost sounds like I'm calling him a shortened form of "masturbator," so my brain short-circuited, and I ended up saying, "See you, babe." And then I hung up right away before I could correct myself, because I was trying to meet a deadline on another job. It was a slip of the tongue of epic proportions. Despite being very busy, I sat there at my desk, blushing and staring at my phone for at least a minute before I recovered and, with shaking hands, went back to work. I made a point of not making eye contact with him for the rest of the day, too.

Tonight, I do a double take when I get a glimpse of my computer clock at 6:30. "Shit!" I mutter, kicking it into high gear. I have thirty minutes to get my butt to FedEx for their latest drop-off. I hop from my chair and look over the partition that separates my desk from Lisa's. She's long gone. A quick sweep of the office tells me everyone else is, too. Except Jude.

Oh, Lord. This is what king-sized fantasies are made of.

But I don't have time for fantasies.

I do a quick spell- and format check of the document and hit print, practically running for the printer on my shoeless feet. "Oh, gosh, oh, gosh, oh, gosh!" I whisper as I run back to my desk to hit "print" again when I realize I forgot to print the first copy in color. When I get there the second time, red lights are flashing, indicating a jam. "Son of a White Sox fan!"

With the precision and efficiency of someone who's cleared about a thousand paper jams, I open all the little hidey-holes that paper loves to get caught in, reaching my hands in spaces and around hot metal parts, tossing the fan-crinkled paper over my shoulder.

"You *will* print for me, you piece of steaming crap!" I say lovingly to the machine as I close all the doors and tap my foot impatiently while it resets my job and sends it through again. "Come on, baby. You can do it. I just need one copy. Just one. I'll make the saps at Kinko's make my duplicates. Just give me one copy."

The last page slides out, and I grab the stack victoriously. "Ha-ha!" I cheer, holding the document aloft as I rush back to my desk for my shoes and purse. On my way past Jude's office, I inform him, "I'm leaving! You're the last one here!"

"Oh, blimey. Mind if I follow you out then? I lost my office key recently." He grabs his jacket from the back of his chair and shrugs it on as he hurries to catch up to me at the door. "Hole in one of my trouser pockets, I'm afraid. Keep forgetting to ask Wanda for a new one. Key, that is. Actually"—he keeps talking when I don't say anything—"I'm a bit afraid to ask her. She's sort of... humorless... and... scary. Am I the only one who thinks that?"

This is the most Real Jude has ever said to me. I wish I were less distracted so I could enjoy it more, but I'm dancing like a woman with a bladder-control problem as I hit the lights and lock the door.

"Right. You're in a rush," he observes.

"Yes," I answer. I put the proposal between my teeth and

hit the elevator "down" button before sliding my shoes on. "I have to get this to FedEx before seven."

He looks at the clock on his cell phone and gives a low whistle. "You're cutting it a bit fine."

"I know," I say shortly, rushing into the elevator when it arrives. I press the button for the ground floor; he presses the button for the parking garage.

"Do you have a plastic sheath for that paper? It's pissing it down out there," says the guy with the lake-view office.

My stomach drops. "No." Shit. I didn't even notice. But I would have known if I had been listening to the rising scream in my leg and hip that alerts me to dips in the barometric pressure.

I shove the document inside my shirt. The FedEx is just about as close as my car, which I had to park in an uncovered lot thanks to running late this morning (fantasies in the shower are especially time-consuming). Either way, the proposal's going to get drenched.

"Ah... I can give you a lift."

My heart starts pounding. Partly because I just got a flash of the fantasy I was having in the shower this morning. Partly because I can't imagine being in a car with him. Of all the things I've pictured us doing, riding together in a car isn't one of them. And for some reason, that matters.

"No! I mean... Oh. Well... I don't know... You don't have to."

He raises his eyebrow at my strange string of replies. "I know. But it's no trouble. Really. My car's in the underground car park." He motions to my shirt. "Come on. That's not going to do the trick. It'll be rubbish by the time you get five feet up the frog and toad, and all your hard work is going to go down the pan."

"It's only three blocks away." I'm not sure if I'm trying to convince him that my shirt will keep the rain at bay or if I'm assuring him that I won't be too much of a bother. I'm too focused on filtering out the parts of his sentence I don't understand (which are many) to examine my motives.

"I think I have enough petrol," he jokes.

"Okay. Thanks."

We bypass the ground floor and descend to the second level of the parking garage. In silence. I'm suddenly very aware that my hair looks like it hasn't seen a brush in several hours (because it hasn't). And I'm also noticing that Real Jude doesn't smell like Fantasy Jude. It's not a bad thing; just different than I imagined. Fantasy Jude smells like books and gin and tonic. Real Jude smells like cinnamon Altoids. And Tide.

We glance at each other at the same time, smile tightly, and look away. Finally, the elevator doors open, and Jude leads the way to his car. When we stop next to it, I start laughing, which he immediately misinterprets.

"Yeah. Sorry. It's a bit of a pigsty," he apologizes.

"No!" I say, even though on closer inspection, it kind of is. As he throws fast food wrappers and bags into the backseat to clear the passenger seat of the compact navy blue import, I explain, "I have the exact same car."

"Stroll on!" he cries.

"What?" *Is he telling me to walk?* "I'm sorry. I didn't mean anything by it," I stutter, thinking he's taken offense to something I've said.

"Come again?" he questions, then seems to realize I'm confused by what *he* said. "Oh! No. I just mean, that's incredible!"

Relieved, I elaborate, "I'm not kidding. Same model year, same color, same everything!" I pat the small spoiler on the trunk.

He comes around the car. "Then you drive. You know where we're going, and we'll get there faster without your having to direct me."

I'm not entirely sure about driving his car, but I don't have time to argue, so I answer, "Okay." I hand him the proposal, which is warm from being up against my body. If he notices, he doesn't say anything.

Other than having to scoot the seat up considerably so that I can reach the pedals, it's eerie how at home I feel in his car. It even smells like my car, thanks to the fast food wrappers scattered around.

I shoot onto Lake Shore Drive, turning on the wipers and the headlights at the same time. Then I weave in and out of traffic, looking in the mirrors and over my shoulder as I drive as fast as legally possible to get to the nearest FedEx. We're there in less than five minutes.

"See? Much faster," he says, smiling shakily. There's sweat on his brow. "You're a very... *confident* driver, Lisa."

While I wait anxiously in line inside the copy store, I fume. Fantasy Jude would never mistake me for someone else. Then I try to calm down by telling myself it could have been worse: he could have called me "Leslie." Of course, he wouldn't make that mistake, since he and Leslie are such bosom buddies. Gag.

After ridding myself of the proposal, I return to the car, where Jude's sitting behind the wheel. I settle into the passenger seat and tuck my company credit card into my purse.

"Thanks for the ride," I say stiffly, all earlier feelings of camaraderie gone, thanks to his gaff. I just want to get to my own little blue car and home, where I can spend some quality time with Fantasy Jude in a hot bath.

As he backs out of the parking space he says, "I got your name wrong just then, didn't I? You're Libby, not Lisa."

I look out the window. "It's no biggie. People do it all the time." It's true; I don't know why I'm being so unforgiving about it. I don't care when Gary does it, which is surprisingly often, given how long we've worked together. And every new person calls me "Lisa" at least once (usually more often) until they get to know us better and realize how very different we are.

"It's difficult to keep the assistants straight; your names all seem to start with the letter 'L.' Was that a requirement of the job?"

"Yeah. I mean, no. Anyway, Zoe ruins your theory."

"Who's Zoe?"

"Short brown hair, glasses, little voice?"

"Ahhh... Hmm," he says, struggling to place her.

"Well, maybe you haven't met her yet." *In the three months you've worked here*, I add silently.

"Right. Well, I mostly work with Leslie."

I like how he pronounces the "s" in her name as if it's a "z." She hates that. I hope he says it like that every time he talks to her.

Snottily, I say, "She's usually the one who has the least amount of real work to do," proud of myself for having the presence of mind to get in a dig, knowing she'd do the same in my position.

He laughs. "I *had* noticed that. The rest of you will be beavering away at your desks, and she'll be wandering around, announcing that she's brewed a fresh pot of coffee or some other such nonsense."

I barely keep from cracking up at 1) his use of the word, "beavering," and 2) his very true observation about Leslie.

"You seem to keep pretty busy yourself," I comment, hoping it doesn't sound too much like I watch him all day.

"Better than being bored, I suppose," he replies. "They have me working on the design for the new wing at the art museum."

I point to let him know to get into the left lane so we'll be in position to turn into the parking lot where my car is sitting. "Wow. That's a big account," I remark about his assignment. "No wonder you're always at work."

He shrugs. "Well, I have nothing better to do, really. New in town and all." Quickly, he adds, "That is, I play rugby with some blokes on Thursday nights, so it's not like I'm a complete and utter loser, but... yeah, I guess I sort of am." He smiles over at me. I fall into that dimple again. "Uh... we're here," he announces, jerking his head toward his car's twin, which he's parked beside.

"Oh! Gosh! I was spaced out or something. Sorry."

I fumble with the door handle, then realize the door's locked. He hits the button to unlock it, while I mumble and stumble over the most inelegant "thanks" and "goodbye" in the history of manners.

He waits to make sure I'm safely in my car and that it starts before he pulls away, giving me a subtle salute. I rest my head on the steering wheel and wait for my heart to return to a normal rhythm before backing out and heading in the opposite direction for home.

❧ 4 ❧

UNDERSTANDABLY, I COULDN'T GET JUDE OUT OF MY HEAD THE rest of the long, rainy night. I went home to my cramped apartment and made a tasteless low-calorie microwave meal for myself, eating it in front of the TV, fending off my cat, Sandberg, until all that was left were the water chestnuts that neither one of us wanted. Then I watched an hour of a chick flick on cable before realizing I'd already seen it and hated it the first time.

I kept wondering what Jude was doing. Judging by what he'd said to me in the car, probably something similar to me, I decided (minus the chick flick). Unless he was playing rugby. *No, that's on Thursdays,* I reminded myself, distractedly worrying a rough edge on one of my fingernails.

What's up with that, anyway? Rugby? Really? I had him pegged for a tennis guy. Or polo. Or soccer, at the roughest. It's not that he's wimpy-looking, but he's tall. And thin. I hear the word "rugby" and I think of stout, fireplug-shaped guys beating the crap out of each other on a muddy field. Jude sits (or stands) in an office all day. Rugby is... brutal. And dirty. I watched part of a game one Saturday when there was absolutely nothing else on TV, and I was shocked. It was like mud-wrestling... with a ball. Guys were bleeding! I turned it off after a guy took an elbow to the face, breaking his nose and sending a fountain of blood arcing onto the field. I made a note to look for bruising on Jude on Fridays.

The car thing had me shaken, too. At first, it was a funny coincidence. And then the more I thought about it, the more sinister it seemed. Okay, maybe not sinister, but creepy at the very least. I mean, what are the chances? (If he'd had a Ryne Sandberg bobblehead doll suction-cupped to his dashboard, I would have really freaked.) Plus I'd totally pictured him driving something like a Mini Cooper or an Aston Martin. Well, maybe not something *that* fancy, but something, well, European. Not a Japanese puddle-jumper. Automatic, to boot. Fantasy Jude likes to use the stick shift. So much more aggressive and manly. In a clean, non-bloody way.

By the time I'd obsessed about every heretofore-known discrepancy between Real Jude and Fantasy Jude, the crappy movie was over, and Sandberg was trying to coax me over to the bed, rubbing against me and purring. It's so sad when your cat is the only guy interested in getting you in the sack.

Today. I'm grumpy. I tossed and turned last night, unable to get a good scene going between Fantasy Jude and me. Real Jude kept butting in, calling me Lisa and babbling about frogs and toads and pans. I kept getting the two Judes confused. And we can't have that. I work with Real Jude. He needs to stay at work. In his little glass office.

Just before I'm getting ready to leave with Lisa and Zoe for lunch, he walks past my cubicle and backtracks. He pokes his head around the partition. "Whatchya," he says simply, smiling, then going on.

"Hey!" Lisa answers to his back, widening her eyes at me.

Zoe squeezes my arm. "What was that?"

I blush but try to hide it by pretending to search for something in my purse. "Nothing. He gave me a ride to FedEx last night."

They both stare at me open-mouthed, so I explain, "It was raining. My car was in the overflow parking lot. I was carrying an important proposal that couldn't get wet. We were leaving at the same time." When they continue to gape, I roll my eyes. "Can we go to lunch already? I'm starving."

"And crabby," Lisa mutters, catching up to me at the elevator.

Zoe's too nice to be the first one to say it, but she nods her agreement.

"I didn't get a lot of sleep last night, okay?" I try to defend myself and close the topic at the same time. But it only adds fuel to the quickly building inferno.

Lisa laughs. "Oh! I see."

"Alone!" I insist. "I had insomnia. Probably something I ate."

"Mm-hm..."

Zoe interjects softly, "That was a really nice smile he gave you. And he made a point to back up so he could give it to you."

Suddenly paranoid that someone's going to hear them, I look around us. "Will you two shut up? If I had known it was going to be so much trouble, I would have just walked in the rain."

The elevator arrives. We step in, although I'm tempted to send them without me.

"'Trouble'?" Lisa questions, pushing the button. "What

trouble? We're just teasing you a little bit. That's nothing unusual. Unless you're referring to something else that happened when Jude gave you a ride…" She holds her hands in front of her like a frame. "I'm seeing steamed-up car windows, body parts pressed up against glass…"

"So!" I interrupt loudly. "Where are we going for lunch? Did we ever decide?" I figure the only way we're going to get off this subject is if I drag us away from it. "I'm in the mood for sushi. Is it weird to want sushi for lunch?"

"It's not a crime to be attracted to someone," Lisa says.

"Especially when he looks like that," Zoe agrees. "He's not really my type, but I have unconventional taste in men."

That's an understatement. The last guy she dated had so many tats and piercings, it was hard to tell what features God had originally blessed him with. And I know she's not meeting these guys at the public library on Friday nights, so it makes me wonder what our quiet little Zoe is like when she's off the clock.

The elevator doors open on the lobby, but I hang back while they step off. "You guys go ahead," I say, hitting the button to take me back up to the office.

"What?"

"Oh, come on! Don't be a baby," Lisa says. "We'll stop bugging you."

But the doors are already closing. I wave at their incredulous expressions, then I'm blessedly alone again. Sighing, I lean against the wall. I don't really want to sit at my desk through lunch, eating a candy bar from the vending machine, but I don't want to go somewhere outside the building and eat alone, either. Maybe I'll find the closest hair salon and get a haircut. I've been thinking about it for a while. My straight hair is halfway down my back when I wear it down, which isn't very often, because it's so hot and heavy. It's going to be unbearable when the summer temperatures really kick in.

"I love your hair. It's so beautiful, the way it catches the light." *He leans close and breathes in.* *"And it smells so good."*

"Thanks." *My freshly cut, silky black hair looks like something in a shampoo commercial.* *"Most guys prefer long hair."*

"You make any length look fabulous." *He fingers the ends, brushing his knuckle against my ear.*

"Well, I thought it was time for a change."

With his lips almost touching mine, he says, "Don't change too much, though. I like you just the way you are."

Real Jude materializes in front of me. I startle and squawk, drowning out and replacing the usual elevator *ding* and making him look up from the floor, where his attention had been while he waited.

"Libby!" His smile turns to confusion as he gets into the elevator with me and presses the button to go down. "I thought you had already gone with Lisa and... blimey, how embarrassing. I can't remember her name."

I'm so flummoxed, I can't move fast enough to get off the elevator. The doors close and we descend, both facing the front. "Zoe," I rasp, then clear my throat. "That was Zoe."

"Oh! You mentioned her yesterday, and I couldn't picture her. So that's her."

Tamping down my irrational irritation at his inability to remember her, I say crossly, "Yes. That's her. Hasn't she done any work for you in all the months you've been here?"

He either doesn't pick up on my pique, or it doesn't bother him. "No. I s'pose not." Then he laughs. "I've only been here three months, though. And I hardly ever leave my office."

"Except for today." I glance at him from the corner of my eye.

"Except for today," he repeats, grinning, rocking back and

forth on the balls of his feet. "I decided to get away for an hour." He says it like it's the most rebellious thing he's ever done. Turning his body toward me, he asks, "Would you like to join me?"

Instead of outright rejecting him, which is my first inclination, I hedge, "Where are you going?"

He shrugs, still grinning. "Dunno. I have no idea what's even close. I thought I might take a walk. It's lovely out today."

We arrive in the lobby before I can come up with a nice way of saying, "no," so I step off the elevator and have an out-of-body experience as I watch myself walk with him to and out the revolving door, onto the sidewalk.

"Where to?" he asks expectantly, as if I'm the instigator of this outing.

"Oh. I don't know. Sushi?" I can hardly believe I'm hearing myself. I was supposed to say, "I don't know... I think I'm just going to get my hair cut." That was the plan, wasn't it, before he interrupted Fantasy Jude and me?

He nods decisively. "Sushi." Then he stands there, waiting for me to lead the way.

And I do. Now it'd look *really* weird for me to back out, so I'm stuck.

My internal hermit is chewing me out, pointing out how unbearable Lisa and Zoe are going to be if they find out about this, when he says, "So, what about Lisa and... Zoe? Ha! I think I've got it!"

Suddenly terrified that he's reading my mind, I falter. "W-What? What about them?"

"Her name! I think I've got it now." He taps his temple. "Sorry. Go ahead."

I shake my head at him, trying to figure out if it's me or him making this conversation almost impossible. I can't help but snap, "I don't know what you're talking about!"

His smile fades. "Right. You left the office with Zoe and Lisa, but then you came back up in the lift. And then rode it down again." The smile returns. "Do you like to spend your lunch hour riding the lift?"

Completely unconvincingly, I lie, "Oh, that. I... uh... er, thought I forgot my... wallet! But then I found it in my purse while I was riding the elevator up."

Turning toward me but keeping in stride with me, he puts his hands in his pockets and squints in the sun. "Do you want to try to catch up to them?"

His question suddenly makes me wonder if they'll be at the sushi place we're heading for. My stomach clenches. "Uh, no! That's okay. I'm sure they're way ahead of us, already eating by now." As casually as possible, I turn a block before the street we'd take to get to our original destination and say, "You know, I'm actually more in the mood for a burger. Is that okay?"

"I'm easy," he replies. "Whatever. As long as it's not a garden burger. That just sounds hideously unappetizing, don't you think?"

"Sure. I guess." I've never spoken to another English-speaking person and had more trouble understanding him. I feel like I'm constantly three seconds behind. Like there's some kind of audio lag going on in real life. It's completely disconcerting and disorienting.

Because of that, other than a recommendation on what he should order when we get to the tiny burger joint, we don't say anything until we're seated with our food. And we only start talking again because he insists on it. My main objective is to make it though this meal without being discovered.

"So... are you originally from Chicago?" he asks after swallowing his first bite. He takes a drink and waits for my answer.

"Yes," I say simply.

He nods, waiting for more, but when I don't volunteer anything, he soldiers on. "You must like it well enough, then, to stay here after... what was it? University? Secretarial school?"

I can tell from the way his eyes are twinkling that he's kidding about secretarial school, but I still bristle a little. "For your information, I went to Loyola," I tell him snobbishly, hating myself for being such an elitist bitch. But for some reason, it's important for me to establish that I'm more than someone who can type and make coffee.

And I don't want to be Real Jude's friend, anyway. That would seriously hinder my relationship with Fantasy Jude, who I *really* like.

Eyebrows raised, he swallows another bite, then says. "Wow. What did you read?"

His question takes me aback. Does he want me to list everything I read in college? "Uh... textbooks?"

He wrinkles his brow, then laughs. "Oh! No. Sorry. I meant what was your area of study?"

Why didn't he just say that, then? "I *majored* in anthropology and sociology," I reply, unexpectedly annoyed by his impressed expression and his obvious reappraisal of me and my intelligence based on my answer. If I'm just a secretary, I must be dumb; but someone with a degree... now *that's* impressive? I get so sick of being stereotyped, especially by these high-and-mighty, nerdy architects I work with (not *for*).

He repeats, "Wow. And how'd you get into, um, administrative work, then?"

"It's a long story," I dodge and feint. "What about you? You went to Oxford?"

Holding his napkin up to his mouth, he closes his eyes and bounces in his chair, obviously laughing and trying not to spit out his food or choke. When he recovers, he answers, "Uh, no. Not even close. Not everyone from England goes to Oxford, you know."

"I know!" I say defensively. "I just figured..." I blush as I realize my blunder. "I must have you confused with... someone else. Anyway, sorry." I take a deep breath to compose myself, then ask neutrally, "Where'd you go?"

"University of Edinburgh. In Scotland. I read Architecture and Design."

"Obviously."

"Well, maybe not. Maybe I studied to be a... secretary."

"Very funny," I say flatly.

He cocks his head. "Sorry. I'm getting the idea that your job is a sore topic."

I don't want him getting any ideas about me, so I force myself to smile. "Not at all." I wave my hand in front of myself and say, "Don't mind me. I'm taking a bad day out on you."

He graciously accepts my half-apology, which makes me feel even worse. If he would just be a jerk and tell me to go screw myself, it would be a lot easier.

To keep the conversation away from me and my background, I go back to asking him about himself. "Anyway, what brings you to the Windy City?"

He looks blankly at me; then understanding lightens his features. "Oh. Yes. Chicago's the Windy City, isn't that right?" I nod, amazed that someone could not know that like they know that the sky is blue.

He plays with his straw, tying it in a knot. "A job."

"Yeah, but why'd you choose to apply for a job in Chicago, of all places?"

"*You* like it here, right?"

"Yeah, but I don't know any better. Unfortunately." I sit back and study his reaction to my probing. "I'm just curious why Chicago got your attention, as opposed to New York or L.A. or, I don't know, St. Louis. Anywhere."

He runs a hand through his hair and makes a noise with his lips that I interpret as being at a loss for words. Finally, he says, "I applied in lots of cities. Not necessarily the ones you mentioned, but others in addition to Chicago. They all seemed pretty much the same to me. I'm not terribly familiar with U.S. geography. This firm gave me a good offer; I took it."

Being the private, guarded person I am, I know a half-truth when I hear it. I also know how annoying it is when someone won't take a hint and keeps pressing you for an answer you're not willing to give. I don't want to find out too much about Real Jude, anyway. The less I know, the less chance I have of getting confused and repeating my earlier stunt of treating fantasy like fact.

"Sounds perfectly reasonable." I dunk a French fry in ketchup and eat it like I don't have a care in the world, including knowing anything personal about him.

He smiles uncertainly at me. I'm content to eat the rest of my meal in silence, but he's squirming in his seat like a naked hairy man in a Velcro chair.

Eventually, he sighs and blurts, "That's really only half the story. About why I came to Chicago."

I raise my eyebrows in the strongest expression of interest I can muster. In reality, I'm silently begging him to leave it alone.

"If you're a criminal, exiled from your home country, I don't want to know.".

He chuckles nervously, and I'm worried for a minute that I might have guessed correctly. But then he says, "Close. Divorced and exiled. However unofficial and voluntary the exile may be."

This is a most distasteful revelation. The Jude I've come to know and—in some twisted way—love has never loved another woman but me. He came to me an inexplicably talented virgin lover. And he certainly doesn't have any baggage as messy as an ex-wife!

"You don't have an ex-wife!" I state confidently, speaking more to my fantasy than to him.

He laughs, obviously thinking I'm kidding, giving him my version of "stroll on."

"You sounded so English when you said that just now. Reminded me a bit of home." Rubbing his eyebrow, he says, "I wish I could deny it. But alas."

He looks pretty chagrined by the fact, but I have no idea what to say to him. All the next logical responses would lead to further disclosures that I'm not interested in hearing. Actually, I *am* interested, but I know I shouldn't be—*can't* be—so, it's best for me to just drop it.

But how do I go on with this lunch? "Oh, that's nice. Ready to head back to the office? Unfortunately, I can't be seen with you, so you leave now, and I'll be about five minutes behind you"? Somehow I don't think that's a socially acceptable response.

"Bummer," I say instead, panicking as the silence drags on. "I'm sorry."

"I'm not, to be quite honest." At my shocked expression, he explains, "I'm sorry it didn't work out, but I'm glad to be rid of her."

"Okay!"

"That came off wrong," he quickly states. Clearly embarrassed, he laughs at himself. "What I meant…"

"You don't have to explain yourself to me," I interrupt him, standing up and grabbing my purse from the floor. "It's none of my business."

He rises, too, coming around the table and following me through the tables crowded into the tiny space. When we emerge onto the sidewalk, he says, "Bloody hell, now you think I'm a right git."

Keeping my eyes straight ahead, I reply, "Whatever that is. I don't have an opinion of you one way or another." For some reason, I'm really mad at him. I wish I knew why. I only know that I am, and that it causes me to spew, "I'm just an administrative assistant where you work. And you're just another one of the guys who orders me around and looks at my breasts when he thinks I don't notice."

"Come again?" he sputters next to me. "I've never... that is, I resent that accusation! Every last word of it!" His tone softens, and he mumbles, "At the risk of sounding completely pathetic, I thought... perhaps... that you and I were becoming friends." When I say nothing but keep walking, he continues, "And it was a bit of a relief, actually. I haven't made many friends since moving here."

I will *not* feel sorry for him. I'll be strong. He can be friends with someone else. Leslie will be the first volunteer, as long as the job comes with benefits.

"I don't really do the whole *friend* thing," I state as matter-of-factly as possible.

"Bollocks," he says. I assume he's calling me a liar, though I'm not sure, until he challenges, "What about Lisa and Zoe?"

Coolly, I reply, "The three of us don't hang out together outside of work. Lisa has a husband and step-daughter who keep her busy. And Zoe... we don't seem to have the same interests. We're just co-workers who don't hate each other."

He slows down, and I find myself adjusting to match his pace, although I can't explain why. I mostly want to get back to work, where I don't have to talk to him anymore.

After a while, he says, "Well, at least you have that."

"What about your rugby team?" I ask, kicking myself for letting on that I retained anything from our contact last night.

He snorts. "Truth be told, most of them are wankers, a bunch of blokes with something to prove, trying to be hard cases. I like the sport, but I haven't really clicked with any of the blokes I play with." He sighs. "And I hate to sound like a whinger, but I don't really fit in with any of the blokes at work, either. A few of them seem downright adversarial, in fact. As if they're trying to set me up for failure."

I wish I could reassure him otherwise, but I can totally see where that might be the case. A gaggle of xenophobic morons, most of them, elbowing their way to the top, resentful of the new guy who lands the big project. Never mind that Jude doesn't have a life and works about five times as hard and double the hours they do.

"You'll meet people," I say lamely. "Outside of work. Who wants to talk shop all the time, anyway? That's all those guys know how to do." I just can't be mean to this guy, no matter how much I realize it would make my life a lot less complicated.

Another huge sigh escapes him. "Right." Hesitantly, he adds, "You're right about them, though."

I try to remember what I've said. "About them talking shop?"

He rolls his hand in a circle. "Yeah, that. But the other thing, too."

I have no choice but to look at him to try to figure out what he's getting at.

Ducking his head, he laughs shyly. "They *do* talk about… you know." He draws a set of breasts on himself in the air in front of him. A big set.

"Oh," I say, trying to sound like I don't care. "Of course they do." Even though I want to, I don't force him to admit or deny that he's right there with them when they do. Instead, I skirt danger by saying, "Well, we talk about them too. Only"—I lift my chin defiantly—"it's the inverse. We speculate just how little their peckers are."

He cracks up, putting his hand on my shoulder to steady himself as he staggers through his laughter. The touch is casual, but it makes me tingle in some serious places. I smile in spite of myself.

We've arrived at the office building. My smile dies. "If you tell anyone I said that, I'll deny it," I tell him, moving away from his touch.

"Same here about the other thing," he says, still chuckling.

I know I can't get into that elevator and walk into the office with him if I want to have any peace this afternoon, so I make up something about needing to look for my MP3 player in the building's Lost and Found and tell him I'll see him later. Thankfully, he doesn't offer to help. Grinning, he stands at the bank of elevators and waits for the next available ride up while I slink over to the security desk, where I paw through the box of junk for a lot longer than it really takes to see everything in it.

Funny thing is, though, I think I found Jude's missing key.

5

I WISH DR. MARSH WOULD CHANGE THE PICTURE IN THAT frame. Or at the very least, rearrange the items on that shelf so that I'm not always looking at the picture. I have the damn thing memorized, and I'm sick of looking at it.

On a whim, I tell him so. I want to keep him off the subject of LFW, anyway.

"Does that picture bother you?"

"It bothers me that I've been staring at it for five years," I answer.

"I like that picture," he says. "It reminds me of a really happy day in my life. Don't you have any pictures like that?"

"No, I don't."

He cocks his head to the side, waiting for me to expound on the subject. I turn my attention to him. "You know I don't."

"Why not?"

He's in full therapist mode today. Sometimes our sessions feel like we're just two acquaintances (not friends, necessarily) having a conversation. But on days like today, it's clear that he's the head doctor, and I'm the head case.

I sigh, knowing it's easier to answer his questions when he

gets like this, even though he already knows the answers. "Because my parents never saw me graduate from college. There was nobody there to take my picture. And it wasn't really a happy day, anyway. It was just… an end."

"What about Hank?"

"What about Hank?" I retort, being intentionally difficult.

"Wasn't your brother there to take your picture?" he asks.

I level my best *you're a moron* look at him. "He was sixteen. And in a foster home. He wasn't there."

"That must have been lonely."

Lonely. That word never fails to make me cry. It's why I refuse to ever admit to myself that's what I am. I say I'm "single," or I call myself a "hermit." I might describe myself as "by myself," even. But never "lonely." It's such a black, plaintive word. And scary.

Annoyed by my automatic response to his saying that word, I roughly grab a tissue from the box on the table next to me, pressing it against my eyes before the tears can spill over. "Big deal," I say, talking tough. "There are worse things to be."

He pulls the corners of his mouth down in a contemplative expression. "I guess." After a pause, he asks, "Don't you have any pictures that you keep around that make you smile? Anything?"

I refuse to admit that I have a box full of pictures of Sandberg that I paw through every once in a while when I'm truly bored. Somehow that's more pathetic than not having any pictures at all. "No. Where would I get these pictures? I don't have friends; my brother lives thousands of miles away; I never go anywhere."

"Any pictures of you and your boyfriends?"

I tap my chin and say sarcastically, "Let's see… Have I ever had a boyfriend? A real one, that is? Whose picture I could take? Hmm, that would be a no."

"How are you and"—he consults his notes—"Jude doing?"

I can't help it. At the mention of that name, I feel my whole face brighten. "Oh, I have a lot of fun with Jude," I state, not feeling ridiculous at all when I say it.

"What kinds of things do you do together?"

I think for a second. "Well, we go to baseball games. And the beach. He takes me for drives in his red MG convertible. He reads poetry to me."

"Are you sexual?"

His question is so matter-of-fact that I'm almost tricked into answering it. My ferocious blush makes a verbal reply unnecessary anyway. Before I can recover and say something to bury my mortification, he asks, "And the real Jude? Still ignoring you? Or vice versa?"

"For the most part," I reply. It's technically true. If one were to add up all the time available for us to interact with each other and divide into it the time we actually spend interacting, it would be a very low percentage. Much less than 50%, for sure.

He closes one eye and gives me a skeptical look, but he doesn't challenge me. Instead, he posits, "Why do you think it is that you've never had a boyfriend?"

"I'm boring," I immediately supply. Then after I think about it for a minute, I add, "And average-looking. And I have issues."

Steepling his fingers under his chin, he says, "'Boring' and 'have issues.' Those are things you don't find out about someone until after you date them. You can't *see* 'boring' and 'has issues.'"

"Well, that's where the average-looking part comes in," I explain. "The cover of the book doesn't lend itself to curiosity for curiosity's sake."

He writes something down. "Mm-hm. And what features

of yours make you 'average-looking'?" When I don't answer right away, he rips a piece of paper off his legal pad and hands it to me. He digs in his desk drawer for a pen and tosses it to me. "Let's do something. I'm going to start listing your physical features, and you're going to write down a word you'd use to describe yourself. Ready?"

I nod.

"Eyes."

I scrawl down, *green*.

"Nose."

I jot, *pug*.

"Ears."

I don't think about my ears very much, so it takes me a second to come up with something. I settle on *little*, for lack of anything else.

"Teeth."

They're *straight*.

"Lips."

I bite them, trying to feel them with my teeth. *Smooth*.

"Breasts."

That one's easy. *Big*.

"Weight."

I tap the pen against my thigh. *Average*.

"Hair."

I know it's my best feature, since everyone's always complimenting me on it, so I feel confident calling it *nice*.

"Okay, now make another list right next to the first. Those will be the words you think your fantasy guy would use to describe those same features."

I quickly write down the eight words, hardly having to think about it. I mean, Fantasy Jude has complimented me a million times.

"Now, read me *your* answers," he demands when I set the pen aside.

At the end of my list, he smiles but merely says, "Okay, now what did you think fantasy guy would say?"

Trying not to blush, I read them quickly. "Captivating, adorable, delicate, dazzling, luscious, fabulous, fit, and gorgeous."

"Which list do you think is more accurate?" he asks.

"Mine, obviously," I immediately answer. "I mean, the other list is based on what a person in a fantasy would say. If it was based on fact, it wouldn't be much of a *fantasy*."

"You're selling yourself short," he claims. "The truth definitely lies somewhere in the middle, I'll grant you that. But it's a lot nearer to his list than yours, I guarantee it. If I polled a hundred guys and asked them which list more accurately described you, I'd say the majority of them would pick the fantasy list."

"Okay, so for the sake of argument," I say, crossing my arms over my 'fabulous' breasts, "let's say I'm a little above average. What good does that do me? Guys still don't ask me out. So maybe you *can* see 'has issues.'" My glare dares him to explain to me why I've never had a boyfriend.

He glances at the clock on his desk and verifies the time on his watch. "I'm giving you an assignment between now and our next session. Two assignments."

I groan like a high school student.

He grins. "Every single day, I want you to spend five minutes in front of the mirror and pretend you're not looking at yourself, but at a friend, and I want you to compliment the woman in the mirror on one aspect of her appearance. You have to say it out loud. With feeling. Now, to keep you honest, I want you to write down the date and the compliment and bring them to me next time."

I roll my eyes but agree.

"Be creative," he urges me.

"Fine, fine! What's the other assignment?"

"I want you to be more aware of the signals you send to men, especially men that you find attractive. And I want you to consciously try to be more approachable. Smile. Keep your arms away from your chest."

I drop my arms, stick out my boobs, and give him a toothy grin. "Like thish?"

He laughs. "Maybe a little more subtle than that. And..."

"Wait! That's already two assignments!" I object.

Holding up a hand, he says, "This is extra credit. If a man asks you on anything remotely resembling a date, you should consider accepting it."

"Even if he's a leering pervert serial killer-in-the-making on the El?"

"You know what I mean. Use your own discretion, of course. Maybe stick to guys you kind of already know; ones you've seen often at the store or... *at work.*"

"Yeah, yeah," I mutter, standing up. "You're really demanding today."

"Just giving you your money's worth," he says. "I expect your compliments and a full report on the other assignment— and extra credit, if applicable—at your next session."

❦ 6 ❦

It's Day 6 of the Dr. Marsh experiment. This morning, I got up, got ready, and stood in front of the full-length mirror on the back of my bathroom door. I've already told myself over the past few days:

1. "You have shiny hair."
2. "That shirt makes your eyes sparkle."
3. "My, what clear skin you have!"
4. "What a stunning shade of lip gloss!"
5. "Hey, Legs! Have you been working out?"

Today, I turned this way and that before settling on "Nice knockers!" *Take that, Dr. Marsh,* I thought as I wrote the statement underneath today's date.

The other part of the assignment isn't going as well. I've noticed that I tense up every time I'm in the presence of a man. And that's a lot, considering I work in an office full of them. I've tried to make myself relax and smile, but that's attracted more questions than offers.

Jude asked me as I smiled at him while we were walking

out of a meeting the other day, "Is everything okay? You look like you're in pain."

I've been working on my smile ever since. I hope to be able to tell my reflection someday, "Your mouth doesn't look like a rictus."

Today, I've come to the conclusion that I need help with this mission I've apparently chosen to accept. Dr. Marsh never said that was against the rules, so I'm going to ask Lisa and Zoe. I'm nervous, but after I give them a little (emphasis on *little*) background information (I tell them I'm trying to get into the dating game and need some pointers), I feel less tense.

"So far, I've tried to smile more and not cover my boobs with my arms," I open the forum.

Lisa says, "You do have a nice rack. Let's go out at lunchtime and buy you some flattering shirts."

"Not low-cut," I stipulate.

She sighs. "Fine. But form-fitting. Accentuate your tiny waist and big tits."

Zoe giggles into her hand then offers, "You should start trying to initiate conversations with people, instead of always waiting for them to talk to you first."

"That's a good one," Lisa says. "But don't be the annoying person who volunteers too much information. Just start with 'Hi.'"

Suddenly, I feel like I should be taking notes.

"But she shouldn't be too closed off, either," Zoe qualifies.

Lisa considers that and nods.

To me, Zoe gently explains, "You know, if someone asks, 'How are you today?' they're generally looking for an answer like, 'Fine.' Don't go into detail about your PMS or anything. But if you're having a conversation with someone, and they ask you something like, 'What'd you do this weekend?' it's okay to give a more thorough answer. Like, 'I went to a ball-game, and it was awesome,' instead of, 'Nothing.'"

"What if I really did nothing, though?" I ask, suddenly worried about the 'boring' part of my personality and life.

Lisa eagerly adds, "Tone of voice is important, too. There's a difference between, 'Nothin' much! How 'bout you?' and 'Nothing. What's it to ya?'"

"Do I sound like that?" I put my hand to my chest, then drop it again for fear that it will lead to defensive arm-crossing.

"Sometimes," Zoe admits, wincing. "Maybe not to us, but definitely to some of the guys."

"Boop-boop!" Lisa signals, busying herself with some papers on my desk. "Here comes Jude. Practice on him," she prods.

"No!" I object, suddenly experiencing performance anxiety. "I'm not ready!"

"Do it!" Zoe hisses before sliding across the 'hallway' to her own cube.

Lisa takes the papers with her and slips into her own space, but not before whispering, "Don't be a wuss. It's just Jude."

I lick my lips, cross and uncross my arms, and try to relax my face into something more inviting than a scowl. "Hey, Jude," I say, then kick myself as soon as the words are out there.

Barely breaking stride, he rolls his eyes and responds, "Nice. That's a new one," before going into his office and closing the door.

I hear Lisa giggling on her side of the partition. Zoe leans back in her chair, her face sympathetic, and says, "You had the right idea…"

"Just the wrong words," Lisa wheezes. "Nice Paul McCartney impersonation."

I drop down into my chair and put my hot face in my hands. "He probably thinks I'm a combination of a nerd and a bitch, if that's possible."

"You can be a nerdy bitch," Lisa confirms. "Or a bitchy nerd. It's possible."

"Don't worry about it," Zoe insists. "It was only Jude anyway."

The novelty—if there ever was any—has definitely worn off with Zoe. He's just another one of the guys. Lisa still looks wistfully at him sometimes, but most of the time she treats him like a kid. And Leslie's convinced he's gay, probably because he hasn't asked her out yet. None of them knows about Fantasy Jude, and I know my behavior toward Real Jude lately doesn't make them suspect I'm attracted to him on a level deeper than that he's nice to look at.

Because I'm not. Of course. It's Fantasy Jude I love, not the loner workaholic divorcé who drives my dinky car's doppelganger and plays in the mud with guys on Thursday nights. Not the Jude who graduated from a college I've never heard of (probably the equivalent of a community college here) and whines about the other guys not liking him. And definitely not the Jude who probably doesn't know a sonnet from a haiku. He didn't even notice when I had ten inches of my hair lopped off. Walked right past my desk without a word.

I've taken to imagining that Fantasy Jude and Real Jude are identical twins who have polar opposite personalities. Fantasy Jude definitely has the better of the two.

Just last night, Fantasy Jude said the sweetest thing. What was it? Oh, it was so cute! What *was* it? Shoot! It's going to bother me until I remember it. It's on the tip of my brain...

"You're my cuddly Cub."

Yep, that was it. Get it? Because I like the Cubs. And we were cuddling on my bed, watching the game. Aw... it was adorable.

Anyway, I bet Real Jude leaves his socks and underwear on the floor. If his car's any indication, his place is likely disgusting. And he probably doesn't even know how to boil an egg. Fantasy Jude cooks for me all the time. And we eat by candlelight.

Screw Real Jude.

7

"YOUR TEETH ARE EXCEPTIONALLY WHITE TODAY."

"Thank you," my reflection tells me. "I've been using a whitening toothpaste."

"You're welcome. And it's Friday. And hotter than hell out there. How about we forego the pantyhose today? Your legs are awesome enough without them."

"Well, that's two compliments in one day! Make sure you write them down for Dr. Marsh."

I don't really know how talking to myself in the mirror is supposed to make me less crazy and less (*gulp*) lonely, but I have to admit, I feel pretty good after my morning "conversations" with me. The little pep talks are getting longer, too. I'm kind of enjoying them. Not that I'm going to tell Dr. Marsh that.

Yesterday, I was able to tell myself that I have a pretty smile. It felt so great that my smile got even prettier.

People at work are starting to feel less uneasy around me, too. I actually had a conversation with Jamie from accounting about Kit Kat versus Twix in front of the vending machine the other day. Then he said, "Hey, I was wondering..." and I noticed when he leaned closer that he had horrible halitosis, so I pretended I heard my phone ringing and rushed out of there with my Kit Kat before he could finish his thought.

I straighten my wrap dress and tighten the tie-belt, being as objective as I can about how I look. It's the first time I've had the guts to wear this dress since Lisa picked it out for me and persuaded me to buy it. It's really pink. No matter. I don't have time to find a different outfit and change, so here goes.

When I get to work, Lisa whistles at me. "See? I told you! You look hot."

"Probably because I'm sweating," I grouse, lifting my hair off my neck and fanning myself at my desk.

"You know you're gorgeous, so shut up."

I stick my tongue out at her and go into the break room, where I stand in front of the open refrigerator for a few seconds after setting my lunch on the crammed shelf.

"Libby," I hear behind me.

Quickly, I close the fridge and turn around to face Gary, who's standing there, cup of coffee in hand. I don't know how he can drink that when it's a hundred degrees outside.

"I need you to work with Jude today on his presentation for the art museum."

"Okay," I answer readily, perkily, and approachably. "When's the presentation?"

"Monday. Clear your workload. Give any other work you have to Lisa, Leslie, and Zoe. This is priority one." He sips his coffee, then pours the rest down the sink. "I'll check on you guys later to see how it's going." He sets his dirty mug in the sink (which is right next to the dishwasher, by the way) and walks out.

Sighing, I rinse the cup and place it in the dishwasher for him. Then I head back to my desk.

I dump a few minor projects in Lisa's and Zoe's laps. A

really unsavory job I was dreading goes to Leslie. When I tell her what needs to be done, she narrows her eyes at me. "What are *you* going to be doing all day, then?"

"I have to help Jude with his presentation for the Art Museum Board," I declare, careful to keep the gloat I'm feeling out of my voice. "I'll be in his office if you have any questions about that." I point to the stack of spreadsheets she's supposed to consolidate into one workbook.

I knock on Jude's office door, which is open. He spins around from his drafting table. "Right. You're here to help, I take it?"

It's not the warmest greeting I've ever received, but I'm used to being treated like a piece of office equipment. "Take it or leave it," I answer cheerfully. "What do you need help with?"

"Everything," he says despairingly. "I'm crap at presentations. I design. I draft. I don't do public speaking."

"Show me what you have so far," I say, going to his computer.

He follows me around his desk and opens a document titled, "Art Museum Presentation." It's blank.

"You're kidding me, right?" I start minimizing things on his computer desktop, trying to find his real notes.

He gulps and scratches his head. "Nope. Not joking. I've got nothing."

"Well, you have to have something!" I try to keep the panic at bay. Nothing will come of both of us breathing into paper bags all day.

"I don't!" He crosses his office and closes the door so no one overhears us. "I don't have a bloody, sodding word. Not even an idea."

"But Gary's going to come in here this morning for a run-through!"

"He is?" His pale face whitens further and takes on a green tinge. "Oh, blimey."

"How long have you had to work on this?" I ask.

"Two weeks."

"And you have nothing?"

"We've already established this," he confirms, growing impatient. "I can get out the thesaurus and give you some synonyms if you don't like the word 'nothing.'"

I drop my hands from my forehead and tilt my head inquisitively, "You say 'thesaurus' funny. Say it again."

"Thesaurus," he says, putting the accent on the first syllable. "What's wrong with that? *You* say it funny. TheSOREus. Bizarre. How do you say 'aluminium'?"

"Not like that!" I crack up. "Al-yoo-MIN-ium? You put an extra 'I' in there!"

"What are we doing?" He grins hysterically. "We don't have time to muck around!"

"No, it's definitely not in our shedyule," I crack.

"Bugger off."

"Whatever that is, we probably don't have time for that either," I say. "Okay, let's get serious. You're in deep shit."

"Whilst that's very helpful information, it doesn't actually solve the problem," he replies.

"Show me your drawing." I walk to the drafting board and stand over the huge blueprint draped over it. "This is bad-ass," I breathe reverently after a few minutes of studying it.

He stands next to me. "Thanks. I mean... well, the thing is, it's a wing that's going to be dedicated to modern art collections. So, I thought it should *look* modern. But the trick was making a seamless transition from the traditional architecture of the original structure. That's the purpose of this corridor here." He points to a part of the drawing, and I notice for the first time how nice his hands are. Slim fingers, clean, short nails, but not girly.

"Also," he continues intensely, oblivious to my study of his hands, "it's not enough for it to look modern; it has to look timeless. I don't want it to be dated in twenty years, for someone like me to walk past it and say, 'Oy, that's so retro-looking.' That would defeat the purpose of having it look modern, if it only looked modern for a decade. So I added a lot of classic elements to it to soften the more contemporary features. I feel it will serve to balance it out in the end." He looks up at me, seeking my approval.

"It's… awesome."

"Seriously? You're not just saying that because I'm bricking myself and have sweet F.A. to show Gary when he comes in here?"

Still staring at the drawing, I answer distractedly, "I have no idea what the hell you just said, but this is really beautiful." I trace a line of the building with my finger.

He laughs. "Well. I can never get enough of flattery, but we really need to figure out what I'm going to say."

"What's wrong with what you just told me?" I ask, snapping out of my trance.

He starts to enumerate all the problems with it, but I interrupt him. "Well, obviously, we'll shine it up. And we'll have to add to it, but we can hide a lot of deficiencies with sweet computer graphics."

I walk to his desk and pick up his phone, calling down to Marvin in Graphic Design. I tell him what's going on and that Gary says it's our top priority. He listlessly informs me that he has nothing better to do today, anyway, and he'll be right with us.

"We're going to take the Museum Board on a virtual tour of your new modern art wing. And they're going to be blown away," I assure Jude. "In the meantime, sit down over there and repeat what you told me." I settle myself at his keyboard and start typing what he says. When we get the skeleton down, we go in sentence by sentence and tweak the language.

I have him come around the desk to read it through. When he finishes, I say, "Plus, let's face it; you could stand up there and recite the alphabet, and they'd be impressed and consider you an authority because of that accent."

"I don't have an accent," he says, still leaning across me. "*You* do."

I've seen that face before. This close to me. At that angle.

"Your eyes are so stunning. I find myself thinking of them at the oddest moments during the day."

"Like when?"

"Constantly. Mostly at work, when I'm supposed to be concentrating on other things. But also when I'm in bed... alone. You drive me to distraction."

"Well, I'm here now. Why don't you do some of the things to me that you imagine doing?"

"What a fabulous idea," he mutters as he slowly and sensuously begins removing my clothing.

Neither one of us seems to breathe. I see for the first time a slight bump in the bridge of his nose, only noticeable at this distance (or lack thereof). He licks his lips. I mimic the gesture without thinking.

"Knock-knock. Someone call a graphics genius?" Marvin asks as he lets himself in.

Jude stands up straight, and I roll away from him on the chair. After I explain to Marvin what I'm envisioning (for the presentation), he complains, "I totally should have known about this a week ago, dudes. What you're asking for will take days. I'd have to work through the weekend to get it done."

"So you'll do it?" I half-joke hopefully.

He stares me down. I stand up and clasp my hands to my chest, pleading, "Please? It'll be so awesome; it'll be worth it."

"Says the girl who's not going to spend her weekend at work."

Suspecting I'm going to regret it, I say, "What do you need me to do to help? I'll work this weekend if it means you'll do this for us."

Jude steps in. "Ah, no. No worries. Never mind. I'll simply... mount the drawing on a backing and frame it, put it on an easel. It'll be fine. You shouldn't have to work through your weekend, mate, because I made a pig's ear of this whole thing." I notice he didn't say anything about how *I* shouldn't have to work on *my* weekend.

I shoot Jude a dirty look. I almost had Marvin ready to agree. I could see it. I place a silencing hand on Jude's arm and say to the graphic artist, "Seriously, Marvin, I'll do what I can to help. So will Jude. We'll all work this weekend, if that's what it takes. And... and..." I desperately search for anything else to sweeten the pot. "And I'll take you to a Cubs game, my treat. Next weekend. I think they're playing the Cardinals. Big rivalry!"

Now I have his attention.

"I do likes me some Cubs," Marvin says in a silly voice.

"Oh!" Jude cries. "Now this is getting a bit ridiculous. If anyone should be bribing the bloke, it should be me. I'm the twit who got myself into this mess."

"No, no," Marvin is suddenly very accommodating. This will work just fine. As a matter of fact, you don't even have to work the whole weekend with me. Just come in for a couple of hours tomorrow so I can make sure everything looks the way you want it to look." He points to me. "You. Call me later and give me your cell phone number. Before you leave today."

I want to cry when he actually winks at me.

I gulp. "Okay."

He waves in Jude's general direction. "You, too, I guess. In case I have any questions or problems."

"Really—"

But before Jude can object any more, Marvin's out the door, a copy of the plans under his beefy arm.

I smile sickly but bravely at Jude. "Well, we still have a lot to do before Gary gets here. Let's get back to work," I say, trying not to think about what I've gotten myself into.

And for what? Some guy who's a procrastinating 'twit.' But it's not really for him. It's for his presentation, for the company.

And I have to admit, this is the most fun I've had at work in a long time.

✻ 8 ✻

Jude was supposed to be here twenty minutes ago. We're going to see what Marvin has so far. I don't know why I'm needed. I'm pretty sure I've already paid my dues by agreeing to go to a ballgame with a freckled, microphone-headed, beady-eyed computer geek who's shaped somewhat like Barney the dinosaur and sweats excessively, which is not going to mix well with the summer sun beating down on the outfield bleachers at Wrigley Field. But you get what you pay for. And I think it's going to pay off. It had better, for Jude's sake.

I'm lingering at my desk in the mostly dark, totally empty office, putting off going down to the graphics suite. I don't want to be alone in a cramped, dark room with Marvin. I think it might not be safe, actually. And a girl can never be too careful.

It's eerie to be at work when no one else is. Due to a new company policy, everyone's computers are off, so there aren't even any screensavers blinking or scrolling or doing all the other things screensavers do. And it's amazing how much quieter it is when the PC fans aren't all whirring. For a second, I'm tempted to go over to Leslie's computer and turn it on so it looks like she broke the rules. But I don't move from where I'm standing. I don't want to chance Marvin hearing me move around out here. Until Jude arrives, I decide to lie low.

I know he's not here yet, because the door was locked when I got here, and I still have his key. I keep forgetting to give it to him.

I unclip it from my keychain and stare at it in my palm.

"What's this?" he asks as I offer it to him.

"A key to my London flat," I answer coyly.

His eyes mist over. "Oh, wow. This. Is. Big."

"I know," I start to get emotional, too, but I smile through my tears, then laugh as he wipes them from my cheeks.

"You're even gorgeous when you cry." He smiles, his white teeth gleaming. Ting! "But I have something for you that's even better." He goes down on one knee and holds a sparkling ring between his thumb and forefinger. Ting-ting! "Will you do me the honor of being my bride?"

All I can do is nod. I'm overcome by emotion. I've found someone who wants to be with me forever. Someone not from the feline family. I watch him slide the ring on my finger. Violins are playing. I lean down and take his face in my hands, kissing him. "You want to marry me?" I ask after a very long, intense kiss.

"I do."

"Wotcher got there?"

"Aggh!" I drop the key, and we both bend over at the same time to pick it up, resulting in our banging our heads together like two people in a predictable slapstick comedy.

He comes up with the key in one hand, his head in the other.

"Sorry," he says sheepishly.

"You scared the shit out of me," I gripe, rubbing my gourd.

"And you have a really hard head!" And I'm the one with the titanium plate in her head. I'm pretty sure I'm going to have a goose egg.

"Better than a soft one, I s'pose, which yours is definitely not, either," he mumbles, holding the key out to me. "Here; you dropped this."

"Really?"

"You don't have to be all snarky! I said I was sorry. I thought you heard me come in. It's not like I was quiet about it."

As I shake off the afterglow of my fantasy and get back into reality, I inform him, "I think that's your key."

"You're pulling my plonker." He holds up and inspects the piece of jagged metal, as if he's going to be able to recognize it on sight.

"I most certainly am not pulling your... whatever." I wrinkle my nose disgustedly, but mostly at myself for kind of liking the sound of that.

He takes in my expression, wrinkling his nose, too. "Ew. It doesn't mean whatever you obviously think it does."

"If you say so."

"I do."

I barely prevent myself from screaming at his echo of Fantasy Jude's exact words. I suck in a gasp, then choke on my own spit. While I sputter with my fist against my mouth, he thumps on my back. After I can talk again, I step away from him and wheeze, "You're late."

Even stranger than seeing the office empty is seeing him in casual clothes. He's wearing longish shorts that are frayed at the hem, but they look like the kind of shorts that you pay big money for them to look like you dug them out of the trash. He also has on a plaid button-up, short-sleeve shirt, unbuttoned, with a plain white t-shirt under it. And he's wearing flip-flops.

He looks like he worked really hard to look like a slob. The idea of him worrying about what to wear today comforts me for some reason.

Concentrating by sticking his tongue out of the corner of his mouth, he slides his key onto a ring that also holds his car and apartment keys. "Yeah. Sorry. Car troubles."

"Oh, you had to take the El?"

"No," he says, shaking his head, "but just about. I called the car club when I barely made it here. They're supposed to tow it to a garage and ring me." At the mention of his phone, he checks to make sure he hasn't missed any calls.

"Well, let's get this over with," I say, sighing. "I have better things to do today." It doesn't matter that it's a lie, as long as he believes it.

Seeming nervous suddenly, he shuffles his feet, putting one hand in his pocket, then the other. "O-okay."

"What's wrong?" I ask him, worried that he's about to deliver more bad news. Maybe Marvin already talked to him and demanded *two* dates with me. No, I refuse to call them dates. Although... then I'd get my "extra credit" from Dr. Marsh...

"Nothing," he quickly answers. "Not a thing. Where does this Marvin fellow hole himself up to do his best work?"

I keep him in my sight as I point the way. His twitchy behavior continues. He takes his keys from one pocket and switches them to the other, then pulls them out again.

"You're acting like a 'tard," I bluntly state.

"Charming. It's a wonder you don't have more friends," he drawls back.

His comment hurts more than I'd ever admit, especially to him. I start walking and snap, "That's not something I'd expect to hear from someone who owes me, big-time."

"I never asked you to take control of this... this... production," he claims.

"What?" I stop in the middle of a group of dark desks. "Are you an amnesiac? You were frantic, panicked, 'bricking' yourself, or whatever the hell you called it. And I rescued you from a crash-and-burn that hasn't been seen since the likes of the Hindenburg."

"'Oh, the humanity!'" he gasps, laughing.

"What the...?"

"I'm only joking!" he explains. "I know I owe you a lot. That's why—"

"Yo!" Marvin calls from down the hall. "What's taking you guys so long? Preparing to be amazed?"

I sigh and whisper loudly to him as we continue on, "Do you *really* understand the magnitude of my sacrifice?"

He scratches his nose. "Yes. I think I do. If I were a woman..."

"Which, coincidentally, there's a rumor going around that you are."

He laughs. "Great. Anyway, if I were you, I would be contemplating the pros and cons of doing something to put myself in traction sometime before next weekend."

"That's not a bad idea," I give him grudging credit. "Need another rugby teammate?"

"Or you could just tell the bloke that you don't fancy him and the game is strictly a platonic thing. That is," he rushes on in whisper, "I think he may be getting the wrong idea..."

Before I have a chance to respond to that ridiculous notion, we turn into the dark editing room, where Marvin's waiting for us. I'm starting to understand why he resembles a mole. Before my eyes can adjust to the dark, I move too close to Jude in the tiny room, my leg rubbing against his, which is warm and fuzzy and immediately conjures a vision of the two of us naked, tangled, and lazily kissing on a bed. I quickly step away and clear my throat to keep a hysterical giggle from bursting out.

As far as I can tell, Jude's not affected at all by the physical contact. He doesn't even glance at me. He's too focused on the computer screen in front of us. It's the size of a giant flat-panel TV and radiating enough heat to make it feel like it's toasting my already-blazing face.

"Are you ready for this?" Marvin asks dramatically.

My vocal cords wouldn't be able to work right now if I wanted them to.

Jude says, "Bring it," in an American accent scarily similar to the graphic artist's.

While I'm openly staring at Jude, Marvin presses the spacebar on his keyboard, starting the animation. I turn my attention to the screen. The video is designed to look like it's from the viewer's vantage point. We "walk" through a set of glass double doors and "look" to our right, through a huge wall of curved windows that look out onto a manicured garden. We look left, where the S-curved wall runs parallel to the windows. Paintings appear to hang suspended from the ceiling, supported by gossamer wires. Sculptures and statues rest on glass pedestals of varying heights, so it looks as if they're also floating in midair. We face forward again and begin to move. It feels like we're on a giant conveyor belt. Then the picture flickers and goes to black.

"Brilliant," Jude breathes.

"A whole lot better than your framed poster on an easel, dude," Marvin brags. "I still have a lot of work to do, but it'll be ready by Monday night's meeting."

The two of them discuss their other ideas for a few minutes; then Marvin turns around and flicks on a dim light, looking me up and down. I'm suddenly self-conscious in my little plaid shorts and V-necked t-shirt. I might as well be naked. "We're still on for next weekend, right?"

"Uh, sure. A deal's a deal." What I meant to sound cheerful actually comes out a little choked.

"You want me to pick you up?" he asks eagerly.

"Oh, uh, you don't have to do that," I fumble. "I mean, let's just meet there. I'll give you your ticket on Friday so you don't have to wait on me. I might be a little late." I'm making it up as I go along, hoping he won't press the issue. The last thing I need is for him to know where I live.

"Right on. But not too late, right? I mean, you'll get there before the first pitch?"

"Sure thing. Absolutely. I mean, I'll try. It's going to be close."

Jude pipes up, "Just tell him already."

I laugh nervously and blush, "What are you talking about?" I glance anxiously at Marvin. "It's cool. I'll see you there."

"Tell me what?"

"Nothing!" I whisper conspiratorially at Marvin, "I have no idea what he's talking about."

"If you don't tell him, I will," Jude insists.

What is he doing? It's so hot in here! "I don't need to tell him anything," I insist, letting out another nervous, barking laugh and fanning myself. To Marvin, I say disbelievingly, "What the fu—?"

"Here's the deal, Marv. Can I call you Marv?"

"No."

"Right. The thing is, Libby doesn't—"

"Jude!" I mean, the guy is gross, but it's just one afternoon, and I don't want to hurt his feelings.

"No, the bloke deserves to know why you're going to be late. It's nothing to be ashamed at."

I stand there with my mouth hanging open. Then I look

down at my sneaker-clad feet as if I'm embarrassed, but it's really to hide my smile.

Jude explains, "Libby doesn't have a proper sofa. And I told her I'd help her select a new one. But the earliest we can go is next Sunday. And the shops open later on Sunday, you see? So, we're going to try to squeeze in our shopping before the game."

"Why can't you do it the weekend after?" Marvin asks, obviously disgusted at the thought of something impinging on his "date" with me.

Jude shakes his head solemnly. "Oh, it's dire."

"Do it Saturday, then."

"No can do, Marv—in. Like I said, we've been over it a hundred times, and Sunday's the only day we can synchronize our schedules." He puts a hand on Marvin's shoulder, one man to another. "You understand, I'm sure."

"Not really."

"Well, we'll be there as soon as we can, hopefully before the first pitch. That's when the guy on the hill of dirt throws the ball at the bloke with the bat, right?" he consults me.

"Yeah," I say, picking up the thread. "Good job." To Marvin, I say, "I'm trying to teach Jude about baseball."

"I'm a bit thick, though, aren't I?"

"Totally," I agree.

"I keep getting baseball confused with cricket—"

"Wait a second! *He's* gonna be there, too?" Marvin stands up, dwarfing me and making even Jude look fairly short. There are sweat stains under his armpits, right at my eye level. I breathe through my mouth, just in case.

"You don't mind, do you?" Jude asks genially. "I figured it'd be okay, since it's just an outing amongst friends. Right?" He chuckles and says, "It's not as if it's a date, after all. Am I right?" He grins and nudges me, then Marvin as if the mere suggestion of it being a date is hilarious.

Marvin backs down. "Well, not really, no. I guess you're right." He looks fleetingly at me.

I smile what I hope is winningly. "I figured you'd appreciate having another guy there to share a beer with," I improvise, again trying to prevent hurting Marvin's feelings. Pointedly I say, "Jude doesn't really have any friends." And though it pains me to say it, I swallow my pride and add, "Plus, I'm sure you'll do a much better job of explaining the game to Jude. I kind of get distracted by the players' butts sometimes."

"Anyway..." Jude grabs my arm and pulls me out of Marvin's armpits. "Give me a ring tomorrow, if you want. I'll buy you a pint or something. I really appreciate this. You're a good bloke."

It isn't until we're standing at the elevators that he starts laughing. "Thanks for the 'Jude doesn't have any friends' comment. Nice."

"You deserved it. The 'players' butts' thing was too much, wasn't it?" I ask self-consciously.

He shakes his head. "Perhaps. But it was rather amusing to hear you say it."

We step into the compartment, and he pushes the button for the parking garage. I rest against the wall. "When did you decide to cook up that story?"

He shrugs. "I felt so badly for you! He was practically licking his lips at you whilst he sat there making his own gravy in that hot, close room. And you were trying so hard to be nice, since he's doing us such a huge favor..."

"You thought of that on the spot? The couch shopping, the baseball game, all of it?"

"Yeah. What do you think I do? Sit around all day thinking of ways to rescue you?"

I blush... again. "No!"

The elevator doors open. I step out and walk toward the place where I parked my car, but I stop short. He stops at the same time, pulling out his phone and gesturing exasperatedly.

"Oh, bollocks. They still haven't come to get my sodding car."

But I'm barely hearing him. I'm too busy looking at the empty parking space where my car was parked less than an hour ago. "Shit!"

He looks up. "What's the matter?

"Somebody stole my car!" I cry, feeling sick to my stomach. I walk to the now-empty spot. "It was right here!" I throw my hands up and put them on my head. Ouch. I'm getting a bruise where I knocked heads with him.

"You've got to be kidding me!" he utters sympathetically. "Are you sure?"

When I nod, he says, "Well, I'd offer you a ride, but..." He motions to his own car, sitting two rows over. "I don't think we'll get very far in mine. It was coughing a fair bit on my way here." He joins me in the parking space, careful not to step in the huge puddle of oil left by the thousands of cars that have temporarily resided here over the years. "I suppose you should call the police, right? I'm going to call the car club and ask them what's taking so long for them to come get mine."

"I can't believe this," I mutter, trying to decide whether to call information for the nearest police station or to just dial 911.

My mind's racing. What am I going to do without my car? Ride the El? The bus? Yuck! Following a train or bus schedule is a real pain in the butt. I like going where I want to go, directly, non-stop. By myself. Riding along with strangers, especially the weird ones, breathing my air, invading my space, makes me feel claustrophobic.

"No, you haven't. I'm looking straight at it right now. ... Madame, I think I know what my own bloody car looks like.... What? ... No, I'm not hurt! I'm English; that's how I express displeasure.... It's a bit shocking, actually, that you think you have my car but don't." He gives me a look that says, *Can you believe this chick?* (or probably more like *bird*, knowing him).

She says something, to which he replies, "Well, then whose car did you pick up? Because it wasn't mine. I'm positive!"

Hope shines through my despair. "Ooh! Maybe they took my car by mistake!" I say loudly to him.

He shakes his head dismissively at first but then seems to think better of it. "Hang on, Miss.... Yes, I know I'm a rude foreigner. Hold that thought. Do you know the number plate of the car you claim to have towed?" He waits while she looks up the information.

I tell him mine: "762-PLO."

His eyes widen, and he nods at me. I hop joyously.

"I think I know what happened," he tells the customer service rep. After he explains the mix-up and goes back to being a "rude foreigner," chastising the car club for not being more detail-oriented, he hangs up. "They're returning your car and taking mine. Supposedly. I don't know why we didn't think of that to begin with."

"Well, you expect them to check license plate numbers before towing off a car, no matter how sure they think they are that they have the right one."

"True."

I walk over to a low concrete wall and sit down to wait for my car to be delivered. After offering to wait with me, he joins me. While we sit shoulder to shoulder, I think about next weekend's baseball game with him and Marvin. I'm trying to picture the three of us in the bleachers, behind the ivy-covered wall. In my head, I'm sitting between the two of them. Wedged, more like. Marvin's dripping relish and mustard from his hot dog onto my head.

"P-L-O?"

"Huh?" I ask thickly.

"Your number plate. That's funny. Easy to remember, but still."

"What's yours?" I ask, suddenly feeling irrationally defensive on behalf of a stupid sheet of metal. I can't see his plate from the angle at which we're sitting to the car.

He closes one eye as he thinks about it. "Uh, let's see. 925-CIA. So, you're in a fair bit of trouble."

"Whatever. You're a dork." I nudge him with my shoulder to let him know I'm kidding.

His laugh trails off with an "Aaah." Then he says, "So…"

"Soooo," I mimic, dragging it out, making it sound like "sue."

"Whilst we're waiting…"

"Yes?" I affect a British accent and flutter my eyelashes 'whilst' I look down my nose at him.

He laughs, but the nervousness is back. "Uh… huh-huh. You looked a bit like my first form teacher just then."

"Yeesh. Sorry."

"No, no. She was totty." At my questioning look, he assures me, "That's a good thing." He blushes. "I digress. Uh… what I was going to say was… I know it's short notice, but… tonight, I—" He stops and laughs. "I'm sorry. Your face… you look terrified suddenly. Are you okay?"

With massive effort, I manage to smile and duck my head, in case the smile came out looking more like a grimace. "Sorry. I'm a little afraid of what you're about to say."

"Right." He pauses. "Why?"

I honestly don't know, so what am I supposed to tell him? I simply shake my head, horrified that I suddenly feel like crying. I'm incredibly frustrated by my inability to have a normal interaction with a man. I keep my head down and concentrate on keeping my voice steady as I say, "You're just being so serious all of a sudden. It's freaking me out."

"Oh. Right. Well, I'll try to be less serious, I suppose." He takes a deep breath but doesn't say anything until, "Now I'm frightened of why you may be frightened."

Confident that there's no evidence of my earlier rogue emotions, I look up at him and try to smile encouragingly. "No, don't be. I'm sorry. I'm weird. Just ignore me."

Shooting me a look that communicates he's unsure of my sanity, he nevertheless says, "Well, what I've been trying to say for about an age is... I have tickets to a concert tonight. A good one. And I was wondering..."

"Who is it?" I ask bluntly, trying to keep it light.

"Come again? Oh. Right. Snow Patrol. I bought the tickets yonks ago."

"Who were you originally going to take?"

He blushes. "I hadn't gotten that far yet."

Coolly, I confirm, "You bought two tickets to a concert that's tonight, and you're just now getting around to asking someone?"

Without answering me, he eagerly asks, "Do you like them? Because if you don't want to go, I'll completely understand. I waited too long to ask you, perhaps."

Part of me wants to pretend I might have to cancel some other plans to go with him, but I dislike playing those kinds of games. And I do like the band. Plus who am I kidding? The only thing I have planned is daydreaming about Fantasy Jude and watching Sandberg chase a laser pointer on the floor.

Of course, I won't be able to count this as a date in my assignment for Dr. Marsh. Dr. Marsh can't know about this at all. That almost makes it more attractive.

He takes my silence as hesitation based on disinterest. "Never mind." He waves his hand dismissively. "You're right. It's too short notice. I've simply been so busy, I almost forgot about them. And I thought I'd surely have someone to take by now, be it a friend or… someone else."

"Oh, so I'm a last resort?" I say lightly. "You just don't have anyone else to go with you?"

He blushes furiously. "Oh, no, that's not it at all. Believe me!" Looking down at his feet, he despairs. "I've made a real arse of myself. I'm sorry."

I can't stand to watch his torture any more. "Jude, it's okay. I was kidding. It actually sounds really fun."

His shoulders relax, but he still avoids my eyes. "Are you sure you don't have something else going?"

"No, I'm free," I tell him. "My social calendar is wide open."

He smiles and squints over at me. "Yeah. Same here."

I stare at his mouth as if it's made of metal and my eyes are magnets. I can't stop wondering what it would be like if he leaned over and kissed me. It would happen… in a movie. And it would be mind-blowing. The parking garage would suddenly smell like freesias, not hot garbage. Music would play (something heavy on the violins). And when we finally pulled apart, he would say something romantic, something along the lines of, "I've been waiting so long for someone like you," or I'd even settle for something a little more gauche, like, "You're an excellent kisser." And neither one of us would be worried about feeling uncomfortable around each other at work.

Already, just because I'm staring at him, I'm thinking about how awkward I'm starting to feel around him. But I can't stop staring. And he's staring back. Of course, I probably have a big zit or a booger hanging from my nose. But at least he's looking at my face and not some region slightly lower than my neck, where guys' gazes usually come to rest.

Our attentions are pulled away from each other by the tow truck pulling into the garage, my car dangling from the back of it.

"Finally!" he exclaims, hopping to his feet. "So, I'll see you tonight?"

We discuss the details, and I pretend I've gone to hundreds of concerts with guys before, but the truth is, I'm anxious to get home so I can do some research on the Internet about where we're going, where Jude lives, and how long it's going to take to get from A to B to C.

When my car is free, I offer him a ride home (it would really help my nerves to know before tonight where I'm going), but he says he has a few things to do before heading home (I try not to think too much about what that means), and that it'd be easier for him to walk or take the bus.

So I get in my car, slamming the door and leaning down to put the keys in the ignition. Ryno bobbles away on the dashboard. Except it looks like he's shaking his head disapprovingly. If it was a Shawon Dunston bobblehead, it'd look remarkably like Dr. Marsh.

9

EVEN AFTER AN EXTRA SESSION OF SELF-AFFIRMATION WITH THE mirror, I still feel pretty shaky about my evening with Jude. I've mapped my routes, and they're fairly easy, so I won't be distracted and stressed out about the driving part, anyway. Just everything else. Why did I agree to do this? There's a *Myth Busters* marathon on tonight. I could have just stayed home with Sandberg and watched that. But no. I had to get all self-confident and accept the invitation of the hottest guy to ever give me a second glance.

Invitation to what? That's probably the detail that's bothering me the most. I mean, is this a date? Probably not, considering he asked me on a whim when he didn't have anyone else to ask. So, it's a platonic thing. Okay. Well, that's not much comfort, since I don't have friends, either. What does one wear? How does one act? What are we going to talk about in the car or in the line as we wait to get in? Will we go somewhere else after the show? Is it okay for me to sing along with the songs, or is that dorky? At least we won't have to talk much during the show, since it'll be loud. I at least know that much about rock concerts.

I try to imagine what it'd be like to go to a concert with Fantasy Jude, but he's more of a symphony/opera kind of guy. I can't picture him rocking out.

But aside from all those annoying, nerve-wracking insecurities, I'm pretty excited about going. It's a group I always sing along with on the radio. I'm not a mega-fan, though, so I don't have a band t-shirt I can wear. I settle on a fresh t-shirt but the same plaid shorts I've been wearing all day. I don't want to look like I'm trying too hard.

At six-thirty, I'm on the verge of throwing up as I stand at my door, making sure I haven't forgotten anything. Sandberg blinks calmly at me from the bed.

"Okay, I'm going," I tell him. "No parties while I'm gone. I won't be late." I pull the door closed and lock it.

Just as I'm getting into my car, concentrating on not hyperventilating, my cell phone rings and vibrates in my pocket, scaring me. "Oh, gosh!" I slide it out, closing my eyes as I hold it to my ear. I see on the display that it's Hank, calling from Florida.

"Hey, sis," he greets me. I hear music and laughter in the background.

"Hi," I reply, trying to moderate my breathing. "What's up?"

"Not much. Whatcha doin'? Watchin' TV?"

"Something like that," I answer, not wanting him to know the truth. I don't want to answer a billion questions about it. I know he doesn't really care, anyway. He only calls for one thing.

"Cool. Hey, I was just wondering…"

"How much?" I know where this is going.

"Just a coupla hundred, to get me through until payday," he answers nonchalantly. When I tell him I'll go the ATM in the morning and wire the money to him then, he hesitates before saying, "Oh. I was kinda hopin' you'd be able to get it to me tonight. Are you busy?"

"I can't do it tonight."

"Why not?"

That's the problem with having no life and setting a precedent that you can drop everything (because "everything" is "nothing") and cater to someone's impulses at a moment's notice: when you suddenly can't, you have to explain yourself.

"I just can't, okay?" I snap. "If it's an emergency, use the credit card, and I'll pay it off with your money when I get the statement."

Grudgingly, he says, "Naw. It's not that important. I was just... me and the guys were goin' out tonight, that's all."

"Maybe someone can spot you some singles to stuff into the stripper's G-string," I can't help but snipe.

"God, Libby! Excuse me for askin'! Sheesh."

I start the car. "Anything else?"

"Yeah. Maybe you should get laid. Would do wonders for your attitude."

"I'm sure you get laid enough for the both of us, Hank."

"Screw you."

"No, screw you!"

"I bet Mom and Dad would be real happy to see what a miserable, dried-up old cooter you've become."

I hang up the phone with shaking fingers. "Nice," I say out loud, trying to shake off his comment. Well, vocabulary never has been his strong suit. I toss my phone into one of the car's cup holders. I will not cry, I will not cry, I will not cry.

I repeat this to myself the entire drive to Jude's. He's waiting for me on the steps in front of his apartment building, adding evidence to my suspicions that he's a slob and doesn't want me to see the inside of his place. He's wearing the exact same thing he was wearing earlier. I'm glad I didn't change into anything special. I would have felt pathetic.

After he slides into the car, he smiles at me. "Hey. How's it going?"

Still stung from the conversation with my brother, I nevertheless swallow and attempt a smile. "Okay. You?"

"Brilliant, thanks."

I pull onto the street to take us away from his building. After navigating a maze of one-way streets to get out of his neighborhood, I feel confident enough to talk without betraying my mood. "Have you heard anything about your car?" I ask, thinking that will be a safe topic.

"Yeah. But I'm useless when it comes to those sorts of things. I only know they have to order a part, and it'll take at least until Wednesday for them to do the repair. But it's under warranty, so I won't have any out-of-pocket expense."

"That's good," I say, concentrating on the other cars as I merge aggressively onto the expressway and cut around the slowpoke in front of me. In my peripheral vision, I see Jude shift in his seat and slowly wrap his hand around the door handle.

I ease off the gas. A little. And I resist the urge to pass the next few cars, because it would require me to cut off some other ones. Normally, I wouldn't hesitate, but I have a feeling my passenger's not enjoying the ride.

"Anyway," he says after a while, "I hear these guys are fantastic in concert. That's why I jumped on the tickets when I found out they were coming to town."

"What were you going to do if you couldn't find anyone to go with you?" I ask what I've been wondering all afternoon.

He stomps on an imaginary brake in his floorboard as I come up quickly on the back of the truck in front of us.

"Aaahhh… I dunno. I s'pose I would have gone by myself. Or not gone at all."

"You'd have let the tickets go to waste? You could have at least scalped 'em," I suggest.

Looking over at me, he says carefully, "That's illegal, though, right?"

"Yeah? So what? People do it all the time."

He chuckles. "Well, not foreign people living here on a work visa. If I got caught, I'd be deported."

"Doubt it," I say. "But whatever. I guess it doesn't matter."

"Right." After another close call with a car, he asks, "Do you often break the law?"

I laugh. "No! Never!" At his silence, I reconsider. "Well… I guess I do a bit of the time when I'm driving—"

"That's sort of what I was getting at."

"Am I making you nervous?" I tease.

"Very."

While I'm amused, I'm not cruel. I make a conscious effort to drive less aggressively.

He explains, "Part of it is that I'm still not used to sitting on this side of the car and not driving. And I'm constantly worried I'm driving on the wrong side of the road. Plus," he adds, "I didn't drive much at all before coming here. Still avoid it whenever possible."

"I like to drive," I state, but it sounds more like a dirty confession.

"I can tell."

"My dad taught me how." The sentence is out before I even realize I'm going to say it.

Jude loosens his grip on the handle now that we haven't had any close calls for a few minutes. "Oh? Is he a Formula One driver?"

I smile at the idea. "No. He tried to teach me to be very cautious."

"So… what? After you were no longer under supervision, you went rogue? A bit of a rebel, are you?"

I don't want to talk about this, I realize. "Not exactly. But you have to die of something…" My tone effectively shuts down the conversation. All conversation. We drive in silence for a while.

Soon, the stadium looms ahead of us, and I position us to exit the highway.

We park, walk to the gates, and take our place in the line. Jude pulls the tickets from his back pocket, inspecting them. We determine we're in the wrong line for the section where our seats are and go to the back of the correct line.

After we've been standing there a while, not touching, not talking, he says, "I believe these are good seats; at least I thought they were when I bought the tickets."

The guy in front of him turns around and cranes his neck to read the ticket. "Dude, those are excellent. Trade ya."

"Ah, no thanks," Jude answers, taking him seriously.

"I was just kiddin' anyway, man. Don't get all worried. There's really not a bad seat in this place. You've never been here before?"

Jude consults me. I shake my head, even though I hate admitting that I've lived in the area my whole life, and this is the first time I've set foot in Soldier Field. For anything. Much less something as cool as a concert.

"No," he answers for both of us. "First time. Soldier Field virgins, both of us."

I avert my face and stare at my shoes, trying not to squirm too much. The line starts moving, funneling us through security and into the stadium. Soon we're working together to find our seats, but the signs are clear, so it's not difficult. Before long we're sitting and waiting for the opening act, a group neither of us has ever heard of, to come out.

He taps his fingers on his knee. I glance at him shyly. He looks down quickly. Then we both look up at each other at the same time and laugh nervously.

"This is a bit odd," he states matter-of-factly.

"A little," I agree. "We're really early. I overestimated how long it would take to get here. Sorry." Really, I wasn't expecting Jude to shell out so much money to park as close to the stadium as we did. I'd figured in at least a mile walk from the car.

"Oh. No worries."

More finger tapping.

I look around at all the people filing in. The crowd is going to be massive. But it still feels like Jude and I are alone. Very alone. And very awkward.

In LFW, I'd know exactly what to say and how to act. More importantly, Fantasy Jude would know what to say.

"You look lovely this evening."

"Oh, this? Just a t-shirt and shorts?"

"Yes. Well, I must admit, it's more clothing than I'd prefer, but since we're in public and all..."

"You're incorrigible."

"I know. And you love it."

"Of course."

I fan myself with my hand.

"It's been rather hot lately, hasn't it?"

"Huh? Oh! The weather. Yeah."

"Is it always this hot here in the summer?"

"No. This is freaky hot." *Like you.* I wish I were the type of person who could pull off saying something like that. But... maybe not. I mean, do guys really like stuff like that? Leslie seems to think so. And I don't ever want to say anything remotely resembling something she would say.

Not for the first time, I get the paranoid feeling that he can read my mind as he looks over my head, a private smile on his face. Then he changes the subject. "You mentioned your father earlier. Do your mum and dad live nearby still?"

I'm saved from answering by the opening band, who's revving up. It's deafening. We stand with the rest of the crowd and cheer, even though we have no idea who they are. Jude inserts his pinkie and forefinger into his mouth and lets rip an ear-splitting whistle. My eyes widen. He wipes his fingers on his shorts.

"Sorry," he mouths.

The look on his face is so comically sheepish that I crack up. He relaxes and grins, putting his arm casually around my shoulders. We hop up and down, like all the people around us are doing, to the beat of the music.

Although I didn't recognize the name of the group, one of their songs has been featured heavily on the radio and in a car commercial, so I know the words and sing along without even thinking about whether or not I should. The band does their job, loosening everyone up, lowering our inhibitions as they encourage us to participate and dance with each other, whether we're total strangers to each other or co-workers who may as well be.

At the end of their act, Jude turns to me. "Programs. Would you like one?"

I shrug. "Should I?"

My response seems to puzzle him. "Uh... Hmm... I don't know how to answer that." He laughs.

The heat from my face could incubate a hatchery. "It's just that"—I try to explain my seemingly inexplicable answer —"I've... never..." I sigh and look away from him as I make my confession. "This is the first concert I've ever been to. So I don't know if it's worth it to get a program. I've never done this before."

He stands up and holds out his hand, wiggling his fingers at me. "In that case, the answer is 'yes.' It's mandatory that you have a program commemorating your very first rock concert."

Uncertainly, I take his hand. It's warm and dry. I stare at our two hands for seconds that seem like an hour. I feel disconnected from my body as I try to remember the last time I held anyone's hand. It saddens me when I can't recall. It was probably the hand of one of my parents, as we were crossing a street when I was a little kid.

Jude pulls me to my feet. "Right. I think I saw a stand right this side of the security check." He lets go of me when he sees me still gazing at our linked hands.

I smile nervously up at him, hoping I didn't offend him. "Okay. Let's go, then."

It takes a good thirty minutes to weave through the crowd, stand in line, and get back to our seats. By the time I've had a chance to do a cursory flip through the little booklet, the lights are dimming, some music starts playing, and the crowd goes crazy. The guy behind me grabs my shoulders and shakes them, even though I've never seen him before in my life. Jude turns around and says, "Oi!" good-naturedly, but I laugh to show that I don't mind. I'm pretty excited too, and can understand the guy's enthusiasm.

The band runs out onto the stage, waving before taking their positions at their instruments and microphones. The lead singer yells, "How's it goin', Chicago?!" in the sexiest Irish brogue I've ever heard, stirring up the kind of scream-fest that makes my hearing distort.

The first song they perform is fairly slow, which I think is an interesting choice, but I guess it gets everyone's attention. I'm not familiar with it, so I listen intently to the lyrics. And I'm a little shaken by how much I can relate to them. Of course, that's what makes a song good, right, that pretty much everyone can find some way to relate to it? But it's still a little spooky, like the lead singer's singing directly to me. When he softly sings the final words, the crowd goes ballistic, screaming, clapping, whistling, and—in some of the girls' cases—crying. I stand there, processing the song.

Jude nudges me. "ARE YOU OKAY?" he shouts, leaning down closer to my ear.

I nod, pasting what I hope is a sincere-looking smile on my face. Then the next song (a fast, catchy number) starts, and the moment passes. None of the other songs take me by surprise. I actually know more of them than I'd expected I would. Jude and I sing and clap along unselfconsciously to the faster songs, even when they're clearly about love or—more often—sex (or is that just where my mind is?). We simply let loose and have a good time.

It's something I've never done before, and I can see now how it could be addictive.

10

In addition to the over-priced program, I walk away from the concert with two t-shirts, ringing ears, and a huge crush on the entire band. And I don't want the night to end... ever.

So I'm relieved when Jude says (shouts) in the car, "I'm starving. Let's go to this great gastropub in my neighborhood. It's open late."

"A what?"

"Gastropub. You know, a pub that serves food."

I shake my head. "Okay, I think you're making these things up now and pretending they're your funny British words. And then when I'm convinced they're real words, you're going to laugh at me if I use them."

He narrows his eyes at me playfully. "Take the piss all you want."

"Maybe when we get to the 'gastropub,'" I say. I guess I just agreed to go.

We park at his apartment, in his temporarily empty reserved spot, and walk the three blocks to the bar. Before we find a seat, Jude walks straight up to the bar, where he talks to the bartender for a while, after introducing me. Their easy conversation makes it clear that Jude's a regular.

"Come here often?" I ask, as we walk to a table with our first round of drinks.

His rejoinder, "Is that a pick-up line or a question?" makes me laugh and blush.

I eventually answer as I slide into my side of the booth, "Just a question," but the real answer is, "Both."

He twirls the cardboard coaster in front of him. "I'm not much of a cook. I come here to feel a little less… lonely."

There's that word again.

I just nod, afraid of talking and admitting how lonely I am, too. Then I say, "But it's good that you're not homesick for England."

"What gave you that idea?" he asks, raising a thick eyebrow. "Most of the time, I feel like a Billy No Mates in this town. I'm terribly homesick."

I cock my head. "But you said…" Oh. No. Not again. "Never mind," I quickly amend.

"What?" he presses. "What did I say?"

"I'm getting you confused with someone else." I hide my face in my glass.

Wryly, he asks, "Hanging out with lots of Limeys lately?"

Our server comes over and takes our orders. By the time she's gone, Jude's forgotten his earlier question and has mercifully moved on.

He takes a huge gulp of his dark beer and says, "Anyway, I'm at sixes and sevens lately. I like my job, and I *want* to like this city, but I feel so out of place here."

"Maybe someone at the embassy can suggest a support group for you," I offer. "You know, made up of people like you who have relocated to the States. It would probably help a lot just to hear someone who talks like you… and understands what you're saying when you say things like 'Billy No Mates.'"

"Friendless loser."

At first, I think he's calling *me* that; then I realize he's defining his earlier statement. "Yeah, I got that from the context of what you said earlier. It was just an example."

"Actually, that's a really good idea," he says slowly. "I know I'll get used to it over here eventually, but it'd help if I had someone to talk to." He looks up at me for the first time in several minutes. "Like this. This is nice. Even though I'm being a whinger and you'll probably never want to go anywhere with me again."

I wish. Wouldn't that make things simpler? Wouldn't it be great if I could say, "This really sucked," and go back to my life as I knew it before? But the thought of going back makes me want to cry. And my advice to him may result in that. Once he gets some real friends, why would he ever want to hang out with me?

I know he's looking for some kind of reassurance, though, so I say, "It's okay. We all have our moments."

"Mine's over," he promises. "Let's talk about something else. Not work, and definitely not exes. Movies. That's safe enough. What's your favorite?"

I perk up. Movies are one of my passions. "Well, I know your favorite is *Casablanca*, but I really love—"

"*Casablanca?* When did I ever say that?" he sputters, wiping beer foam from his upper lip. "Blimey! That's not a bloke's movie at all!"

Quickly, I cover, "I could have sworn you mentioned that before..."

"No! Never. We've never even had this conversation."

"I know that!" I quickly reply. "I just thought you said it in passing."

"How would that come up? I hand you a drawing to put in the post and say, 'Here's lookin' at you, kid. By the way, *Casablanca* is my favorite movie of all time, because I'm an insufferable wanker'?"

I laugh to cover my embarrassment. "Sorry. Simple mistake!"

He glares skeptically at me but lets it go. "I interrupted you. You were saying your favorite movie is…"

"No. You go first." I need a second to compose myself.

"*Psycho.*"

Again I think he's name-calling, but when I realize he's answering the question, I'm even more disappointed. "Really? *Pyscho*? Of all the movies ever made, *that's* your favorite? What about *The Great Gatsby* or… or… *The Godfather* or…?"

"What's your favorite, then, Miss Clever Clogs?"

"*The Natural,*" I answer promptly.

"A Redford fan, then?"

"What about it?" I challenge him defensively. "He's a great actor. And it's a great movie."

"It's about baseball," he complains, pulling a face.

"Only the greatest sport ever invented."

"I beg to differ."

"Of course you do, Mr. Rugby."

Our food arrives, but as soon as the server is gone, he picks up the conversational thread seamlessly. "For your information, I don't think rugby is the best sport ever invented. But"—he points at me with his fork—"it's ten times better than bloody baseball."

"You're crazy."

"Like a fox." Suddenly, he dissolves into laughter.

"You're just saying all this to push my buttons," I finally realize.

He takes another bite, swallows, and grins. "For someone so smart, you can be really thick sometimes."

Keeping my eyes on my plate, I reply, "Thanks and ouch."

"You're so easily excitable. It's hilarious."

"Glad to be entertaining."

"Oops. There goes the wall."

I glance up at him. "What?"

"I've gone too far; you've put up the wall." He raises his flat hand in front of his face. "The Great Wall of Libby," he intones ominously.

"Whatever." He thinks he's so smart, like he knows me.

"Don't be angry at me. I'm sorry." But he's still grinning. "I'm just taking the piss. Having a little fun."

"At my expense."

"Yes. You're right. It's not very nice."

He finishes his food and leans back in his side of the booth with his beer, which he drains in two long, smooth gulps. I watch his Adam's apple bob once, twice. Pushing my plate away, I put my chin in my hand. Then I signal to our server to bring us two more drinks.

A couple of hours later, at closing time, I'm feeling no pain. And Jude's giggly and silly, at best; drunk at worst. We've discussed every superficial subject two people can touch on and have had several good-natured arguments about music, books, and movies.

As we walk back to his apartment and my car, he says, "I know you like to drive dangerously, but you're not going to attempt driving home like this, are you?"

"I told my cat I'd be home tonight," I say truthfully, making both of us laugh so hard we have to stop walking and support each other on the sidewalk.

When we can move again, he says, "Seriously, let me call you a cab."

"I'll be okay in a few minutes," I insist, not quite sure that's true. If worse comes to worst, I decide I can sleep it off in my car for a few hours. "I just need some water. Or coffee. Or something." It's hard to talk when your teeth are numb, I've discovered tonight.

"You're slurring your words, Libby," he points out.

"Remember when you called me 'Lisa'? That made me so mad!"

We laugh about that for a while, too.

At my car, he says, "I really can't let you drive home like this. I'd feel terrible if something happened to you."

"I wouldn't," I blurt.

"You don't know what you're saying," he says, smiling. "In any case, you're a menace to other drivers when you're sober; I can only imagine how you'd drive now."

"Whatever."

"Whatever," he mimics. "Come upstairs for a minute. I'll pump you full of fluids and send you on your way."

"I like the sound of that."

"Saucy minx!"

I have no control over my mouth. And I don't care. It's not like I've never been drunk before (give me a *little* credit), but I've always been alone. No chance for embarrassment there, until it comes time to admit to someone that you often get drunk alone. Sandberg's not spilling any of my dirty secrets. I'm probably going to be mortified—and sick—in the morning, but right now, it's fun to let myself go for once.

While he unlocks his door, I lean against the wall, which doesn't really feel like it's completely upright. Just as I'm sliding backwards, toward the stairs, he grabs my arm. "Oi! You *are* sozzled. In you go!" He pulls me into the apartment.

Once I get my bearings, I observe aloud, "Whoa, it's clean in here!"

"You expected a pigsty?"

"Like your car," I say, in defense.

"Well, I guess I should admit that I did a little clearing up this afternoon. It's not usually *this* clean. But I'm not a complete scruff. I manage to keep my manky pants and socks off the floor." He helps me sit on the couch.

I grab a throw pillow that has the Union Jack on it. "Nice pillow."

"A little bit of home." He holds up the other one. It's white with a narrow red cross on it. "Flag of England. St. George's Cross."

"Cool," I breathe. On a whim, I hit him softly across the face with the Union Jack pillow.

He blinks for a second, then, without hesitation, hits me over the head with his pillow. Harder than I hit him, I think.

We go back and forth like that until we're swinging away with abandon, hitting each other in the face, chest, shoulders, and back. At first, we're laughing, but as the blows get harder, all we're doing is grunting. I've never had a pillow fight with Fantasy Jude. I think he's probably too refined for that. I can't even imagine it. But this is a blast.

He stops first, so I get in an undefended strike before he grabs the pillow, wrenches it from my relatively weak grasp, and tosses it aside. His hair is mussed in a most sexy way. I'm sure mine just looks mussed. I tuck a strand behind my ear.

During the pillow fight, I've sobered up a fraction. Not much, but enough that I'm more aware of my surroundings. And how Jude's looking at me. Or more accurately, how he's looking at my mouth. He leans forward slightly, so slightly that I'm not really sure if it's true or if my drunkenness is making my eyes play tricks on me.

"I'm a virgin," I reveal oh-so-unsubtly. I don't shout it, but I don't say it quietly, either (my ears are still sort of ringing from the concert). In any case, there's no mistaking what I've said.

He looks completely sober now. Then again, I still feel like I'm wearing goggles made of wavy block glass, so it's hard for me to read his expression.

"That's... Well... Bully for you," he murmurs, standing up and putting as much distance between us as he can in the narrow living room.

I'd definitely be more self-conscious about my confession if my blood-alcohol level was anything below point-one-oh. But right now I'm treating it as if I've just told him, "I've never seen *Psycho.*"

Matter-of-factly, I continue, "I know, it's kind of weird. I'm twenty-eight. But the situation has never presented itself."

"That's difficult to believe," he says, turning his back on me. He tinkers with something on his fireplace mantle.

"You don't believe me?" I ask.

Quickly he answers, "No, no. I believe you. That's not what I meant." Suddenly, he puts down the object he's been fingering (a metal tourist trinket of the Sears Tower) and crosses to a closet. "Uh... I'll make up a bed for you on the sofa."

Stung, I stand up. And fall back on the couch. And stand up again. "Well, I wasn't implying that you should know because you were about to... *de-flower* me."

"You need to sleep it off," he merely replies, not defending his intentions at all.

"Never mind. I'm going home."

"No, you're not. You're pissed."

"Damn right, I'm pissed! Everything was fine until I told you I've never had sex. Then you got all weird. Like I'm a freak."

"Drunk. You're drunk. And now's not the time to have this conversation." He unfurls a blanket and drapes it over the couch. "Please. We can talk about it tomorrow, right? When you're clear-headed."

It's amazing how sobering mortification is. If only it could be sold over-the-counter for its instant effects. "I'm sober now, unfortunately," I insist.

I pat my pockets to make sure I have everything, that nothing has fallen out during our pillow fight. Then I head for the door. He blocks my way.

"Move!" I demand.

"I... I don't want you to go," he states quietly.

I think I know what he means, and it makes my heart race, but I'm too proud to stay, so I obtusely reply, "I'm fine. Really. I won't hurt myself or anyone else; you won't have that on your head."

I side-step him. He lets me go.

But I don't get far. Because when I get down to my car, I'm greeted by the sight of a bright orange traffic enforcement boot on its back driver's-side tire.

11

I EXPERIENCE PLENTY OF FIRSTS WHEN I WAKE UP THIS
morning.

1. Waking up in a man's apartment.
2. Waking up to see a man openly staring at me.
3. Waking up in the presence of a man, period.

I sit up gingerly, evaluating just how bad my hangover is.
Not as bad as I'd imagined it would be. My head only *feels* like
it's going to explode, not that it already has. And I'm less stiff
than I would expect after sleeping on a couch all night. It's a
fairly nice couch, after all.

From his stance in the kitchen, Jude asks casually, "Would
you like some coffee?"

I nod and wince at the pain it produces. "Oh... You
wouldn't happen to have some pain reliever, would you?"

He brings me a cup of coffee and drops two ibuprofen
tablets in my upturned palm. I ignore my screaming liver and
down them.

To my annoyance, he doesn't look hung over at all. Just to be sure, though, I ask, "How drunk were *you* last night?"

He shrugs. "Not. Squiffy, at the most."

I'd roll my eyes at his incomprehensible terminology, but it would hurt too much. Instead, I infer that he means "tipsy," and say, "So you remember... everything?"

He half-smiles. "Uh, yeah. Do you need help remembering?"

"Unfortunately, no," I answer, sliding my feet into my shoes. The shades are mercifully drawn shut in the room, but I can see the sun peeking around the edges. It's going to hurt like hell to walk out there. I hope I have a pair of sunglasses in my car that I can snag before walking to the nearest bus station.

The gracious host has a never-been-opened toothbrush he lets me use. After I spit and rinse, I chance a glance at myself in the medicine cabinet mirror. Bad idea. "You look like ass," I whisper to myself. Obviously, that won't be going onto the list that goes to Dr. Marsh. Before I can overthink it as gross or inappropriate, I take Jude's comb and run it through my flyaway hair. Now I have bloodshot eyes, sallow skin, an upset stomach, and a lot of regrets. But my hair looks sleek. And my breath is minty fresh.

As I emerge from the bathroom, I decide to confront what we're both thinking about. "Sorry about the TMI last night. I was really drunk."

"I know," he replies. "No worries."

I laugh mirthlessly so he knows I feel exactly the opposite. "I wish."

"About that," he begins.

"Please," I beg. "No. Let's not. Talk about it, that is." Then I blush at how that sounds. "I mean, let's just drop it. Period."

He looks down into his coffee cup. "Right."

"Thank you."

I go to the door, unlock it, and open it. With my hand on the doorknob, I say, "And thanks for last night. Mostly it was fun."

He comes around the counter and approaches me. I open the door wider, stepping through it so that I'm standing out in the hallway with easy access to the stairs.

"Right. Well, sorry about the parking ticket mix-up. I'll take care of that first thing tomorrow, when the parking authority opens."

He goes on to explain, now that I'm sober enough to understand (and care), that he and the neighborhood parking enforcement officer "have a bit of a feud running." He claims she tickets him for the "most minor of infractions. This time, I suppose it was because you'd parked slightly over the line separating my space from the one beside it. She must have mistaken your car for mine."

"Give me a break. Nobody gets booted for that."

"I don't think the boot was for that particular offense." He rubs the back of his neck. "It may be that... Well, let's just say I haven't quite gotten around to paying all of those other tickets. In fact, I've been meaning to contest them, considering some are a blatant abuse of her power." He attempts a justified chin-lift, but his sheepish expression gives away his guilt.

I sigh and roll my eyes at him, irritated that I'm caught between him and some meter maid on a power trip. Not to mention it's getting extremely old dealing with the inconveniences that keep sprouting up related to the great misfortune of driving a vehicle virtually identical to his.

And the arrogance of him, not paying the tickets! He probably thought he'd charm his way out of them with his plummy accent. Cheeky bastard.

But I can't summon the infuriation this situation would

normally induce, because I'm too worried about the much bigger pachyderm practically prancing around the room.

As if reading my mind, he says, "Libby... I hope you won't feel uncomfortable around me now. Because of what you told me."

I laugh nervously. "Well, I think that's unavoidable. Sorry."

He looks deflated. "Oh. It's only that... I hoped you wouldn't think so little of me that you'd think I'd think differently about you because of... that."

"I *thought* we weren't going to talk about this." I fish my car keys out of my pocket. When I glance up at him again, he looks so sad that I take pity on him. "Listen, forget about it. Really. Please. You're the only other person in the world who knows that. So I'd appreciate it if you kept it to yourself."

Nodding once and briskly, he says, "Of course. You don't even have to ask."

"Just making sure." With that, I turn and limp stiffly down the stairs, marveling at how I haven't been completely desensitized to humiliation in the past eight hours.

Other than when I wire the money to Hank, I spend the rest of Sunday in bed, listening to Snow Patrol on a continuous loop. Fantasy Jude tries to cheer me up, but not even I can reconcile the reality of my predicament with the ideal of him.

Sandberg gave me the cold shoulder for the first hour after I got home. I gave him a few extra treats, though, and that seemed to placate him. I also told him, "I would have rather been here with you, buddy, believe me." Who cares that it's a lie?

Monday, I have my hand on the button to call in sick to work, but I know I can't drop the ball on my part of the

Museum Board presentation. Instead, I call Wanda and tell her I'll be late, since I have to get this thing with my car straightened out. When I call the city, though, they say that Jude's already been there to pay the tickets, and the boot has been removed.

I do make it a point to tell the person on the phone that it was really irresponsible of them to boot my car just because it's the same color, make, and model of the offender's car. And was parked in the personal parking space registered in his name. After saying all that, I feel pretty sheepish, so I say, "Never mind. I understand how it happened," and hang up quickly.

I take the El to the stop closest to Jude's apartment and walk to my car. Someone, obviously when the orange metal contraption was still clamped on my tire, has stuck a note on my window that says, "Loser."

"Pretty much," I can't help but agree as I tear it off, crumple it, and throw it into my backseat.

Jude lives a little further from work than I do, so by the time I get there, it's close to 9:30. I put my purse in my desk drawer and sit down to check my voicemails and emails. But first, I peek over at Jude's office. He turns from his drafting board right then, sees me, and waves his pencil in my direction as a greeting. I act like I didn't see him. I'll have to talk to him soon enough. But I want it to be on my terms.

Lisa pokes her head over our shared wall. "Hey. What's going on? Everything okay?"

I jump about a foot. "Shit," I mutter. "Nothing! I'm fine!"

"Yeah, that's convincing," she says. "Seriously, why are you late?"

I'm annoyed that I have to explain myself. The least Wanda could have done was send out a lousy email to the other admins that I'd be in eventually. "I had a personal errand to run," I say shortly.

She accepts my answer without question. "So... what's the latest with you and Jude?"

"What?" My head snaps up to look at her. She seems completely innocent, but she's obviously heard something.

Marvin. Anyone who says men aren't as gossipy as women is delusional. "Nothing happened, okay?"

Lisa furrows her brow. Zoe, hearing my tense voice, comes across the aisle. "What's going on? What'd you do this weekend?"

"What is this, twenty questions?" I huff, grabbing my wallet and stomping in the direction of the break room. Of course they follow me, Lisa filling Zoe in on the way.

As I look for something in the vending machine to eat for a late breakfast, Lisa says, "Well, I *was* just asking about the Museum Board presentation tonight, but now I'm curious. What were *you* talking about?"

I don't know how to get out of this one. Silence can only work for so long. She's going to come up with more outrageous scenarios than what the reality is, anyway, so I answer (however minimalistically), "We worked together on it this weekend. I thought you were assuming something happened between us when we were here alone. But we weren't alone. Marvin was here too."

"Why would we assume that?" Zoe asks.

"Because you guys are always trying to make something out of nothing."

"The preemptive denial," Lisa muses. "Always a sign of guilt. I know that from being a step-mom."

I shoot her a dirty look. "Or a sign that someone's friends make her paranoid."

Just then, Jude walks in. He sees Lisa and Zoe with me and

says, "Oh. I thought... Never mind." He runs his hand through his hair. "When you get a minute, can you come with me... er, I mean..." He blushes and punches his fist against his leg. I want to punch him for being so obvious. "Marvin wants us to look at the video when you get a couple secs—minutes!" He turns and mutters disgustedly at himself, "Oh, fuck me," as he walks away, in the direction of Graphics.

I'm so annoyed by his display that I'm not even blushing, like I normally would be.

Lisa exchanges a glance with Zoe, but neither one of them says anything to me. Instead, they scurry off together, whispering. The most I can hope for is that it's not all over the company by the end of the day that Jude and I are sleeping together. That's the best I can hope for. The worst? I don't even want to think about it.

Abandoning my breakfast mission, I stomp to Graphics, where Jude and Marvin are deep in discussion about the video.

"There you are," Marvin says. "I was just about to show Jude the animation."

I give him an expectant, impatient look that clearly communicates, "Roll it, already, Numb-Nuts."

"Alrighty, then," he replies, turning out the lights and hitting the button to start it. We wait through the stuff we've already seen, and then it continues with us "looking" up at the glass-and-beam vaulted ceiling.

After that, I don't pay much attention. I don't care. I'm just the admin. I know I'm only here because Marvin needed an excuse to look at my boobs. And he's too lazy to walk past my cubicle, so he decided to have them come to him. I'll be glad when this is over so I don't have to talk to him again for a while. Until Sunday, that is.

"Buh-ruther," I grumble aloud at that mental reminder.

"What?" Jude and Marvin ask at the same time, all eyes on me.

"Nothing," I answer. "Sorry. It looks fine. I was thinking of something else."

The two of them return their attention to the monitor. "See, I had the animation 'walk' in a circle, cutting through the gardens to get back to the entrance, so we can just loop it and play it behind you while you're describing your design. That way, there aren't any awkward jump-cuts or tiresome fades or other transitions that have been way overused."

Jude nods, his finger curled on his chin. "Nice. Very good," he says distractedly. I swear he's looking at me out of the corner of his eye.

"'Nice?' 'Very good?'" Marvin mocks. "I worked my ass off on this all weekend, and that's what I get? It's fuckin' awesome, dude!"

Snapping to attention, Jude says, "Oh. Right. Completely. I agree. I was merely thinking of... what Libby said, er... wrote for me to say... My script! And how it's going to sound in addition to this."

He points at the animation and takes a deep breath. The intake of oxygen seems to help him concentrate. He looks straight at Marvin and says, "I doubt people are even going to be listening to me. Which is good! You did a brilliant job. I can't thank you enough."

Grudgingly, Marvin says, "Yeah. Well, okay." Then he adds, "You know, you could show your appreciation by staying home from the baseball game Sunday. Huh-huh."

Jude levels a steady look that makes Marvin take it back with a "Just kidding, dude."

But then Jude quickly says, "No, uh... if that's what you want. I mean, it's the least I can do."

"What?" I jump in, panic rising in my chest.

Ignoring me, Jude tells Marvin, "I have loads of other things I should probably be doing then anyway. Maybe I *will* stay home. Watch the game on the telly instead."

With that, he thanks Marvin one more time for his help and walks out.

"That was easy," Marvin says to me. "Looks like it's going to be just you and me, babe."

Without replying, I rush from the room, chasing after Jude. I don't even care how it looks. "Hey, J— you!" I call, stopping myself before I sound like a lame Beatles cover band (again) but not before I sound like I'm broadcasting his religious beliefs. He half-turns but keeps walking. I catch up to him and fall into stride at his side just as we're passing Leslie's desk.

"What the hell was that about?" I demand in hushed tones, conscious of her nosy stare.

Without looking at me, he says, "I thought that would be preferable to both you *and* Marvin."

"Are you kidding me? What made you think that?"

"You don't seem to want to have anything to do with me. I'm saving you the discomfort of uninviting me." We turn together and go into his office.

"I never invited you in the first place," I point out, then rush on, "But I was glad you invited yourself, because it meant I didn't have to be alone with Marvin."

He shuffles some papers on his desk. "Well, invite someone else, then. I'm sure Zoe or Lisa wouldn't mind being your buffer." Abruptly, he changes the subject (sort of) but still refuses to look at me. "I thought you weren't coming to work today."

I abandon the comeback I was going to give him about his former remark and close my mouth at his latter statement.

Finally, I say, "I had to get my car. Thanks for paying your tickets."

"Not at all," he replies formally. "Sorry about the mix-up... both of them." He sits down at his computer and starts clicking his mouse, his eyes on the monitor. "Anything else?"

I can't believe it! I'm being... dismissed!

"I... I guess not," I stutter. "Unless you need help with your presentation?"

"Nope. Everything appears to be sweet as a nut, thanks to Marvin."

His cold tone gives my heart the equivalent of brain freeze. But I lift my chin. "Okay. Good. I'll just... uh..." I back through the doorway.

"Shut that, please, if you don't mind," he requests.

"Sure." I pull the door closed and go directly to my desk, where I stay the rest of the day without talking to anyone.

❧ 12 ❧

I SLEEPWALK THROUGH THE NEXT FEW DAYS, SUFFERING FROM insomnia at night, LFW an annoying haze of TV snow. By the time my session with Dr. Marsh comes around, I'm in an epically foul mood.

As soon as I sit down, he asks, "So? How did the assignment go?"

"Fine," I answer shortly, handing over my list of compliments.

He takes the paper but doesn't take his eyes from my face. "You don't sound or look fine."

I shrug petulantly.

Letting it go for the moment, he puts on his glasses and peruses the list, laughing out loud at a few of the statements. Finally, he sets it aside, along with his glasses. "Very good. I'm glad you took to heart my encouragement to be creative."

I say nothing.

"What about the other part?" he prods. "Have you noticed a difference in the way people respond to you when you modify your body language?"

"Yeah, it's been great. I've been hit on by a guy with halitosis, and I have a date this Sunday with another guy who has a garden hose hooked up to his armpits." I cross my arms over my chest. It's the most comfortable I've been in days.

"I'm sensing some sarcasm here."

My response is a narrowing of my eyes.

He sighs. "Okay. Well, let's start with this date. A guy asked you out, and you said, 'yes'?"

"That's usually how it works," I answer. I don't tell him that I was the one who actually offered the tickets; nor do I tell him the circumstances surrounding the offer. I just want to get Dr. Marsh off my back about my issues with men.

"Why did you accept, if you find him physically repulsive, as I'm getting the impression you do?" he asks, jotting something down in my file.

I stare at the college graduation photo. "Because I wanted to fulfill the assignment."

"But that was extra credit. You didn't *have* to do it."

"I didn't *have* to do any of it, really. But you know me well enough to know that if an authority figure gives me an assignment, I'll do it. It's hardly even fair."

Not acknowledging that, he states, "Well, this date is a start. And it's only a date."

"Except I work with the guy. And he's a leech. It's not going to be easy to shake him." I pick at a thread on my pants.

Dr. Marsh tries another subject. "Speaking of guys you work with—or their fantasy alter-egos—how are things going with you and Jude?"

"Which one?" I slip up and ask.

He raises his eyebrows. "You have a status report on both?"

"Never mind," I reconsider. "Fantasy Jude and I broke up." I'm painfully aware of how dumb that sounds.

More note-writing in my file. "Oh? What happened there?"

"He was too perfect. And he always agreed with everything I said. I got bored." I chew on a hangnail.

"So does that mean you're getting to know the real Jude a little better?"

"What is it with everyone's obsession with me and Jude?" I ask hotly, shifting in my seat.

"Is everyone obsessed?"

"It feels like it! I can't get any peace. If it's not Lisa and Zoe, it's Leslie. If it's not Leslie, it's Marvin. 'What's going on with you two?' Nothing! A whole lot of it!"

"And this is upsetting to you?"

I'm not about to fall into his trap. "That people won't leave me alone? Yes. That nothing's going on with me and Jude? No. I just wish my life would get back to the way it was before."

"Before what?" He leans forward.

I hadn't planned to tell him. As a matter of fact, I had a specific plan to *not* tell him anything about last Saturday. But now I need a second opinion. Quickly (we've already eaten up several minutes of my one-hour session), I recap the events of Saturday, starting with meeting up with Jude and Marvin at work (which means I had to come clean about the "date" at the Cubs game this weekend) and ending early Sunday morning, with the pillow fight and my revelation. He listens intently, only interrupting when something's unclear.

When I finish, he folds his hands in his lap and asks, "So... now things are strained between the two of you?"

"Ha! That's an understatement. He wants nothing to do with me. He's not even coming to the baseball game Sunday, like he promised. I'm stuck alone with Sweatstains McGee."

Dr. Marsh stifles his laughter.

I ignore him and ask expectantly, "Well?"

He clears his throat. "What?"

"What do you think?"

"About what?"

"About Jude's reaction to my confession."

"Oh. You want my opinion?"

I nod, suddenly nervous.

"Well, I can't tell you for sure what he's thinking. His reaction could be interpreted two ways: he's either turned off or he needs time to think about it."

"I already know that. Which interpretation do you think, as a guy, is more likely?"

He shakes his head. "It's hard to tell. I don't know him."

"You're useless!" I practically explode. "And frankly, I think you're lying. You know exactly what he's thinking. You're just protecting him. Because you guys all stick together."

I stand up and pace the room. Anything to avoid looking at that damn picture on Dr. Marsh's shelf again. "You know he's totally freaked out by the prospect of being the person I lose my virginity to. Not that I even asked him to be. I think it's pretty presumptuous of him to think I *was* asking that, just because he took me to a concert and got me drunk. As if it were a foregone conclusion that I'd sleep with him! The joke's on him, of course, because I've already slept with Fantasy Jude *lots* of times, and I'm sure he couldn't compete with that." I turn my back to Dr. Marsh, unable to say the next thing while looking at him. "Because *that* was fabulous." I put my cool hands to my burning face.

And then I start crying. Because I know what I've said is pathetic. I know it's not reality; I know it would only make Jude—or any man, for that matter—run faster and farther if he knew how out of touch with reality I can be. I'm not just a virgin; I'm a crazy, delusional virgin. Not too long ago, I would have been shut away in a home for insane spinsters.

Dr. Marsh lets me take my time as I blubber in the corner.

Finally, when I'm moderately composed, he asks, "Have you ever thought of telling him some of this?"

I whirl around. "Are you kidding? That's not even funny!"

He puts up a hand. "Now, just hear me out—"

"If you're going to make an assignment out of this, consider it an incomplete right now," I warn him. "I *won't* do it. It's bad enough that I got drunk and told him... that. The subject is closed."

"What I meant is, maybe you should open up to him a little more about your life in general. Your background. Maybe then he'd understand."

"I don't care if he understands! I don't have to justify anything to him. Or anyone else."

I can tell by the look on his face that Dr. Marsh doesn't believe a single word of that statement. And even though he's right that I'm lying, the fact still remains. "He's moved on. Decided I'm not worth the trouble. If he ever even entertained the thought that I was."

I glance at the clock. Time's up.

13

"The record-breaking heat wave continues, with highs today and tomorrow in the upper 90's, heat indexes in the low 100's. But there's some relief in sight. Showers and thunderstorms, some potentially severe, on Tuesday evening and into the overnight hours should cool things down a bit, as well as bring us some much-needed rain. The high on Wednesday is only expected to reach 91. That's your latest look at the forecast; now here's the latest from some guys who put on an awesome show here in the Windy City last weekend—"

Eff me. I quickly switch off the radio before I get sucked into the song, which I happen to like a lot. Unfortunately. But I don't need any reminders of Jude. Especially now, as I'm on my way to the dreaded baseball game.

I've never, ever, ever dreaded going to a Cubs game. Ever. And I'm pretty pissed off that I've put myself in the position I'm in right now. I should have just let Jude fight his own stupid battles.

I watched the first pitch from the comfort of my own couch and contemplated calling Marvin to tell him I was sick. But I already had my ticket. And it's one of the only games I've had a chance to go see at Wrigley Field this season. *And* they're playing the wretched Cardinals. The pull of the ivy is stronger than the revulsion I feel for my date.

By the time I park and climb my way to my seat in the outfield bleachers, it's the bottom of the third inning. When Marvin sees me, he stands and waves both hands over his head. As if I don't know where my seat is. And as if I needed a reminder that he keeps two of the Great Lakes under his arms (Superior and Michigan, by the look of things today).

"It's about time you got here," he greets me as I sit down. "I was starting to wonder if you were gonna stand me up."

"Sorry," I mutter, motioning to the beer man that I need a drink. Now.

Marvin retakes his seat, brushing up against me. At the risk of invading the space of the person next to me, I move over a little.

"Yeah, well, Jude told me you got a phone call as he was dropping you off after your couch shopping, and that's probably what was making you late."

I pay the beer man and take the first wonderful sip of my ice-cold drink. Then I say caustically, "Oh, Jude told you that, huh? What'd you do, call him to find out where I was?" What a stalker!

We all stand up as the batter hits one hard toward center field, right where we're sitting. But it drops well in front of the wall, caught by the Cardinals' outfielder. After we're seated again, Marvin says impatiently, "No, I asked him when he showed up here without you." He mops his brow with his t-shirt sleeve, which is already sweat-soaked.

I resist the urge to:

1. gag;

2. spit my mouthful of beer onto the head of the
   person in front of me;
3. shout, "Jude's here?!";
4. look around frantically for him; and
5. punch Marvin in the face for the implied "dumbass"
   at the end of his sentence.

Instead, I manage to swallow my beer and say coolly, "Oh. Right. I didn't realize he beat me here."

The next batter strikes out, ending the inning. Marvin turns his full attention to me as the sides switch out. "He went to the bathroom. So what's the deal? I thought he said he wasn't coming to the game."

"I guess he changed his mind."

Marvin rolls his eyes. "Yeah, well, thank God you're here. The dude's been asking me so many questions about the game that it's embarrassing. I've hardly had a chance to watch."

I hide my smile in my plastic beer cup. "Sorry. I got here as soon as I could," I manage before drowning my grin in another swallow.

The people immediately to my right stand up, allowing someone through. Jude edges past me and moves to retake the empty seat on the other side of Marvin, but Marvin willingly scoots over to make room for him between the two of us.

"Go ahead, man. Sit next to Libby. She's the one teaching you about baseball, right?"

Jude hesitates for a nanosecond, then takes the seat. "Right. Excellent. Thanks, mate."

Marvin's absence is literally a breath of fresh air. I can breathe through my nose again without getting a snootful of sweaty man. And there's enough room between Jude and me for a slight breeze against my left side.

"Thank you," I whisper to Jude.

"Not at all," he answers, smiling. "What'd I miss?"

I know he's talking about the game, but I say quietly, "You missed my finding out that you covered for me, probably knowing that I was sitting at home, bribing myself with season tickets next year to get myself out the door."

He laughs out loud, then covers his mouth as he murmurs back, "I actually thought it was a huge bag of Kit Kats you were promising yourself, but I was spot-on with the rest of it."

Marvin startles me by standing up right as I'm about to say something about his sweat glands. I quickly close my mouth and smile up at him as he announces he's going to the bathroom and slides past us.

As soon as he's gone, I inform Jude, "He's really mad you're here. He's already bitched to me about it. Why'd you change your mind?"

Hiding behind his sunglasses, Jude watches the action on the field, a routine ground-out by the other team's hitter. "Already had the ticket. Had nothing better to do. Etcetera, etcetera..."

"But you told Marvin—"

"He can bugger off. He did a great job on the animation, and he really saved my bacon, but he's been a bit of a wanker about it, holding this over your head when it's obvious you don't fancy him." Now he looks at me. "Right?"

"Right!" I agree readily. "So right!" More quietly, I say, "I'm glad you changed your mind."

He gently bumps against my side. "Me too."

Suddenly a ball comes rocketing toward us. I put my glove up, but Jude's taller and manages to catch the opposing team's homerun bare-handed.

"Mother fu—" he hisses, tossing it into his other hand so he can shake off the sting.

"Throw it back!" I shout at him.

"What?"

"You have to throw it back, to show the other team we don't want their homerun ball!"

Quickly, as if the ball has cooties, he tosses it over the wall, where it lands on the centerfield grass. Everyone around us cheers. He grins so brightly his smile could have been used to illuminate a night game before Wrigley got lights.

"Yeah!" he yells, forcing a vein to pop bulge the middle of his red forehead and shaking his arms over his head. "Screw you, Cards!"

This outburst makes him the prince of our section. Guys around us slap his back and tousle his hair. I can't stop laughing. The excitement eventually dies down as it sinks in that we're still down one-zip, thanks to that homer. But I feel as happy as I would if we were winning with two outs in the ninth inning of Game Seven of the World Series. Well, maybe not quite *that* happy, but pretty close.

Marvin left in the middle of the eighth inning, claiming he wanted to beat the traffic, but we'd largely ignored him since he returned from the bathroom, so I have a feeling it had more to do with that than anything else. After we said goodbye to him, I told Jude, "By the way, true fans don't worry about the traffic. We stay until the bitter end."

Jude nodded. "Damn right!" he concurred. "I can easily see us coming back and getting eight runs in our next two at-bats. We're not ready to jack it in just yet!"

He cracked me up pretty much the entire game. He knows a lot more about it than he was letting on, but I can tell he thought it was funny to be the clueless foreigner, especially around Marvin, who was visibly annoyed by his questions and ignorant comments. After his bare-handed snatch, I gave him my glove and said, "Here; if you're going to be a hero, you'll need this." I knew any ball coming our way would meet his reach much sooner than mine anyway, and I hated the thought of him breaking his hand at his first (maybe?) baseball game.

Now the game's over, and we're sitting in the bleachers, waiting for the crowd to clear. A few other fans have the same idea, but we're pretty much alone up here.

"This is how you do it," I tell him. "You stay *later*, not leave earlier. *Marvin.*"

Jude laughs. "Absolutely." He stretches his legs, resting his feet on the empty bleachers in front of us.

"This is my favorite place in the whole world," I say, tucking my hands under my legs and shrugging my shoulders up near my ears. I don't know why I feel the need to tell this guy such personal details.

He looks around. "Good memories here?"

I nod. "Yep. Never had a bad time in this park. That's why I was dreading today so much. I couldn't believe that Marvin was going to break my streak. And it was my own fault. Speaking before thinking, you know?"

"Yeah, but I really do appreciate your speaking up. I didn't have anything to bribe him with. I don't think he would have helped us as readily if I'd offered to get him into one of my rugby matches. Not quite the same attraction as this." He motions to the field in front of us.

"You're welcome." I play with one of the laces in my ball glove. "Thanks for helping me keep my happy streak alive. Here. Today." After an awkward pause, I add, "And I heard that the presentation went well Monday night, so I guess it was all worth it?" I don't divulge that I only know this from eavesdropping on him and Lisa the day after the Art Museum Board meeting.

"Yeah. Definitely. For me, that is. I hope it was all worth it for you, too."

I actually mean it when I say, "For sure. I wouldn't change a thing."

"Really?" he quickly asks, pulling his knees up and anxiously turning toward me. "Nothing? Even... what you told me?"

I swallow. "Even that. I guess. It's kind of pointless to regret it."

"Because I feel like you hate me for knowing."

"I don't hate you, Jude." I stand up to lead the way down the bleachers and out of the ballpark, but he snags my hand. "What?" I ask, turning to look down at him. *Why won't this topic die?*

"Did someone... hurt you?" Despite the slight sunburn on his cheeks, he looks pale.

I blink a few times, then laugh nervously. "If you're asking what I think you're asking, the answer's no. Nobody hurt me... in that way." I tug on his hand. "Come on. We should get going."

And although it's not necessary by any means, we continue to hold hands all the way to the street, where we reluctantly part ways.

❧ 14 ❧

"AT THE RISK OF GETTING MY HEAD BITTEN OFF, WHAT'S GOING on with you and Jude?" Lisa asks me quietly in the bathroom.

Calmly and pleasantly, I answer, "Nothing. Why?"

"He's been at your desk five times so far today. And it's only"—she consults her watch—"10:12."

I smirk at her but respond mildly, "Don't you have anything better to do than count how many times people visit my desk?"

"Not really." Now that she knows I'm not going to be defensive and angry, she moves closer to me. "Come on. Spill it. I know something's up."

The reality is, though, that it's still not much. Definitely not enough to dish about in the ladies' room. Despite my instincts to keep it to myself, I answer, "I don't know. We've just been... hanging out. A lot." That's when the smile that's been making itself quite at home in my chest breaks through to my face.

"I knew it!" she says triumphantly. "I told Zoe there was an electric current between the two of you strong enough to light up the greater Chicagoland area. Ha! I love it when I'm right!" She faces the mirror and reapplies her lipstick. "So... when you say 'hanging out,' do you mean 'hanging out with your clothes off'?"

"That," I reply, "is none of your business. But no. Just hanging out."

"Do you want it to be more?"

I blush. "I guess."

"I don't blame you. He's a cutie."

LFW is open for business again. Only this time, Fantasy Jude is pretty much the same thing as Real Jude. I have to fill in the blanks sometimes on things I don't know about him, but there's no longer an Oxford-educated, tennis-playing, MG-driving, gleaming-toothed, satin-tongued Brit residing in my mind. The Jude in my fantasies plays rugby, uses weird terms and phrases that I don't really understand all the time, drives a car identical to mine, loves *Psycho,* and makes me laugh. He's... well, dreamy.

There's a knock on my apartment door. I open it and there's Jude, standing in a pool of light that has no obvious origin. But it makes the blondish highlights in his light brown hair stand out. And it makes him look like an angel.

"Hey, Libby. Can I come in?"

"Yes. How did you know where I live?"

"Corporate directory. I just had to see you tonight. I'm sick of talking on the dog and bone all the time like two spotty teenagers." He walks in and looks around. "This flat is the business!"

"Thanks. I think."

"Well, I didn't come here to compliment your apartment. I came here for a bit of a snog, actually, to be quite honest."

"Oh. If you insist..."

"...I say, 'good for you!' This is exciting!" Lisa trills over her shoulder in a silly soprano, breaking into my daydream as she pushes the door open and exits the bathroom.

I must say, beaming at myself in the mirror, that I agree with her wholeheartedly.

~

It used to be that I dreaded the weekends. Even more than weekdays, which I also didn't really enjoy. So, in other words, it used to be that I hated my life. But especially weekends. They were long, boring, and—yep—lonely. And then after suffering through two full days of doing nothing with no one, I'd have to go to work and endure everyone asking me, "How was your weekend?" or "Did you do anything fun this weekend?" You can only say "Fine" and "No" in so many ways. Then, after surviving the Monday inquisition, I'd have three measly days of peace before people would start asking, "Have anything fun planned this weekend?" Two hundred times a year (at least), I'd find myself answering something having to do with my empty weekends.

Well, not anymore. I have (dare I say it?) a boyfriend. Well, kind of. In a sort of Victorian definition of the word. He's definitely a boy, and I'm pretty sure we'd consider each other friends. Okay, so I'm a little confused about what we are to each other, since I'm not very experienced with this sort of thing, but what I'm getting at is that Jude and I make plans to do things together. And then we actually do them. That's called "dating," right? I'm almost certain it is.

Only… don't people our age who are dating do more than hold hands? Well, Jude and I don't. I think once he may have given me a peck on the cheek when he dropped me off at home at the end of the night. But it was a kiss very similar to the one my brother gave me when I took him to the airport to return to the University of Florida last semester. And since the pillow-fight/"I'm-a-virgin" fiasco, I haven't set foot inside his apartment again. Neither has he been inside mine. I think I'm destined to turn thirty without ever having been French kissed. What a dismal prospect!

I've determined that if anything's going to be done about this, however, it's going to have to be my doing. It's obvious that Jude's taking things slowly (what's a word for "so-slowly-that-three-toed-sloths-are-passing-us-while-making-out"?) because I'm a virgin, and he doesn't want to freak me out. How nice. But it's just a kiss, right? Am I missing something? The only thing stopping me from going for it is that I may be missing something. Now would be a good time to have *real* girlfriends.

Tonight we're sitting in a bar (*not* a gastropub) after seeing a movie that almost required a meeting of the Geneva Convention for us to agree on. Jude didn't want to see a chick flick. I didn't want to watch an action/adventure/thriller/mystery/the-end-of-the-world-is-here blockbuster. Neither one of us wanted to sit in the middle of a bunch of kids and their parents watching the latest animated piece of fluff. So, after researching our choices all week, we decided to see an independent drama at one of the smaller art-house theaters. It seems, after talking it over, that we both actually liked it, although Jude criticized it for being somewhat pretentious and a little too earnest.

Now he's in the restroom, and I'm plotting how I'm going to plant one on him before the end of the night. Easier said than done when you've never done it before. My strategy so far is:

1. Drink enough to lower my inhibitions without getting drunk (I actually want to remember my first kiss ever).
2. Eat and drink things that don't make me self-

conscious about my breath (I had Junior Mints at the movie; I'm drinking fruity girl drinks at the bar).

3. Picture some of the most romantic kisses in my favorite movies (unfortunately, though, most of them were initiated by the men, so it's difficult to reverse the roles in my head).
4. Pretend like I do this all the time (maybe if *I* can forget I'm inexperienced, he'll forget it, too).

Jude returns from the bathroom but doesn't sit down. Instead, he tosses some bills on the table and says, "Are you ready?"

What a loaded question! But I answer confidently, "Yes." Then, beating back the butterflies, I propose, "Would you like to go back to my place for a while?" I would bolster my suggestion with, "It's still early," although it's really not.

It doesn't matter, though, because he casually accepts, as if that's what he expected all along.

When we get to my apartment, I use my body to shield his view from my shaking hand as I unlock the door. After we step inside, I busy myself with hanging up my purse and petting Sandberg so that Jude can look around without my staring at him and waiting for a reaction.

My bed suddenly seems ten times bigger than it usually does. And under a spotlight.

He sits down on the couch.

"Can I get you something to drink?" I open the fridge. "I have beer—but not the kind you normally drink, sorry—wine, water—"

"Water's fine," he answers easily. He leans forward and looks at the magazines on my coffee table. While I open his bottle of water and pour myself a (large) glass of wine, he flips through the *Entertainment Weekly*, laughing at the "Bullseye" in the back and declaring it, "Very clever."

I down half my glass of wine and top it off before joining him. I have another thing to add to my strategy:

1. Don't puke on him (I'm so nervous that I think it could be a possibility).

When I sit down next to him and hand him his water, he smiles and says, "Thank you." After drinking half the bottle at once, he sets it down on a coaster on the table and wipes his mouth on the back of his hand. "You have a nice place."

"Thanks," I reply. "It's small."

"Suits you perfectly," he insists.

Pointing out what I perceive to be the elephant in the room, I joke nervously, "You expected my apartment to be all bed?"

He turns around and glances at it. "Oh. Until you said something, I hadn't even noticed it. It's so tidy and tucked into its own little corner."

"It seems like it's always in the way," I mutter, trying to cover for my awkwardness. I take a huge drink.

He watches me, then when I pull the glass away from my lips, he takes it from my hand and sets it on the table. He doesn't say anything, but I can tell by the amused glint in his eyes that he knows I'm nervous.

"I was just thinking," he says after grabbing my hand, "that maybe you and I..."

"Yes?" I scoot closer to him, trying to send him plenty of signals as I lick my lips and look at his mouth.

"...might reconsider our plans to go to that outdoor art festival tomorrow. It's supposed to rain." His lips move closer to me. I can't stop staring at them. "Libby?"

"Huh?" I ask distractedly.

"May I just…" He leans in, but instead of kissing me when I close my eyes, he rubs his thumb against the side of my nose, where it meets my cheek.

My eyes snap open. I pull my head back.

He grins and holds up his thumb, which has a tiny piece of glitter stuck to it. "This was on your face."

"Oh. I wonder how that got there."

But he's leaning closer to me again, peering into my eyes. "Your eyes…"

I hold my breath, waiting for the compliment that precedes the kiss.

"…are the oddest color. I've never seen anything like them. I suppose you'd call them green, but there's some gray and blue in there, too."

Frustrated and disgusted, I back away from him. "What's it going to take to get you to kiss me?"

Looking genuinely surprised by my outburst, he says, "Did you want me to kiss you? I thought we were talking about other things."

"Who cares? Do you need a written invitation?"

His face clouds over slightly. "No. I don't suppose I do. But if I kiss you now, it will seem like I'm merely doing it because you asked me to, not because I want to."

I sigh. "Just forget it. I've waited twenty-eight years; I guess I can wait another decade or two."

He laughs, then stops abruptly. "Wait a minute. You've *never* kissed a man?"

"Or a woman, for that matter," I clarify. Might as well get that annoying question out of the way.

"Blimey," he breathes. "That's… sort of… incredible."

"Yeah, I'm a living relic," I say, trying to keep the bitterness from my voice.

He looks at me long enough that it starts to make me squirm. I reach for my wineglass again. "Stop staring at me like I'm a sideshow oddity."

Blinking and shaking his head slightly, he says, "Sorry. I'm merely trying to sort something out in my head."

"Can I help?" I ask fake-solicitously. I might as well be of some use.

"I'm sorry if this is rude or forward, but what, exactly, have you experienced and... *not* experienced... when it comes to, erm, romantic endeavors?" he queries. When I fidget even more, he says, "I'm not trying to make you feel self-conscious; I really want to know."

"This is going to require more wine," I declare, getting up and filling my glass almost to the point of overflowing. For good measure, I take a swig straight from the bottle. His laughter at my behavior loosens me up a little. It suddenly seems silly for me to be shy talking about sexual matters with a guy I'd really like to have sex with.

I sit down again, this time very close to him. He's turned sideways, so his arm is resting on the back of the couch. His hand moves up, his finger wandering up to play with a strand of my hair near my ear.

"Please don't make me explain in detail to you how this is possible (I know you're a smart guy and don't need it spelled out), but I've never been kissed; I've never made out with anyone; and I've never had sex, in any form. *However*, I have experienced orgasms."

While he processes this information, I pause, begging him again—this time silently—not to make me explain it. I don't look at him. When he honors my requests, I continue, "I know it's backwards; I know what *that* feels like, but I don't know what it feels like to be kissed... romantically." I manage to utter without dying of embarrassment.

After he's been quiet for what feels like forever, I can't stand it anymore. I look over at him. He's studying me.

I swallow loudly.

"So," he recaps finally, "You've done the things you don't need anyone else's assistance to do; but anything that requires more than one person will be totally new to you?"

His use of the word "will" gives me chills and makes me break into a sweat at the same time. I gulp. "Uh… yeah."

"No pressure?" He tries to smile, but one side of his mouth doesn't quite make it.

I stop waiting. Turning quickly, I brush my lips up against his, careful not to jam my mouth into his face. His eyelids droop, but he keeps his eyes open. As do I. It seems wrong to close my eyes and rob myself of the memory of what he looked like when I took my first kiss from him. His arms go around me; my arms rest against his chest then slide over his shoulders so I can press my breasts against him. Only when he deepens the kiss and closes his eyes do I close mine. And when his tongue thrusts into my mouth, I almost melt out of the kiss, sliding down his body and off the couch. Only his tight grip on me keeps me in position.

This is the most intimate thing I've ever experienced; at least, in real life. I seriously underestimated its magnificence. And I think he's a good kisser, although I'm not sure how I would know for certain. It sure feels good. Not slobbery. Not too much tongue, choking me (I always kind of wondered how that worked). Maybe my future fantasies *will* involve a satiny-tongued Brit, just not in the way that the old Fantasy Jude was. No talking necessary, please. Did that moaning noise just come from me?

I pull away and wipe my mouth. My eyelids feel like they weigh a hundred pounds each, but I manage to open them. After just a few seconds of heavy breathing, staring at that mouth and remembering what it was doing to me, I throw myself at him again, this time not worrying so much about mashing my face into his. That's kind of the idea, actually.

I think a lot less during the second kiss. My lizard brain kicks in, I guess. And all it keeps saying is, "More, more, more."

Then my hands receive some signals that tell them to unbutton Jude's shirt. They do so, remarkably dexterously. I slide my hands against his surprisingly furry chest, which is very warm to the touch.

When my palms brush against his nipples, he makes an "Mmmphh" sound and wrenches his lips from mine with a wet sucking noise.

Smiling, I open my eyes. And freeze at the horrified look on his face. "What? What did I do wrong?" I ask, retreating to my corner of the couch and instinctively folding my arms across my chest.

Words don't seem to be forming well in his brain. He shakes his head. "Uh... no. Nothing wrong. On the contrary," he finally manages.

"Then why'd you stop?" I question him disbelievingly.

As he buttons his shirt, he replies, "Because I'm afraid that's as far as I can go before I *can't* stop."

"So?" Relieved, I crawl across the cushions and rub against him. "Who asked you to stop?"

He lets me kiss the corner of his mouth but says, "Right. Well. I don't think you should have your first kiss and your first... time... at the same... time."

"I'm okay with it," I assure him, trying to unbutton his shirt again.

Gently, he pushes my hand away, then the rest of me. "I'm not," he insists, standing up. He shakes one of his legs and straightens the front of his shorts, showing me his back. Well, at least I know *his* lizard brain is on *my* side.

"You're overthinking this," I try persuading him. "Really. Lots of girls lose their virginity the same day they have their first kiss. They just happen to be a dozen years younger than me. Which is so much worse, when you think about it. I'm a grown woman; I know what I want. I know what I'm getting into."

Apparently composed enough to face me again, he turns around. "What if I told you *I* wasn't ready? That it has nothing to do with your being a virgin?"

I find that hard to believe, I think but don't say. Instead, I tilt my head and wait for him to elaborate.

He runs his hand through his hair. "I don't know... I feel like I don't really know you, as odd as that sounds."

I scoff. "You know me better than any other person on this planet!" I'm not including Dr. Marsh in this statement, but he doesn't need to know anything about Dr. Marsh, period.

"I seriously doubt that." Then he rushes to add when I start to assert the veracity of my claim, "Anyway, even if that's true, it's still not much. We seem to talk about me all the time, but when it comes time for you to reciprocate, you clam up." He rubs his chin. "And I'm not really comfortable using a conversation with you about your sexual *inexperience* as foreplay."

"So it *is* about my virginity!" I accuse.

"Partly," he admits. "I'd be lying if I said it wasn't. I've never consciously been someone's first. It's a bit daunting."

Tears of frustration are building in my head. "Someone has to be the first," I mumble, knowing it's one of the lamest arguments in the world and that I've lost.

He sits on the arm of the couch, facing me. "Libby, I don't want to be merely 'someone.' We've established that you don't even need me in order to, well, get the job done, for lack of a better way of saying it." When I avert my eyes, he says, "So what I'm trying to get at is that I think we need to be intimate in other ways before... that way."

"You're not normal," I state, defeated. "What kind of guy passes up such an easy opportunity?"

"One who wants to sleep at night? With sore tackle, granted..."

When I figure out what that means, I burst into involuntary laughter.

He smiles, relieved. "It's not that I don't want to. Trust me. I *want* to."

"Stop mollycoddling me," I demand lightly.

"Stop pressuring me," he jokes in return. "No means no."

"Who hurt you?" I mean it in jest, but his expression turns serious. "I was just kidding," I hurriedly say. "You know, because you asked *me* that once."

He nods. "Of course. Right. Sorry. Only... I wasn't kidding when I asked you."

"I know. That's what makes it funny. Or not. Just forget it."

He seems to do so fairly easily. "So." He stands up and stretches. "I should probably get going."

My disappointment is complete. True, I started out the night with my only goal being to kiss him, but I got greedy in a hurry. Now I'm dissatisfied to the nth degree. But I can hardly argue one minute that I'm an adult, then pout like a child when I don't get my way. So I rise and say, "Okay," brightly, as if I really am okay with it.

He grasps my upper arms and bends his knees a little so he can look me in the eyes. "Do you want to brave the predicted thunderstorms tomorrow?"

The thought of not seeing him the next day fills me with melodramatic despair. "Yes! If it rains, we'll figure out something else."

Fortunately, he agrees. Then he catches my mouth with his. It's a lot less frantic than the last kiss, but it has the same effect on my insides. I'm not sure if I'm glad or disappointed that it's short.

"Go away," I tease.

"Absolutely." He walks to the door, which is about three steps away. "I'll, uh, see myself out."

After he leaves, I catch Sandberg staring at me from the foot of the bed, where he's waiting fetchingly for me. If a cat could roll his eyes, he would.

❧ 15 ❧

I cancel my next two appointments with Dr. Marsh and screen his calls to check up on me. I'm not ready to talk to him about Jude, now that he's really my boyfriend (I'm confident about that fact now—we definitely do things that people don't do with their friends). I don't want him to say anything or ask any questions that would put a damper on what I'm feeling, which is near-constant euphoria mixed with a little bit (okay, a *lot*) of sexual frustration. And Dr. Marsh has a real knack for putting a damper on things. I think it's one of the first skills he lists proudly on his resume.

About the only thing that could make my life more perfect right now would be if the Cubs had a chance of making it to the post season. But not so. Fall is almost here, and my team is well out of it, as usual. The boys'll be hanging up their pinstripes for a few months with the usual promise of "Wait till next year." But for some reason, it's not as disappointing as it usually is.

I'm more interested in rounding some bases of my own.

Unfortunately, I'm not a sprinter. By any stretch of the imagination. I'm more like the veteran catcher trying to run on two bum knees. And Jude's the pitcher who has a mean throw to second and is keeping me close to the bag.

He's also a crafty guy when it comes to not giving me many chances to tempt him. At least that's the construction I'm putting on it so that I don't take offense and assume he just doesn't want to sleep with me at all. I'm choosing to trust his original statement that he wants to get to know me better before taking that step. And I'm trying not to think of the possibility that he won't want to take that step after he gets to know me better.

Fortunately, he's keeping me too busy to sit around obsessing, like I normally would. We've been to more Chicago venues in the past few weeks than I've been to in my entire life. There are plenty of places that I've never visited because it's no fun to go there alone. It's a blast experiencing these things for the first time together. It's especially funny when Jude assumes I'm the all-knowing local and I end up being just as clueless as he is.

And I hope I'm giving him what he wants: insight into my personality. I think I am, anyway. The other day, as a matter of fact, he got out of the car after I drove us home from the Medieval Times Dinner and Show (which was non-stop hilarity, by the way, even though I don't think it's intended to be as funny as we found it) and said proudly, "My testicles didn't try to re-ascend once during that drive."

"You're getting to *know* me and trust me," I replied pointedly, putting plenty of emphasis on the word "know."

"I think it's because you're actually driving more safely. But you may be right about the other," he admitted, smiling at me over the roof of the car.

"I know I'm right," I boasted.

He grinned even more broadly and fingered the radio antenna. "Don't get too confident yet, though."

I rolled my eyes. "Oh, I won't. I know you're right there to knock me a down a few pegs and dash my hopes."

But I really thought he was getting to know me better, on my terms, and I couldn't help but get my hopes up.

That's why it's so disheartening when he turns to me tonight after we've finished watching a movie at my place (on my bed!) and says, "So, when do I get to meet your parents?"

My heart races, but I manage to calmly toss out this rejoinder: "When do I get to meet yours?"

He acts like he's jumping from the bed. "Let's go. I'll meet you at O'Hare in one hour. Maybe they can get more information from you than I've been able to get."

"What are you talking about?" I ask incredulously, pulling him back down next to me. "I tell you everything!"

"Liar." His tone is light, but I can tell he's serious. "I know all sorts of things that anyone who sends out those ridiculous 'get-to-know-me' email forwards can find out: your favorite color, athlete, song, wintertime activity, the name of your first pet, who you think is most likely to keep the forward going, etcetera, but do I really know anything deeper than that?"

"You know one thing deeper than that, that's for sure," I point out and add under my breath, "not that it matters or that you care."

"Not fair!" He props himself on his elbow, trapping Sandberg's tail under his arm in the process. The cat yowls at him and jumps down with an indignant hiss. "Sorry, mate!" he says, leaning over the edge of the bed to try to make amends. "Your mum made me do it." When he sees the cat's forgiveness is a hopeless cause, he returns his attention to me. "Anyway, you know I care, so don't play that tired card."

"Why don't you tell me why you're so damn virtuous?" I turn it around on him, expecting him to dodge the question and give me a bunch of crap about not wanting to cheapen the experience for me.

He sighs. "We've already been through this."

"Lie to me again, then. Or tell me half-truths. Same thing."

The irony of my statement isn't lost on either of us, but he's gracious enough not to call me on it. Instead, he sighs and says, "Fine. I'll give you the whole reason. Because I think you deserve that after all this time. And then I don't want you to accuse me of holding back anything ever again."

I give him a look that lets him know I'm not impressed with his big talk.

He chuckles at himself but makes good on his offer. "I really don't like talking about this, because I hate even thinking about her, but my first wife, Kiersten, was a very secretive person. About big things, little things, *every* thing. It didn't matter if she had nothing to gain by keeping something from me; she did it for the sake of having secrets. And it drove me bonkers." He frowns and picks at the bedspread.

"Give me an example," I urge, wanting to compare myself to her and come out looking better.

He thinks about it for a second. "Okay, here's a good one: when we were first married, she had her post sent to her parents' house so I couldn't look through it."

I wrinkle my nose. "What did she have to hide? Credit card bills? Porn?"

He shakes his head. "Absolutely nothing. She just wanted me to wonder."

"How do you know? Did you ever see her mail for yourself?"

"Loads of times," he affirms. "Her parents didn't know it was a big secret, so if ever I was at their house without her, they'd give it to me to take to her, moaning about not understanding why she didn't have it forwarded to our address. I'd go through weeks' worth of post, searching for whatever she could possibly be hiding. Nothing. A bunch of junky catalogues and maybe the occasional postcard from a friend on holiday."

"That doesn't make any sense," I say, shaking my head at her and getting annoyed on his behalf.

He raises an index finger. "But it never failed to wind me up. And that was the whole idea."

Sandberg jumps suddenly onto my stomach from the floor, startling me. I think he's trying to tattle on Jude for hurting his tail. I pet his head distractedly. "Did she ever have any *big* secrets? Secrets worth hiding?"

"That bloke she kept on the side was probably the biggest secret," he reveals nonchalantly, scratching an itch on his knee. "At least, that was the final straw."

"What a slag!" I cry, outraged for him, using my favorite English insult he's taught me to date.

He laughs. "Right. Well, I was the one who acted the fool, marrying someone I barely knew. Because I confused being on the pull with choosing a life partner, and it all went tits up."

I only understand half (maybe) of what he's said, but I get the gist.

"Which one are you doing now?"

Tilting his head, he sticks his tongue into his cheek and shakes his head in a gesture of confusion.

"Are you 'on the pull,' or looking for a life partner?" I ask, my heart pounding.

He narrows his eyes and answers casually, "I dunno. Who wants to know? I only share that kind of information with someone who's willing to share alike."

"Well, I'm not hiding anything major from you," I promise. "I'd never torture you that way."

"But you're hiding *something*," he says, quickly picking up on my proviso.

"No," I lie. "I'm not. You know everything there is to know about me right now. Do you want to know what brand of underwear I wore in the seventh grade? Or some other pointless detail about my past? Why?"

He shrugs. "No. I don't care about your adolescent knickers."

"Do you care about my grown-up knickers?" I set Sandberg aside so I can roll over and lie half on top of Jude, kissing his mouth.

He smiles and returns my kisses. "Perhaps. Especially if they're lacy."

I unbutton and unzip my jeans, giving us both a sneak peek. "Will you look at that? They are!"

He chuckles against my mouth. "You are just gagging for it! What would your mother say?"

I know this is his way of distracting me while at the same time trying to get information from me, so I pretend to give him half of what he wants. Between kisses on his neck, I say, "I don't talk to my parents."

Rubbing my back, he asks seriously, "Why not?"

I won't be deterred this time as I unbutton his shirt, then his shorts. "I just don't. It's a long, boring story. They haven't been there for me." Sliding my hand down the front of his pants, I look up at him beseechingly. "I promise I'll tell you about it some other time, but I've heard it's bad form to talk about your parents during sex."

He flares his nostrils, his eyes drooping as my hand curls around him. It's the first time I've ever made skin-to-skin contact with... it. He's hard and bigger than I thought he'd be. Not that I thought he was hiding a baby carrot in there, but I'm trying to picture him fitting inside me, considering how many times bigger he is than, say, a tampon. Before I lose my nerve (and his attention), I pull off my t-shirt one-handed. I rub my chest against his and suck on his bottom lip.

"Wibby…"

"Shh… You're only allowed to talk if it's dirty. Or you're moaning," I say playfully.

To my satisfaction and delight, he grunts what I take as his agreement, and he becomes an active participant in the deed. "God," he breathes in my ear as he removes my bra. He sounds tortured almost, which I'd feel bad about if I could feel any emotion other than lust. "I can't say 'no' anymore!"

I laugh a little. "Good. I'm… uh… ready. Don't move. Unless you're going to take your clothes off, which would be a great help."

He complies while I reach into my nightstand for a condom. I can't believe this is really happening. I see my hand close over the foil packet. I watch it pass the packet to Jude, who quickly rips it open and pulls out the rolled-up piece of latex. As he unrolls it down his… oh, gosh! I can't watch that! Instead, I busy myself removing my clothes, tossing them away.

Jude's fingers flutter against my belly as he places his hands on my waist. "Are you sure about this?" he asks one last time.

Careful to keep my eyes above waist level, I nod. He pushes me onto my back and guides himself into me slowly. Instinctively, I tense. He stops. "No?"

"Keep going," I beg. I squeeze his shoulders, gripping them harder as the pressure increases. I'm really scared, suddenly, that this isn't going to work. We're not the same size, maybe. I've read about people being sexually incompatible, which is one of my biggest arguments against abstinence before marriage. I mean, what if you get to the honeymoon, and the key doesn't fit into the lock? You can't just replace the cylinder or grind down the key. And then you're stuck. For life.

He stops trying to go in, backing out a fraction. "Aaah-hh…" I'm trying so hard not to react to the pain, because I don't want him to give up. I don't want to fail my first time out. This has to work! And "work" it is. It's definitely not turning out to be the magical fireworks display I'd envisioned.

"Relax," he says softly, withdrawing completely.

"No! Where are you going?" I can't believe he's abandoning me already.

Touching his nose to mine, he smiles. "Nowhere. But you need to relax some more."

"I am. I will. I promise. Try again."

"What's your rush?" He kisses my nose, then my mouth, slowly, deeply, gently. I arch my back as he kisses my breasts, then my belly. I thread my fingers through his hair and play with it as his mouth travels further and further down my body. When he kisses one of my inner thighs, I feel a *zing* in my core that almost brings me off the bed. He kisses the other one after making a comment about possibly needing a helmet for this job.

"You have to get back inside me," I plead.

"Not yet," he answers. "Almost."

He wraps his hand around my ankle and pushes on my foot until I bend my knee. He could probably twist me into a pretzel right now without any resistance on my part.

But I'm a little worried about what's going on down there, suddenly. I think he might be about to do something that I've read about and seen on HBO, but I'm not sure I prepped correctly for that. Plus, there are things he may see in that region that would raise even more questions. Some of the psychological tension I'm feeling transfers itself into my muscles near his face, because he looks up at me through his eyelashes. "You're not relaxing."

"What are you doing?"

"Trust me. You'll like it."

"Okay. But will *you* like it?"

My question catches him off-guard, and he starts laughing. When he stops, he says, "Would I be down here if I didn't like it?"

Mousily, I answer, "I guess not."

"I thought the rule was no talking unless it's dirty or moaning."

"I'm just not sure about this part," I defend myself. "I was expecting something a little more... basic... my first time."

He joins me up on the pillows, brushing a piece of hair away from my face. "Libby?"

"Yes?"

"Shut up."

I smile shakily. "Okay."

"Before I come to my senses and put my clothes back on."

"Don't do that," I urge him, grasping his upper arm, just in case.

"All right, then. I'll be back in half a mo."

He resumes his earlier position, and I try to focus on what I'm feeling while at the same time clearing my mind of any doubts. In a matter of seconds, I don't have to try at all to do either of those things. It becomes an involuntary, physiological... thing.

"Oh, God," I moan. "That's just... Oh! God!" Repeat that about fifty times, and you get the extent of my vocabulary for the next several minutes. Then I mix things up a little bit at the end, when I pepper in a few f-bombs, "oh yeah"s, and an "Oh, baby!" I'm so dizzy and elated when he lies on top of me again that I almost can't breathe.

He grabs my hands and threads his fingers through mine, pushing my arms over my head.

"Thank you!" I gasp at him in the same surprised tone of voice I'd have for someone who's picked up and returned a fifty-dollar bill I've dropped.

It amuses him. "You're very welcome."

"You were right."

"You have no idea how much I get off on hearing that."

He moves, and I realize he's inside me again. When did that happen?

"How come it doesn't hurt anymore?"

"Who cares?" he retorts, thrusting gently.

"Good point."

"You just needed to relax, like I said." He buries his face in my neck, nipping at the skin there while he moves in and out, going slightly deeper with each thrust. As he quickens his pace, he says, "I'm sorry if this hurts."

Before I can even steel myself for it, it's over. I jerk a little, but I'm distracted by the kisses Jude's placing up and down my arm as he experiences his orgasm. When it's over, he kisses my mouth and says up against it, "Are you okay? You flinched. I'm sorry."

"I'm fine," I reassure him, rubbing the back of his neck. "I'm *so* fine. Let's do it again."

He laughs and rolls onto his back, catching his breath. "Give me a few moments. It's not quite like in the movies."

"I know that!" I reply defensively. "I'm not a complete moron."

When he pats his chest conciliatorily, I scoot over and put my head on it. I doze as he plays with my hair. I don't know how much time passes before he wakes me up by shifting under me.

Panicked at the thought of him leaving, I sit up, clutching

the sheet to my chest. "Where are you going? You can stay here tonight." Despite my best intentions, it comes out sounding about as pathetic as a mewing wet kitten.

Smirking, he looks over his shoulder at me as he sits on the edge of the bed. "I thought I'd go to the toilet, if that's all right with you."

"Oh. Sorry."

I give him the courtesy of not staring openly as he walks stark naked to the bathroom, but I do watch him from the corner of my eye. He tiptoes his way through his clothes, almost tripping on his bunched-up shorts, the used condom dangling from between his thumb and forefinger.

After he's shut the door, I realize something very important: there's no going back. I've crossed one of those thresholds that the door slams shut behind you and locks from the other side. My old life is dead to me, no matter what happens next. I'll never again be content to sit home alone on a weekend, watching WGN, petting Sandberg, and eating crappy frozen dinners. I've seen how other (a.k.a., "normal") people live.

And I like it. A lot.

❧ 16 ❧

I'M HAVING A REALLY HARD TIME AT WORK. I HAVE THE attention span of someone who's just discovered sex (that's a little shorter than the attention span of a flea). I don't think it's affected my work performance yet (otherwise Lisa would have pointed it out), but I leave work every day exhausted from the effort I've had to put forth to keep my back to Jude's office windows. The other day he was wearing a suit with a vest and he had his jacket off, his back to me as he stood at his drafting table. I finally had to go into his office, close his blinds, then leave again.

He immediately IMed me.

MONDAY, AUGUST 17, 2:36 P.M.
Jude.Weatherington:
??

Libby.Foster:
Never mind. It's for the good of the entire company, trust me

Later, back at my place, I let him in on the whole story, and he laughed. "Well, I can't very well sequester myself all day so you can do your job."

"Yes, you can," I argued. "You used to stay in there for eight hour stretches; you'll just have to go back to doing that."

Things are a little better now that we're not keeping our relationship a secret. Not that we were ever very successful at it. But now that it's official with both of our bosses, I feel a lot less paranoid about every visit he makes to my desk. Since there's nothing to speculate about anymore, people have stopped staring so much at us and have gone back to their own lives.

Except for Leslie, of course. She likes to make snide comments as often and as publicly as possible, the jealous whore. Jude thinks it's funny and just laughs it off, but I'm a little more self-conscious about what people are thinking. Half the time I feel like I have a blinking sign over my head that says, "Freshly laid."

It doesn't help that *everything* seems to be about sex. I mean, I thought it was bad before, when I was sexually frustrated, but now it's ten times worse. Songs that I never interpreted to be sexual I now understand to be basically lyrical porn. I look at the billboards around town, whether they're hawking shoes or hair care products, and blush, picturing whatever Jude and I did the night before (or that morning or afternoon). I'm afraid I might be a sex addict.

Of course, I keep most of my thoughts to myself. And I try to play it cool with Jude, restraining myself and allowing him to make the first move at least half the time. I don't want him to know he's created a monster.

Speaking of monsters, Marvin emerges from his cave today for the first time I've seen him in weeks. He stops by my desk, standing next to Jude, who's leaning against my cubicle wall, waiting for me to collect my things so we can leave for the day.

"Uh... hey," he says to Jude, "Gary told me he wanted me to do another animation for one of your projects. You got a minute to talk about it?"

Jude stands up straight. "Ace. Right now?"

Marvin nods. "Yeah, dude. I gotta get started on it right away. You guys are really starting to annoy the piss outta me with your last minute shit. Always on Fridays."

"Did you tell Gary that?" I tease.

He shoots me a dirty look. "No. But I can say it to you two."

"Whaddya say?" Jude asks me. "Can we postpone sofa shopping for a few minutes whilst I have a chin wag with Marv, here?"

Marvin stares disgustedly at us. "Sofa shopping? Again? What is that, like, a euphemism, a cute little inside joke for you two?"

"I wish," Jude mumbles.

"Go," I say, pushing his shoulder. "I'll wait for you here. The couches can wait until tomorrow."

In an effort to get out of bed more often, I've started manufacturing errands for us to run. The latest is the quest for a perfect couch—for real this time (sort of). I've dragged Jude to half a dozen furniture stores; we've sat, bounced, lounged, and cuddled on more than fifty sofas; but I haven't found the right one yet. Probably because it's a bogus mission designed to curb my carnal urges. I guess I'll either have to pick one or come clean sooner or later. But for now, it's a decent distraction.

As they're walking away, I hear Jude say to Marvin, "I owe you one again, mate. This sofa business is getting on my wick."

I feel guilty, but it's either couch-hunting or *I'll* be on his wick.

~

It's so cold. The snow is melting under my cheek, which is quickly going numb. But I can't move. Well, I can, but when I do, everything hurts.

Where are Mom and Dad? I can't move enough to look for them, but I know, deep down, where they are without seeing them. I can sense them seeping into the soil.

Maybe this time is different...

"You're going to be okay. Here comes the ambulance. Over here! She's still breathing!"

The red, white, and blue lights lend an almost celebratory mood to the scene. Like patriotic strobe lights at a Fourth of July party. They're also mesmerizing, and I find myself unable to keep my eyes open.

"Stay awake, now! What's you're name, honey?"

"'Lizbeth." My voice doesn't sound like mine. It's gravelly, raspy, and wet.

"Elizabeth?"

"Uh-huh."

"That's a beautiful name, Elizabeth. Now, you just stay awake for me."

"Sleepy..."

"I know, I know. But it's important that you stay awake. Does a pretty girl like you have a boyfriend, Elizabeth?"

"Jude."

"Very good."

"Where's Jude?"

"Was he with you? There may be another one somewhere!"

"Dunno." I'm so confused...

"Stay awake. Dammit, I need a board over here! What's taking so goddamn long?! Elizabeth, wake up! Libby, wake up..."

Jude's nudging me in the small of my back with his foot. "Libby... wake up," he groans more than says. "You're dreaming again."

I'm curled up in my usual ball on the extreme side of my bed. It doesn't matter how snuggled up we are when we fall asleep; by the morning, I've edged as far away from him as possible. More than once I've woken up as I'm falling onto the floor. I can't explain it. When I'm awake, I can't seem to get close enough to him. But something about sleeping brings out the mostly dormant hermit in me.

Now his gentle foot-bump is making me totter dangerously on the edge of the mattress. I slide the extra inch it'll take me to not be in the bed anymore and set my feet on the floor. "Sorry," I say, twisting a little to look at him behind me, but he's already asleep again, his mouth half-open and his hands tucked angelically under his head on the pillow.

The cold sweat is drying on my skin, making me shiver in my t-shirt. I groggily shuffle to the bathroom, where I turn on the shower, mixing as little cold water in as I can without scalding myself. I can't stop shivering. It's always like this, though. I'm used to the dream and its after-effects—how I feel worse than I did even on that first day I woke up in the hospital—because at least then I was on a cocktail of narcotics and couldn't really process the truth.

What I'm not used to, however, is the presence of Jude in the dream. Or at least the notion of him. That's new. And terrifying. A blending of my past and present into one horrifying psychological stew. My hands shake as I squeeze shampoo onto my upturned palm. Nausea claws at my stomach until I fear I'll throw up in the shower. Chills run up and down my arms and the backs of my thighs. The feeling only abates after several minutes of steady, deliberate breathing.

It's going to be fine, I tell myself over and over as I scrub my hair and body. The two things *aren't* related. They're completely separate. One has nothing to do with the other. It's just my brain getting a little confused, piling all the important things in my life into one "bin," if you will. That's all. It's time to 'fess up to Dr. Marsh so he can help me work through some of this.

After my shower, I feel much better, but as I'm toweling off, I freeze, hearing voices on the other side of the door. Two men, one of whom is obviously Jude. The other I also recognize immediately: Hank.

"Shit!" I whisper. Quickly, I wrap the towel around me. Not expecting company, I hadn't brought my clothes into the bathroom with me. And this isn't the biggest towel in the world, but I make do, ensuring everything important is covered before I rush from the bathroom.

Both of them look at me accusingly as I stand in the doorway, but I don't think it has anything to do with the fact that I'm still dripping from some places.

"Hey," I greet them, smiling sheepishly.

Hank says, "I had no idea you had a boyfriend, Libby."

"I had no idea you had a brother," Jude states.

"Uh… now you do?" I try, crossing to my dresser and pulling out the first clothes my hands touch. "Jude, this is Hank, *who didn't tell me he was coming up for a visit.* Hank, this is Jude."

"I thought I'd surprise you."

"Oh, you did that, for sure!" I chuckle nervously, taking my clothes into the bathroom. Before I close the door, I say to them half-kiddingly, "Don't talk about me while I'm not in the room."

I dress with my ear practically pressed against the bathroom door. I'm terrified about what Hank might say.

I barely hear Jude ask, "So... are you going to visit your parents whilst you're here?"

I'd whimper, but I don't want to miss Hank's answer, which is a hesitant, "Uh, I might swing by there, but it's not really my style."

"You don't think they'd be happy to see you?" Jude presses.

Hank pauses, then says, "Not that it's any of your business, but I don't believe in that shit."

I barely have my jeans over my hips and my shirt tugged down before I crash back in on their conversation. "Hey! Uh, we should do something together later today, just the two of us," I say to Hank as I zip my fly and button my pants.

"Jesus, Libby," he gripes, looking away. "You could have finished getting dressed before coming back out here. It's a little early in the morning to be seeing my sister's snatch."

Jude's eyes widen, but he doesn't comment. Instead, he grabs his keys from the counter. "I'll get out of your way, then." Quickly, he finger-combs his hair.

If he's expecting me to object, he's overestimated my ability to act coolly under pressure. All I can think about is getting these two away from each other, and his voluntary departure fits well into that plan. When he spins his keys noisily around his index finger, I say meekly, "Call you later?"

He raises his eyebrows on his way past me. "Whatever," he replies. "Good meeting you, Hank." With that, he's gone, the slammed door vibrating the walls.

"Leave it to you to find a weird one," Hank remarks in Jude's wake.

"He's not weird," I say to defend him.

"He has an interesting notion of the afterlife, that's for sure."

I busy myself making coffee as my little brother takes a seat on one of the barstools at the counter. "He doesn't know they're dead," I say matter-of-factly. "Let's keep it that way for now."

"You're such a freak," he grumbles.

Whirling around, I object, "No, I'm not!" At least not as much as I used to be.

"Then why don't you just tell him, for Christ's sake?"

"I will, okay? I just have never found the right time."

"'Dude, my parents are dead.' How hard is that to say to someone? It's a lot easier than keeping it some big stupid secret."

I roll my eyes at him and change the subject. "So, what brings you to town?" I decide to give him the benefit of the doubt and not come right out and ask how much money he needs.

The goofy grin he shoots me reminds me of what he looked like when we were kids, and I realize I've missed him.

"Just thought I'd take a week off before the fall semester starts, come up here and check on my big sister. I didn't think you'd be... busy."

I pull two cups from the cupboard and set them in front of him. Leaning on my elbows on the countertop and wiggling my butt, I smile devilishly. "Yeah. Well, normally I'm not. But I *have* been lately. Very busy."

"Took my advice to get laid, huh?"

Instead of being touchy, I stick my tongue out at him. "Maybe. But not because you told me to. You're not the boss of me."

He reaches across and pulls my hair. I playfully slap his face.

After we go back and forth like that a few times, I turn and grab the carafe of freshly brewed coffee. As I pour each of us a cup, he says, "You're a lot different than the last time I saw you. I like your hair like that. Did you hire a life coach or something?"

"A what?"

"Life coach. Someone who works with you on your issues and kind of gives your life a makeover." He sips his coffee, then dumps about seven tablespoons of sugar in it. "A miracle worker, in other words. At least in your case." He pokes his tongue out of the corner of his mouth and stifles a smile, waiting for me to object to his diagnosis.

Instead, I simply ask, "There's such a thing?"

He nods enthusiastically. "Yeah, man. I'm thinking of becoming one." He stirs what must be something close to coffee syrup.

"I thought you were studying to be a pharmacist." I cross my arms.

Keeping his eyes on his swirling drink, he replies. "Yeah. Well, I don't know. I can't imagine counting pills for the rest of my life. And giving old people advice about how to stay regular." Then he looks up at me and smirks. "You're just disappointed you won't be getting any free dope."

Suddenly I realize I never combed my hair after my shower. I walk into the bathroom to do so, saying, "If I'm disappointed about anything—which I'm not; it's your life— I'd say it's that you're changing your major—again—right before what would be your senior year. Are you ever going to graduate?"

"What's it to you?" he says loudly, so I can hear him. "It's not your money."

I pause mid-stroke as I drag the comb through my hair. I don't want to fight with him (he fights dirty, for one thing), but I can't resist pointing out, "I just want you to have some money left to get settled after you graduate. That's all."

"Just because you live like a nun—well, strike that. Anyway, just because you have some kind of oddball thing against spending the money our parents left us doesn't mean I'm wrong because I don't have a problem with it." Sulkily, he adds, "It's not like I'm out buying fast cars."

"No, just pissing it away on fast women," I blurt. I come out of the bathroom with my hand over my mouth. "Sorry," I muffle, meaning it.

He grits his teeth. "Whatever, Libby. If I didn't have to beg you for every cent, you'd never know, and it wouldn't be any of your business what I spent it on. It *shouldn't* be, anyway. I'm an adult."

In two steps, I'm next to him, putting my arms around his shoulders and squeezing. "I'm sorry. Really. It just slipped out."

Reluctantly, he replies, "Yeah, yeah. I know you only nag the shit out of me because you care."

"Exactly. Let's not fight. What do you want to do today?" I let go of him and return to my cup of coffee.

"What about your boyfriend?" he asks. "He seemed pretty pissed off when he left."

My stomach clenches at the thought of Jude being mad at me, but I say lightly, "All the more reason for me to avoid him for a while."

❧ 17 ❧

It was fun for an afternoon to pretend like Hank was really in Chicago to see me. We talked over lunch, and I even allowed him to reminisce a little bit about the days before the accident. But he got sick of hanging out with me at about the same time I wrote him a big, fat check ("for books and shit").

So after he leaves to go catch up with some of his old high school buddies, I sit alone in my apartment, staring at my cell phone, wondering what I'm going to say when I call Jude.

"Hey, my big-mouthed kid brother's gone, so it's safe for you to come around again."

Probably not.

In the end, I decide to call and pretend like nothing's wrong. When in doubt, denial works wonders.

He seems completely normal until I say, "So, you wanna do something tonight?"

"Is this what you Americans refer to as a 'booty call'?" There's no mistaking the chill in his voice.

"Of course not," I answer, twirling a piece of my hair nervously. "Huh-huh. One track mind."

"So we're going to go out somewhere with Hank, then, I

take it?" He waits for me to answer, and when I don't, he adds, "Because I'd like to get to know him better. Or at all. Now that I've adjusted to the fact that he exists."

"Are you finished?"

"Finished what?"

"Passive-aggressively chewing me out."

"Is that what I'm doing?"

"Yes."

"So you're a shrink now? Because one would have a time with you."

This is the first time he's ever been seriously mad at me. I don't like it. He's… he's… "You're mean," I finally manage after swallowing and trying to steady my racing heart.

"I'm sorry," he says sarcastically. "Do you have the monopoly on that today?"

"When was I mean to you?"

"How about when you tossed me out on my arse this morning?"

"I didn't mean to be mean. You said you were going to leave; I didn't stop you. *That's* being mean?"

"No, first you very deliberately excluded me from your plans; then you were obviously relieved when I said I'd leave."

"You can read minds?"

"It was written all over your face! You didn't want me in the same room with your brother for another minute. Afraid he might tell me your big secret, whatever the hell that happens to be?"

Quietly, I ask, "Why are you being like this?"

"Because I'm sick to the back teeth of women who refuse to be upfront with me, maybe."

"I'm not your ex-wife!"

"That's about the only thing keeping me from jacking it in when it comes to you!"

"What does that mean? Speak English!"

"It means I'm going to put down the phone now, before I say something I regret. I'll see you Monday at work."

My phone beeps at me to let me know I've been dropped, in more ways than one.

"Asshole," I mutter to the phone. Well, I'll be damned if I'm going to sit around my apartment all night, alone. Unfortunately, I don't have any other friends to hang out with.

Impulsively, I grab a jacket and my keys and head for a place I haven't dared visit in nearly six years.

The face. That's what I'm dreading most when I tell him the story. Because I *will* tell him the story, I promise myself as I sit on the ground in front of my parents' double headstone. It's the first time I've seen the large piece of granite. I haven't been here since the day I was released from the hospital and had to watch them lower the caskets into the ground. And I didn't bother coming back after that, even when they told me the headstone had been installed. As a matter of fact, I almost couldn't find the gravesite today, because it looks so different now than it did that awful day. Other grave markers have popped up over the years, not to mention that there's grass here now. And that tree over there is a lot bigger than I remembered.

Anyway, now that I'm here, I wish I'd never come up with this stupid idea. Because now I really *have* lied to Jude. Before, I could get off on a technicality. "I don't talk to my parents." Well, that's not true now. I've been sitting here talking to them like a crazy person for the past two hours.

At first I was unsure what to say. "Hey. How's it going?" is a ridiculous thing to say to two dead people, no matter how unclearly one is thinking. Then I jumped right in, like we've been having an ongoing conversation for six years, and I was just continuing where we left off last time. I talked about Dr. Marsh like he was an old family friend they'd know. I let them know that Hank was visiting and looked good and that he was thinking of changing his major... again. I told them about Jude and how I thought they'd have liked him.

"Anyway," I say now, shivering a little in the cool dusk, "I'm dreading the face. You know the one. The 'oh-my-gosh-I'm-so-sorry' face, the 'you-poor-dear' face. It seems like only recently I've finally stopped running into people who know me from back then. That's why I don't tell anyone. It just makes everyone uncomfortable." I sigh and pick at the grass. "And I know—well, hope—that Jude will be different and won't treat me like the poor, pitiful orphan, but... why can't he just let it be? I mean, isn't it enough to know I don't want to talk about it?"

I throw a handful of grass at the headstone. "You guys really fucked me over, you know that? I wasn't kidding when I told him you haven't been there for me. You haven't. And you got your way, by the way. I've never been anywhere. Just how you wanted it. I spent the semester I wanted to spend overseas undergoing surgery after surgery. And by the time I was finished and ready to go back to school, Hank had been in foster care long enough. I had to get my diploma and get a real job. To support the two of us. Like some kind of tragic heroine in a book, only there's been nothing heroic about my life. It's just been pathetic."

I pause and sigh. "Until recently, I've been pretty ambivalent about life, actually. If it weren't for Hank, I probably wouldn't be here. What's the point?" Annoyed at my own theatrics, I mutter, "Oh, who am I kidding? Even if it were just me, I'd still be here. I'm too squeamish to kill myself. Even with pills. The closest I've gotten to suicide is with my reckless driving. You'll probably be glad to know that I drive a lot more carefully lately. Not as much of a death wish now that Jude's around." I consider that for a second and don't say anything for a while.

"Miss!" someone calls, making me jump. I look over my shoulder. It's a security guard. As I stand, he says, "Cemetery's closin'. You got to leave."

I brush my hands against my damp butt. "Okay!" I call back. To the marker, I say, "Well, I guess I should go home and figure out how I'm going to make it up to Jude for being so… me… this morning." I go to leave, then turn around as I say, "Bye. Again."

Before I let that statement get to me too much, I jog for the gate, where the security guard is waiting.

❧ 18 ❧

THE SHINY BLACK KEYS BLUR AND MERGE, BLUR AND MERGE IN my unfocused stare as I widen and narrow my eyes repeatedly. Blur and merge. Blur. Merge. Jude's office was dark and locked when I arrived at work a little earlier than usual. I've been sitting here staring at my computer keyboard for at least ten minutes, willing myself not to turn around every thirty seconds and check to see if he's arrived yet. I still don't know what I'm going to say to him anyway.

Part of me is really hurt and pissed off at some of the things he said on the phone Saturday. Part of me knows I deserved it.

Yesterday was hell. It felt like I had stepped into a time machine and transported myself six months into the past. I think Sandberg was diggin' it, but by the time I'd flipped through all 260 television channels for the twenty-fourth time, I was ready to scream my head off. I don't live in the best neighborhood, though, so I was afraid someone would call the cops if they heard a woman screaming. And then I'd have to explain myself to one more person.

Suddenly, someone is standing behind me, rubbing slightly

against my right shoulder. "What are you looking at?" he whispers.

I turn around, and Marvin takes a step back. "Get away from me!" I snap. "What the heck is wrong with you?"

He looks hurt. "Wha…? I was trying to see what you were staring at!"

"Why do you care?"

"I dunno. Sheesh!" He glances over his shoulder as if he's looking for someone or making sure they're not around. "Yo. Not cool what you did to Jude this weekend. Not telling him you had a brother, then dissing him so you could hang out one-on-one with your bro? That's cold, man."

At my crazy, angry-eyed expression, he says, "I know, you're probably pissed that Jude told me all that, but he was hurtin'! Came to work to see how I was coming along on that thing I was making for him, that's how desperate he was for something to do to take his mind off it."

I'm going to kill Jude. And I'll be on the news… again.

Oblivious to my thoughts but not to my twitching eye, Marvin continues, "And he wouldn't have told me anything, babe, but we went out for drinks Saturday night, and he had a few too many—although it's *amazing* how well that skinny dude holds his liquor—and that's when he told me why he was such a loser, being at work on the weekend, which I didn't take offense to, you know, considering I was at work, too."

"Shut up!" I hiss. "Just… shut… up, Marvin."

He puts his hands in front of himself and backs away. "Peace. Man, you are one scary bitch," he calmly declares as he turns and strides down the hall away from me.

Funny, now I'm not at all unsure about what I'm going to say to Jude when he gets here. First off, nothing. I refuse to have some kind of public lover's spat for all the gawkers to witness, especially those like Leslie who have been hoping for us to fail spectacularly. Next, if he comes to me to try to start a conversation, I'm going to coldly tell him that he'll have to wait until after work. Then... well, let's just say I hope he knows something about self-defense.

I almost get through the entire day without him trying to say anything to me. Without anyone trying to say anything to me, actually. I think I have "Bite me" written all over me. But at 3:00, he's lurking at the vending machine, knowing too well my addiction to the late-afternoon Kit Kat, especially when I'm stressed out or upset. Instead of being smart and turning right back around when I see him leaning up against the machine, holding an already-purchased Kit Kat as a peace offering, I continue in. But I don't take the candy bar from his hand. Instead, I feed my own money into the machine and press the button to buy my own.

"Now, what's the point in that?" he asks dolefully.

Ignoring him, I rip open the wrapper and turn to walk out.

"Libby!" he beckons.

I stop in my tracks, turn on my toe, and shoot him the dirtiest look I've ever given him (and that's saying something, going back to his first few months of employment here). He brings his head back, his face wary.

"Don't you *even* talk to me," I dictate. "Not here."

I'll give him credit; he has the balls to scoff at me. "That's what I love about America; it's a free bloody country."

"Not for you," I retort. "You're just a big-mouthed... redcoat."

So I'll have the last word, I make my exit right then, but behind me I hear him mutter, "Gormless twit Marvin."

I storm back to my desk, where I begin to annihilate my candy bar.

A couple of minutes later, Jude stops by my cubicle. To my back, he says, "At least let me take you to dinner, so we can talk."

"No," I answer succinctly. Crunch, crunch.

He whispers, "This is ridiculous. How am I supposed to apologize if you won't even give me an audience?"

"We have the technology," I reply cryptically. "Figure it out. Now, go away. I'm very busy and important." I return to openly surfing the Internet.

"Son of a—" he grumbles. But he leaves.

When I'm sure he's gone, I peek over my shoulder and see him stalking to his desk and sitting down at his computer. Pretty soon, an instant message pops up on my screen.

Jude.Weatherington:
is this wht you meant? you wnt me to aplogize to you in an instnt msg?

Libby.Foster:
You're right. That's stupid
Your typing is horrible. I understand it even less than your dumb colloquialisms

Jude.Weatherington:
Pardon, yr highness. I'm not a secretary

Libby.Foster:
Neither am I, a-hole

Then I block him from sending me any more messages. "Come off it!" I hear him yell from his office.

Several people look up from their work and over at him, but I continue to appear busy.

Lisa pokes her head over the wall. "What's the deal with Jude today? You been withholding sex?" She takes in the Kit Kat on my desk next to my keyboard. "Oh… that time of the month?"

"For Jude? Maybe. For me? No."

She laughs. "Oooh. Are the office king and queen having a row?" she asks in an English accent.

This is exactly what I *didn't* want to happen. But he had to make a scene.

I blink innocently up at her. "No. I don't know what his problem is. Why don't you go ask him? I'm sure he'll tell you."

"Never mind," she says, sighing. "I swear, sometimes I don't know why I even bother with you." She disappears, and I hear her typing at her desk, no doubt IMing Zoe to complain about me.

Yes, why does anyone bother with me? It seems like I'm just a high-maintenance, secret-keeping, brother-nagging, gravestone-chatting, sex-starved, back-biting, shrink-seeing waste of space. At that self-pitying thought, I grab my purse from my desk drawer and slink down to Wanda's office, where I tell her I feel sick and that I'm going to take the rest of the day off.

It took him a while, but once Jude realized I was gone for the day, he drove to my apartment and banged on my door, trying very unsuccessfully to get me to let him in. That is, until he said the magic words:

"Libby, please! I love you. And I'm sorry."

I yanked him into the apartment so fast he left skid marks out in the hallway.

I have to say, I don't agree with all the hype about make-up sex. I mean, it was nice, but I would have much rather skipped the fight and had regular sex without the drama. Post-"I-love-you" sex is much better.

Now we're lying peacefully tangled together, playing with each other's hands. I nudge the arch of his foot with my toe, and his leg pops off the bed. "Grrr," he growls, as I giggle at how ticklish the bottoms of his feet are. Since I've discovered that trait, it's never ceased to amuse me.

After a languorous quarter hour, I tilt my head up so I can see his face. He angles his head to better look into my eyes.

"Yes?" he asks expectantly.

"Nothing. I was just making sure you're still awake," I reply.

He brushes his thumb against my hip. "Quite. Actually, I was just wondering for about the hundredth time what this is from." He circles the long, faded scar on my hip with his index finger.

"A freak accident," I say honestly, but don't offer any other information. When he purses his lips, and his eyes darken, I hurry on. "I *will* tell you someday. Everything. I promise."

"When is 'someday'? You know, just a—what do you Americans call it?—ballpark figure?"

"Soon," I answer non-committally.

"Right," he agrees uncertainly.

"But you can go through my mail anytime," I offer.

He smiles. "Thanks. And you promise you're not seeing Marvin on the side?"

I crack up. "I think I speak for all women when I say, 'I'm not seeing Marvin on the side.'"

"Well, I think we're good here, then," he utters, his voice filled with satisfaction.

"Jude." I twist and support my weight on my arms, kissing his chest.

"Hmm?"

"I'm sorry about how I acted when my brother dropped in."

He nods. "Forgiven. Of course."

"Really?"

"Yes. Really. That's how this love thing works, you see. You're not allowed to stay mad at the person you love for long."

I beam at his use of the "L" word again. "Ah. I see. That's how it works?"

"Indeed."

My heart pounds with the knowledge of what I'm about to say, but I try to be as casual about it as possible. After kissing him again, I drop, "Well, then, I guess that explains why I can't stay mad at you." I run my hand under the covers and up his leg. "Because I'm pretty sure... I mean..." Now I'm sweating. So much for playing it cool. "I think I love you, too."

Fortunately, he looks more amused at my uncertain declaration than disappointed. "You think so, eh?"

"No, I know it. I love you." I feel a physical lightening at having said it.

He feigns relief. "Whew. You had me going for a moment there." Suddenly serious, he shifts so that he's on his side. He wraps his arm around me. "You don't have to say it, though. That's not why I said it."

"I know! I mean it!" I insist.

"I know," he echoes. "I've known for a long time."

I roll onto my back, gazing up at him, wishing I had one

tenth of his confidence, wishing I knew what was going on in my own head as much as he seems to know. "You have?"

Now he looms over me. "Yes. I have."

"Since when?" I want to know if he's right. And if he really can read my mind, as I've suspected all along.

He delays answering by kissing me slowly, almost making me forget my question. Almost. But he's not avoiding answering. As soon as the kiss is over, he says, "There wasn't a specific, single moment, if that's what you're asking. But it was close to the same time I knew I loved you."

"And when was that?" I keep digging, my voice nearly a whisper.

"The day of the baseball game."

The jaw on the little Libby in my brain drops. "You knew *that* long ago?!" I can't help crying.

"Shhh," he requests, brushing his lips against my collarbone. "Yes. I did."

"Before we ever..." I trail off, more because I'm suddenly distracted by what he's doing to me than because I'm embarrassed to say it.

He nods, his forehead brushing against me. "Oh, yes. Much before. Otherwise..."

When he doesn't seem in any hurry to finish, I prompt, "Otherwise?"

Lifting his head, he looks me in the eyes. "Otherwise, it never would have happened." He pauses, then verifies with me, "Right?"

After wondering if I'll ever find my voice again, I respond, "Right."

He grins. "See? I knew it."

Then he makes love to me as if to prove it.

❧ 19 ❧

"So that's where we are," I tell Dr. Marsh, after getting him up-to-date on what's been going on.

Dr. Marsh taps his lips with his pen and consults his notes. "Okay. Let me get this straight, then: you haven't told him about your parents, which means you still haven't explained your career choice, but he's met Hank, and he knows you have *some* issues with your past, just not what those exact issues are. You've been intimate, you've exchanged 'I love you's,' and you're basically happy. And you've promised him you'll give him the full story at some point, but you haven't committed to when that'll be?"

I nod. "Yep. I think that's it."

"So... he probably has no idea you come to see me, right?"

"Definitely not!"

Sighing, he sets down his pen. "Why not?"

"I see you because my parents were killed in a horrific accident that I managed to survive. I can't tell him about you without telling him the other part, which I'm not ready to tell him yet." I pluck each part of the sequence from the air and place it into its own little imaginary compartment in front of me. "Get it?"

"Lots of people see mental health professionals, and very few of them because of an incident as traumatic as the one you experienced." He leans forward and puts his elbows on his knees. "Do you see how much you're backing yourself into a corner with all these lies of omission? Where does he think you are right now?"

I brush my hair out of my eyes. "We don't keep tabs on each other."

"Do you know where *he* is right now?"

"At work, of course," I answer flippantly.

"Where did you tell him you would be at this time?" he persists.

After licking my lips, I answer, "The doctor. It's not a lie."

"For what?"

"Routine check-up. Still not a lie."

"What're you gonna tell him next time you have an appointment to see me?"

I shrug. "I'll come up with something. Or maybe I'll have told him everything by then, and I won't have to..."

He raises his eyebrows, waiting for me to finish my sentence. When I don't, he does for me. "Lie?"

Defensively, I respond, "Be as vague."

"Ah." He straightens and folds his hands over his belly. "You're being vague, not lying?"

"Exactly."

"Okay. Let's turn it around so you can see what a double-edged sword ambiguity can be." He points to himself. "What am I, in my most basic form?"

A douche, I want to answer, just to lighten the mood. Instead, I answer, "A man."

"Yes. And what do you do when you have an appointment with me? You come to…"

"See you?"

He points at his nose. "Yes!" He thinks for a second. "Okay, and when you come to see me, a man, do you do it openly or in secret?"

"Secret," I whisper.

Biting his lips, he looks away from me while he gives me a minute to process that.

I see a man secretly, behind Jude's back.

Dr. Marsh is my guy on the side.

When I leave Dr. Marsh's office that day, I sit out in my car for a long time, staring at a vacant lot next to his office building. The cracked pavement has sprouted weeds, some three or four feet tall. Even though we've already had a couple of nights in which the temperature has dipped below freezing, they're hanging on. Winter's on its way, though. I'd know it even if I never went outside or looked at a calendar. I can feel it in the dread that slowly builds all year long and reaches its undeniable crescendo every twelve months.

But in addition to the usual sinister note always sounding in the back of my mind, there are other notes pealing, and they're actually starting to drown out the original one. It's not a pretty song. I know I'm running out of time and Jude's patience. I also know that some of what I have to tell him might send him running, no matter how soon I get up the nerve to tell him.

So I choose a date, a deadline if you will, right here and now in this parking lot. I promise myself—and Jude, silently—that I'll tell him everything, risking "the face," risking his wrath, risking just about everything I've come to care about, on The Anniversary. It'll arrive sooner than I'll be ready, I know that. But I also know I'll never be ready, no matter how long I give myself. The Anniversary will be just as good a day as any to do it.

❧ 20 ❧

I'M SICK. FOR REAL. NOT IN THE HEAD THIS TIME, BUT IN THE body. I'm pretty sure it was something I ate at that Indian place last night. I didn't even want to go there, but Jude kept going on and on about not having had "a good curry in yonks," so like a good girlfriend, I let him pick the restaurant, and he picked that one. It looked like one of those places that often appears on the health violations list in the newspaper. But I've been accused of being a snob, so I didn't say anything. I picked at my chicken curry and focused more on the conversation than the food.

It doesn't matter that I ate like a bird (who was eating a bird, which is wrong); the vomit seems to have the same type of source as the sweat under Marvin's arms: infinite. The first time I thought that, I puked so hard, I pulled a muscle in my ribs.

I called Jude between sessions with my toilet. He offered to come over, but I could tell it wasn't an offer he was relishing. (Oh, relish! Gotta run!)

And I don't want him to see me like this. I've been holding

back my own hair for years; I'm cool with continuing that job without an assistant. Or an audience.

Back in bed. Shivering from chills. Skin hurting. Rib throbbing. Head booming.

And, joy of joys, I have nothing better to do than think about my looming deadline. As predicted, the weeks have flown by, and I've almost arrived at The Day. It's so much more than The Anniversary now. It has the potential to redeem the date forever or confirm its status as cursed.

Though the date has remained the same, I've changed my plan a hundred times. It always starts out the same. I'm going to take the day off, like I always do, but then things get fuzzy. Do I invite him over for dinner? I won't want to eat, that's for sure. I suspect I'll never want to eat again after today, anyway. Do I tell him in a public place so he won't react too badly? Well, he's proven that he's not shy about making scenes, so that's not a foolproof plan. Do I take him some place that has personal significance to us? To me? To my family before the accident? I don't know. It's getting to the point that I'm paralyzed by indecision. I have too many options. The only thing that's a given is that I have to tell him everything. The setting is up in the air. I try to envision where we are when I tell him, but I can't picture us having the conversation at all.

Maybe that's because I won't tell him.

Yes, I will.

I wish I could tell him on the phone. At least then I wouldn't have to see "the face." But it's not really an over-the-phone conversation. If only it were that easy. I'm actually thinking of "the face" as my just due for waiting so long to tell him.

I finally fall into a fever-soaked sleep, and when I wake up I can tell by the light that it's late afternoon. I've missed three calls on my cell phone, all from Jude. After forcing myself to slowly drink a full glass of water, I call him back. And get his voicemail.

"Hey. Returning your calls. I'm still alive, barely. And you never get to pick where we eat again. Love you. Bye."

Bed again. I'm dozing in front of an infomercial about a compilation of footage of the British Royal Family, since the dawn of moving pictures (the only thing I could find that I could be reasonably assured wouldn't make any mention of food) when my phone buzzes on the pillow next to my head.

"I was in a meeting," he says, surprisingly tersely.

"Oh. I'm… sorry?" I'm not sure why I'm apologizing, but his tone tells me I should be.

"No, no," he catches himself. "*I'm* sorry. I… that is, I'm a bit distracted."

"Everything okay?"

"I think so," he answers vaguely. "How are you doing? You think it was the food? I'm fine today."

"We didn't have the same thing."

"Still chicken. I dunno. It's bizarre."

I can tell he's not completely focused on our conversation, so I say, "Listen, I was just returning your calls so you didn't picture me dried up like a raisin on my bathroom floor. I'll let you get back to work."

"Right. Sounds good. Cheers."

Speaking of bizarre… I stare at the phone for a second but then shrug the whole thing off. He's juggling more projects than anyone else there right now; he's entitled to be a little scattered. I wouldn't be holding up under the pressure as well as he is, that's for sure.

Now, how can I order these videos?

～

I'm barely at my desk two minutes, trying to catch my breath and holding onto my chair while the stars dance in front of my eyes, before Lisa hops into my cubicle. "Thank God you're back."

Touched by her concern, I sit down and say, "Aw, thanks! Yeah, I'm okay. A little weak, but—"

"Yeah, yeah. Good." She waves her hand in front of her face. "No, what I really mean is that I've been dying to know what all the meetings were about yesterday. I thought if I had to wait another day to get the scoop, I'd lose my mind."

"What?"

"Don't tell me you're sworn to secrecy. If you say that, we're not friends anymore," she says seriously.

I open my email to see if there are any hints in there as to what she's talking about. Nothing. Just the usual "Can you help me with this?" "Can you update this in our address book?" "Can you order lunch for ten?" Oops. I hope they found someone else for that.

I finally have to turn to her and admit, "I have no clue what you're talking about. Why don't you give me a hint?"

Even though it's obvious she doesn't believe me, she rushes through an explanation about yesterday's constant meetings, all of which were attended by Jude, Gary, and the really big bigwigs. "Rumor has it that the company is opening another branch, but there's no word on location yet. In the rumor mill, that is. I'm sure the people in that meeting know exactly where it'll be." She scoots closer to me. "So? What'd Jude say to you about it last night?"

I shake my head and whisper, "This is the first I've heard of it. I mean, I know he was in a meeting yesterday, but I only talked to him on the phone, and he never said what it was about. We mostly just talked about my budding relationship with my toilet."

"Eww! TMI! You talk to your boyfriend about that stuff?"

I give her a look that conveys "Big deal," and she says, "Gosh, I don't think Steve knew I even had bodily functions until after we were married!"

"Then you're deranged," I declare. "Anyway, now that you mention it, Jude *was* really distracted when I talked to him. It was like he couldn't get off the phone fast enough."

"Well, with the conversation you were having, I don't blame him," she states. "Ick. But didn't he come over to at least bring you soup or something? That's kind of cold."

I go back to cleaning out my emails. "I didn't want any soup. And let's not talk about food in general. Hey, did you help Brandon with this permit application yesterday?"

"Yes." She leans against the cubicle wall. "I wonder where the new office will be. Do you think they're asking Jude to transfer, head it up? What will you do if he has to move to another city?"

My finger freezes on my mouse button, and I get vertigo again. "Uh… do you really think that's what's going on?"

"Why else would he be in that meeting?"

"Minutes transcription?" I offer weakly.

Lisa snorts at me. "Nice try. He's been in charge of or a part of every single major account in this department since he joined the company. They've been grooming him."

"If they have, he doesn't know anything about it," I say. "He's never mentioned that before. As a matter of fact, he always calls himself 'a cog on the wheel.'"

"He's just being modest. Brandon, Heath, Jake—*they're* cogs. Jude's his own wheel, especially ever since he nailed that Art Museum design."

Mr. Modesty himself walks by, slowing down when he sees us.

"Blimey, I didn't expect to find you here today," he says,

looking pleasantly surprised. He steps in and kisses the top of my head. "You sounded like Death yesterday when we spoke."

Lisa says, "'Morning, Jude. You look chipper today. Although you might want to put some cukes on those eyes tonight. Having trouble sleeping?"

He smiles at her. "Not really." Then he looks down at me, "Well, maybe I was a bit worried last night about you, but I know you're tough. A little food poisoning wouldn't keep you down for long."

"Hmm. Well, I guess I should get to work," Lisa murmurs, slipping out.

Although I know she's standing right on the other side listening to everything we say, I quietly ask Jude, "What's going on?" in a bemused tone.

He shakes his head, still smiling. "What?"

"You know… the meetings yesterday. Mingling with the corporate muckety-mucks." I keep my tone light, a verbal elbow nudge.

He transfers his coat to his other arm and avoids my eyes. "I'm afraid I don't follow."

"Jude!" I pull on his pants leg so he has to come closer.

"Libby…" For a second, I think he's going to tell me something, but then he pauses, obviously thinking better of it.

"Are the rumors true?" I ask, regretting the dry toast I ate for breakfast.

He shrugs. "I haven't heard any rumors, so I wouldn't know."

I look up at him disbelievingly. After an informal staring contest, I stand, my eyes still locked on his. "Can we go into your office and talk for a second?"

"Uh… Well…" He backs away from me. "I don't really have time. And I'm sure you have a lot to catch up on from yesterday. Wanna go to lunch later? Grab a burger?"

My stomach buckles. I edge closer to my trashcan and nudge it towards me with my toe, just in case.

"Ooh," he winces. "I guess not. Still have a case of the collywobbles? I'll come back to check on you in a bit." He turns and walks quickly into his office, where he closes the door and shuts the blinds.

Lisa pops up. "Oh, my gosh!" she gasps.

"What the fuck?" I agree.

Jude Weatherington is keeping secrets! From me!

21

JUDE MANAGES TO "WORK LATE" OR ATTEND OFF-SITE MEETINGS the rest of the week, effectively avoiding me. I haven't seen this little of him since before our first lunch together. When he's in his office, the door and blinds are closed. He answers my IMs politely but shortly, then logs off so that he shows up "unavailable." Sometimes, he'll call me when he's on his way home from work in the evenings, but he never talks about work, and if I try to bring it up, he says, "I thought you detested talking shop." The closest I've ever come to getting him to admit something's going on is when he told me, "I really can't discuss it; I could get sacked. You understand, right?"

What can the girl with unshared secrets galore say about that to her extremely understanding boyfriend? I have no choice but to accept it and try to learn to live with not sleeping until all can be revealed.

But the weekend is here, and he has nowhere to hide. I heard Gary saying today on his way out of Jude's office (after yet another closed-door meeting), "Get some time away from here this weekend, rest, and think about it."

"Think about what?" I wanted to shout at the V.P. from across the hall. "It's not nice to make guys keep secrets from their girlfriends!"

But at least I know Jude won't be "working" this weekend (unless it's on his back; I'm feeling much better, and I'm sick of being ignored).

When he stops by my desk at the end of the day, like old times, pulling on his coat, gloves, and knit hat, and says, "Let's get cracking," I can't resist giving him a hard time.

I turn to face him and point at my chest in a "Who me?" gesture. I look behind me, as if I think he may be talking to someone else, then I say, "Surely you're not talking to me, are you?"

He holds my coat out for me. "No need to be cheeky."

Going to him, I spin so I can slip my arms into my coat. "Thank you. I'm sorry. It's just... I'm having a hard time remembering your name. I think it starts with a 'J'..."

"Ah, clever," he remarks resignedly, offering his arm for me to take.

"I don't normally go home with strangers, but since you're so cute, I guess I can make an exception. Just don't tell my boyfriend. He's been a little neglectful lately, but I know he still cares." In response to his cheerless expression, I nudge him with my hip while we walk to the elevators. "I'm just kidding, by the way."

He tries to smile. "I know. You're very funny. But I'm knackered."

I kiss his rough cheek as we get into the elevator with several other people. On the way down to the parking garage, we're both silent, neither one of us caring to have the rest of the occupants listen in on our conversation.

Brandon and Heath exchange glances and smirk at one

another. Brandon looks over his shoulder at us; Heath nudges him. "What?"

Heath mutters something I can't hear, but it makes Brandon laugh and say, "Right?"

Jamie from Accounting and Bruce from the mailroom snicker at what's being said at the front of the elevator.

Ours is the last stop, and we hang back to let three others out before us. As they walk in front of us a few feet, Jude mumbles, "Bunch of nosy parkers."

I laugh. "I thought I was being paranoid; I'm glad it wasn't just me."

"No, they were saying something about us. Or me, more like."

We've arrived at my car. It's frigid down here. I scrunch my shoulders up around my ears to try to keep them warm with my scarf. "Who cares?" I ask, even though I'm wondering the same things they are. Squinting at him, I posit, "My place or yours?"

Once inside his warm apartment, in the blinking glow of the tiny Christmas tree down the hall in the living room, we start the arduous task of taking off our wrappings.

"I hate winter," I grouse.

"Then you made a crap decision about where to work and live," he points out, helping me unwind my scarf.

"Stop being so logical."

He laughs, and I realize with a pang that it's the first time I've heard that sound in days.

When we're standing sock-footed in the kitchen, looking through his collection of take-out menus, I move a piece of his hair behind his ear and kiss his earlobe. "Your hair's getting long," I whisper, making him shiver.

He brings his shoulder up to his ear but keeps his eyes on the menus. "I know. I can't faff around with haircuts lately. Barely have time to use the gents most days."

"Poor baby," I say semi-sincerely. If he wants me to be truly sympathetic, he'll tell me exactly what's going on. I don't complain to him when my hip hurts. Or when I miss my parents. I know I don't have that right until he knows everything.

Finally, he holds up a flyer for the sandwich shop around the corner. "Does this sound okay for your delicate constitution?"

Oh, food.

"Whatever." I take the paper from his hand and give it a cursory scan. "I'll take the number seven with no onions, add pickles, olives, and banana peppers."

He gives me an amused glance. "That's a lot of salty, sour garnish."

"I like salty, sour stuff," I say. "Oh, that reminds me: add mustard."

After he puts in our order, I sit on the couch, gesturing for him to sit on the floor in front of me so I can rub his shoulders. While I'm rubbing and he's moaning, I wonder how long I'm going to have to wait before he tells me what's going on at work. Is this how he feels every day and week that passes that I don't tell him my secret? If so, then I've been torturing him for months. He hasn't seemed tortured, but he's not the easiest person to read. Maybe it's been killing him. Maybe that's the reason for the dark circles under his eyes.

And maybe he's going to take a job in a different city to get away from me, just like he did his ex-wife.

I stop rubbing. "Hey."

"Huh?" He flops his head back and looks up at me. I can see the Christmas tree reflected in his eyes.

"I have to tell you something."

The tone of my voice gets his attention right away. He twists so that he's sitting perpendicular to me but still on the floor. "What is it?"

"I've been trying to figure out for a long time how to tell you this... And I was going to wait another few days, but... but I don't think it's fair of me to keep it from you anymore, even if I haven't come up with the best way to say it." Oh, gosh. I'm really going to tell him. Right now. Not on The Anniversary. Not after meticulously planning every action, word, and moment.

"Oh, fuck," he mutters.

This reaction puzzles me, but a lot of what he says confuses me, so I continue, "I love you, and I want you to know I'd never do anything to intentionally hurt you or... or even so much as inconvenience you. Well, that's not really the right word, but you know what I mean. So, right off the bat, I need to say that I'm sorry."

He rubs his face, his hand swishing against his five o'clock shadow. "I can't bloody believe this. This is just sod's law, isn't it?"

"What's 'sod's law'?"

He misinterprets my question and says, "Well, *this*, of course."

"I haven't even told you what I need to tell you yet."

Standing, he paces in front of me. "You don't have to. I know this talk."

"You do?" Suddenly, I wonder if he's done some research about me. A simple Internet search would probably bring up some old articles about what happened. Or he could have been talking behind my back with Hank.

"Yes. Oh, God!" He puts his hands on his head, really despairing.

His reaction is not at all what I expected in any of the 5,000 scenarios I've dreamt up over the past few weeks. "Okay... But how did you find out?"

Taking his hands away from his face, where they were squishing his cheeks into his mouth, he says, "I had no idea, until just now. No clue. This is a real kick in the dangly bits. And now, of all times!"

I'm about to suggest that we're not talking about the same thing when he takes a look at me, seemingly for the first time in the conversation and says, "I'm so sorry, Libby. I know I'm acting like a right git. But this is a real blow. And I know it's not your fault, and I want to be supportive, but I just need to wrap my head round it. Please, don't think me an insensitive bastard." He sits next to me on the couch. "We'll figure this out."

"What the fuck are you talking about?" I finally interject.

He seems a little less sure of himself when he says, "I'm talking about what you're telling me."

"No, you're not," I say confidently. "I haven't told you anything."

"You don't have to. As a matter of fact, please don't say it out loud. I don't know if I can bear hearing the actual words. But I know. I know." He puts his hand on my shoulder.

"You know that my parents are dead?"

He temporarily loses the anguished expression he's been wearing for the past five minutes. "Wha...? W-When did that happen? Oh, crikey! And whilst you were estranged from them?"

"No, six years ago. Almost exactly."

"I'm *terribly* confused."

"Me too!" I cry. "What are *you* babbling about?"

He jabs his thumb and forefinger into his eyes. "Oh! Thank God!"

"Excuse me?"

"No! Not about your parents!" He quickly grabs my hands, which I immediately pull away from him. Then he lets loose a hysterical giggle and stifles the rest of his laughter. "Not that. Sorry. That's tragic!"

And there it is: the face.

"Spare me," I spit, before he can say anything else. I jump up and away from him. "What did you think I was telling you?"

He laughs at himself. "I thought you were going to say you were… you know, up the duff."

"Up the what?"

"Duff. You know… pregnant!"

"*What?*"

"I know! Imagine how *I* felt! I'm so worried about work, and everything, and then you tell me that, or what I thought was that, and I just started having kittens!"

I stare at him while he jabbers on for a good three or four minutes non-stop about how great it is that I'm not pregnant and that he's so glad I was telling him my parents are dead, not that I was pregnant, and that he's so relieved I'm not pregnant and that it's just that my parents are dead.

Thankfully, the sandwich delivery person interrupts his nonsensical monologue. He pays for the food and tosses the bag on the kitchen counter, pointing to it, as if it contains a dead mouse. "And your sandwich! All those pickles and peppers and things! It all just started making sense. You've been to the doctor recently… You were sick earlier this week…"

"I had food poisoning!"

"So you said, but you could have been covering with that

until you could get up the nerve to tell me. Oh!" He puts his hand on his forehead. "I can't even begin to tell you how relieved I am!"

"I think the past ten minutes have been a good start." I cross to the coat rack and begin re-draping myself.

His forehead wrinkles in consternation. "What are you doing? Where are you going? The food's here."

"I'm *so* not hungry right now, Jude." With shaking fingers, I button my coat.

He rushes to me. "Wait! Why are you angry?"

Hot tears form in my eyes, dripping unchecked down my cheeks as I jam my fingers into my gloves and tie my scarf. I can barely speak coherently, but I manage to say (although how much of it he can understand is another story), "I can't believe you! I try to tell you about how my parents died and how it nearly destroyed my life, so much so that I can hardly bring myself to tell *anyone*, and you..."

I can't finish. I don't even know where I was going with it, honestly. "Just... eat your fucking sandwich and enjoy the fact that you're not going to be a father and that I'm not having your baby and that my parents are gone forever."

I might as well have smacked him across the face.

"But... I... That's not at all how I feel!" he stutters.

"I don't want to hear another word about how you feel," I declare. "I've heard enough for one night."

He stands with his hands hanging limply at his sides while I grab my messenger bag and unclip my keys from its strap. "I'm sorry. Really. I merely got caught up in the moment. And... and... it's really rather funny, when you think about how I cocked it up so badly."

I open the door. "Hilarious. I'm sure I'll be laughing all the way home."

22

OF ALL THE THINGS JUDE GAVE ME TO THINK ABOUT ON THE way home, I spent the majority of the trip worrying about leaving him stranded at his apartment without a car. But by the time I crossed my own threshold (darkened it, more accurately) I was done worrying about anything having to do with the problems he'd brought on himself with his behavior. I collapsed on the bed, fully clothed, still in my winter wear, and really let myself cry.

If Sandberg were a dog, he would have been all over me, trying to figure out what was wrong, licking me and nudging me with his nose. But that's why I like cats. I didn't want to be bothered, touched, or even looked at. Sandberg may have done the latter for a second or two, but I must not have been entertaining enough, because he soon curled his body away from me, tucked his face under his back legs, and resumed his nap.

I was really too stunned and hurt to process everything that had been said at Jude's; all I could do was feel. And it hurt. A lot. So I tried to cry the pain away. But sleep, rather than tears, was the eventual reliever.

This morning, I wake up, my eyes puffed to slits in my face, my mouth dry, and my body covered in a fine glaze of sweat from all the layers of clothing still piled on me. As soon as I got in my car last night, I turned off my phone, but now I pull it from my coat pocket and turn it on. Twenty-four missed calls. And the little envelope that signifies unheard messages seems to be blinking more furiously than usual.

I feel the tears building again, so I quickly delete all the messages without listening to them and drag myself from the bed. Must keep myself busy. Or angry. But not hurt. And definitely not compassionate.

What if I really had been pregnant? How would I have felt after watching Jude practically rend his clothing despondently at the prospect? It's hard to conjure the right words to explain the feeling, but "pretty shitty" comes close enough for now. It's all fun and games to have sex with me and toss out the words "I love you" when it suits his purposes, but when it comes right down to it, he's obviously more interested in the path his career's taking than the path our relationship is headed down.

Of course, it's really not fair for me to resent him for caring about his professional life. He's doing what he loves to do, not just some job. But he's never acted like it mattered *that* much; definitely not more than I matter to him. Maybe this latest development—whatever that may be—has shifted the order of things.

I think of Lisa saying, "They've been grooming him," and I shiver. That terminology hearkens to mind the mafia. Maybe I've been watching too many *Sopranos* reruns. If I had been let in on this "grooming" from the beginning, it probably wouldn't feel like such a threat, but because it's obviously some big secret, something that Jude doesn't want me to know about, it's scary. Like he's compartmentalizing everything in his life so that he can easily lop off certain segments when they're no longer useful to him. Maybe I've been a mere diversion while he's been in Chicago, waiting for his life to *really* take off.

And now it is, and he's ready to move on. I can see how the news he *thought* I was giving him could have put a serious hitch in his plans. His being ready to move on also explains why he was so dismissive about what I was really saying. He doesn't care anymore about my past. Like his ex-wife, I'm about to be a faint memory in a distant city, part of *his* past, someone he laughs about with his next girlfriend on lazy weekends in bed.

That's probably why he's been avoiding me. I thought it was because he wanted to resist any temptation to tell me things he's not allowed to tell me; but really, he's distancing himself. He's getting ready to dump me. Ditch me. Toss me aside.

He may be surprised to find out that I have a little experience with that, believe it or not. Not by a man, obviously, but I know what it's like to lie on the frozen ground, pitched away, waiting for someone to rescue me.

Not this time. And I doubt I'm even going to tell him about the last time. Why bother?

Something else has been bothering me, but I can't quite put my finger on it. It's something Jude said last night, but my mind is such a fog of anger and hurt that I can't remember exactly what he said or why it bothered me. At the time, I was struggling to understand what he was saying in the context of what I was trying to tell him, so nothing made sense. But now, knowing what I know, something he said is throwing up a red flag. If only I could remember what it was.

Due to all the time I spent alone during the week, my apartment is clean, so there's no housekeeping to keep me busy. I do a cursory tidying, including refreshing the litter box and gathering up some dirty clothes to take to the building's laundry facilities in the basement. My phone rings twice, but I don't answer it when I see "Jude" flash on the display. If he keeps calling, I'll turn it off.

I don't have anything else to do, so I stand in front of the washing machine while it goes through its cycles. As I watch the water and soap swishing, my underthings and t-shirts slapping against the little round window, I hear him say it, almost as if he's in the room with me. *"I know this talk."*

I furiously finger the scar in my eyebrow, the one that I painstakingly cover each day with eyebrow pencil, combing the rest of the hairs over it to hide it. It's the only clearly visible physical reminder of the accident. Nobody knows that my leg aches from my hip to my ankle when the barometric pressure drops to a certain level. Jude's seen the surgical scar on my hip, but he knows it's part of my secret. He also knows I have bad headaches sometimes, but he doesn't know it's because I have a titanium plate in my head from where they had to reconstruct part of my skull. Those scars are well hidden under my thick hair.

"I know this talk."

When was that, in the sequence of events? Had I told him my parents were dead? No. We were still talking about two different things: me about my secret; him about unplanned pregnancy. Or pregnancies, more like it, if he "knows this talk."

I drop heavily into one of the plastic chairs in the dungeon-like laundry room. Jude has a kid? Maybe he's not just running away from bad memories in England or a wretched ex-wife. Maybe he's running away from responsibility in general.

No. I don't believe it. Not the guy I know. There's another

explanation. I can't think of one right now, but there is one. Has to be. He's never breathed a word of this. No pictures of the kid, no unexplained phone calls, no nothing. I can't believe the guy I love, the Jude Weatherington who can't even bluff when I ask him if something makes my butt look big, could lie about something that major.

Of course, according to my definition of lying, he hasn't, I remind myself. I've never come out and asked him, "Did you and Kiersten have any children?" It seemed so obvious that they didn't. There was no evidence to the contrary.

However... he never lied to me about being "groomed" for bigger things at work, either. Unless you count calling himself "a cog" lying. Which I kind of do, especially if he knew that wasn't the case. But still, he's not any guiltier of lying than I've been for the duration of our relationship.

That doesn't mean I don't have the right to be upset, though. Especially if he has a kid he never told me about. I mean, what if we had started talking about marriage?

Wait for it, wait for it...

Oh, I see.

She's got it!

That was never in his plan. Of course not. I'm such an idiot. To think the first guy to pay any attention to me would actually like me enough, once he really got to know me, to marry me. I should have known that this was a fluke. My spinster card has *not* been revoked. I'll be digging that out any day now.

And I haven't even begun to probe the open, weeping wound that is the subject of the car accident that changed my life and ended my parents' lives. I finally—finally!—trust someone enough to tell them about it after all these years, after he's begged and pleaded with me to tell him, after I've agonized with the guilt of keeping it from him, but it turns out I grossly misjudged him. So not only can I not trust *him*, I can't trust myself to correctly judge someone's character.

The only one winning in all of this is Dr. Marsh. I'll be padding his retirement quite nicely for the next several years.

~

I've moved on to supervising my clothes in the dryer when Jude appears in the laundry room doorway. I hop down from my perch on the dryer and turn my back to him. "Why are you here?"

"Because you won't return my phone calls," he answers simply.

"That's usually a good sign that someone doesn't want to talk to you," I explain.

"But we *need* to talk. I know you like to run away when things get nasty, but—"

I whirl around. "*That's* a really interesting statement from you."

He eyes me warily. "Oh? I don't recall running from trouble."

I want to know, but I don't want to know. "Never mind. It's not like I'm going to get you to tell me the truth, anyway, so what's the point?"

Sighing, he says, "I didn't come here to have a row with you."

"Well," I scoff, "you'd better turn around and leave, then, because I kind of want to scratch your eyes out."

"Libby..." He comes closer, his arms open.

"Don't!" I insist, pressing myself up against the dryer as far as I can. "I'm serious."

He drops his arms. "Right. Tell me what you want from me. I'll do whatever you want, except leave without talking about this."

I close my eyes, unable to look at him without crying. His image is etched on the back of my eyelids, though, so the tears are unstoppable. "Damn it," I mutter. "Damn *you*."

"I know," he says resignedly. "I made a fist of it last night. And I'm not saying this to excuse it, but I've been under so much strain at work of late." His voice moves closer to me, but I keep my eyes closed. The dryer vibrates soothingly against my lower back.

"Why are you under so much strain?" I ask, figuring this is just as good a place as any to start.

He pauses. When I open my eyes to see why he's not answering, he opens his mouth, then closes it before saying, "I really can't discuss that." Before I can object, he continues, speaking louder to drown out any complaints from me, "You know what it's like... Only in my case I could lose my job if I told you. I'm not really sure what you thought the consequences were to telling me about your parents." When the only reaction he gets from me is a stony glare, he offers, "About work... you'll know soon."

"When everybody else finds out?"

He nods, clearly uncomfortable with his own answer.

"That's just great." I'll probably have to order lunch for the announcement, too. When I'm dumped, it's a public, catered affair.

"I'm sorry. It's not ideal," he admits. "But I promise we'll talk about it alone as soon as we have a chance. I have a lot to say..."

"Whatever," I sigh, dismissing his offer. "I'm just a cog. On the Jude wheel."

"How can you say that?" he asks, slumping into a chair.

I resume my perch on top of the dryer, where it's warm. "That's the reality, isn't it?"

"Absolutely not! Where are you getting that?" Pulling his knit hat from his head, he drops it into his lap, then tries unsuccessfully to press his hair down against his head. It looks unwashed.

Actually, upon closer inspection, he looks terrible, in general. I experience a small twinge of satisfaction from that. I'm not sure how much credit I can take for it, but I'm sure it's a little bit.

"All signs are pointing there," I reply vaguely.

"You're reading them wrong."

I shrug as if it doesn't matter to me one way or the other. "Doesn't seem like I am."

His jaw tightens, then he says, "I guess we'll have to table that one for now, because I'm not at liberty to tell you anything that would change your perceptions."

"How convenient."

"Speaking of... I have to say... your use of the word 'inconvenient' last night really threw me off."

"What?"

"Yes. You said you hated to inconvenience me, or some such thing, and it reinforced my suspicions that you were giving me the, 'I'm pregnant' speech. Again, I'm so sorry I misunderstood."

Coldly, I reply, "Well, since you're so familiar with it, I can see how you would think you could name that tune in two notes." Suddenly, my heart is pounding. This is it. I can tell by the caught look on his face.

"Oh, that. Well. Yes."

"Do you have a kid?"

"No, I haven't," he answers calmly and quietly.

"You and Kiersten don't have a child together? Or you and anyone else?" I feel like I have to ask every possible question so he can't slip through any honesty loopholes.

He shakes his head once. "No."

"Just 'no'?"

He throws his hands up. "That's the answer to your question. I don't know what else you want me to say."

"I want you to explain the sentence, 'I know this talk,' which you said when you incorrectly assumed yesterday that I was telling you I was pregnant." I cross my arms over my chest and wait.

His nostrils flare. He rubs the back of his neck. "Right. When we were getting divorced, Kiersten came to me and told me she was pregnant. I reacted a bit more maturely with her than with you,—again, sorry—but still not as well as I should have, looking back…"

"Maybe you can perfect your technique with subsequent girlfriends," I snipe.

He grits his teeth, then continues, "*Anyway*, the more I thought about it and did the maths, the more I realized that something wasn't adding up. I knew about her boyfriend, of course, so I was legitimately suspicious the child wasn't mine. I told her I wanted a DNA test done when the baby was born. It turned out to be unnecessary, however."

"Why? She decided it would be easier to just raise the kid alone than drag you kicking and screaming into fatherhood?"

"The child was black."

That shuts me up. "Oh."

"The best thing about it? Her boyfriend wasn't."

I catch myself snickering with him about that and immediately stop. I clear my throat and play with my shoelace. "That still doesn't excuse the way you acted last night."

"I didn't say it did." He flaps his hat against his knee. "To my credit, though, I never once asked if I was the father."

"You're kidding, right?"

"What? I think that's important."

"That you didn't add insult to injury? That makes you a prince, huh?" The dryer stops, so I jump down and open it to retrieve my clothes. I'm so ready for this conversation to be over. All I need to do is collect my things and go upstairs, where I can lock the door in his smug face. "You're disgusting."

"I only mean that I could have been a bigger jerk, believe it or not."

"You were still inappropriate."

"Granted."

"Especially because... never mind. My feelings were really hurt by the whole thing. Your reaction to the possibility of my being pregnant is an infinitesimal part of it." I slap the last pair of panties on top of the pile in the basket, then impulsively bury them under some other clothes.

When I turn around to leave the laundry room, he stands, too. "I reacted badly all round. I admit that. I feel especially badly about giving you the impression that I'm glad it was merely your parents' deaths you wanted to talk about and not the other thing." He reaches out to touch my shoulder as I pass him. I shrug him off.

"Don't. You can tell a lot about a person by the way he reacts under stress. I found out a lot about you last night. A lot I didn't like." He turns his head and juts out his jaw. "So... I hope it's a relief to have one less thing to occupy your mind during this stressful time in your life."

His eyes snap back to me. "What do you mean?"

My eyelids flutter as more tears gather behind them, but my voice is steady when I say, "If you think I'm going to sit by like a pathetic… virgin… and wait for you to leave me behind while you move on with the rest of your fabulous life and career, you're nuts." I flip the light switch and head up the four flights of stairs to my apartment. He's right on my heels.

"Wait! Are you… *chucking* me? Because I was an arse and hurt your feelings during a moment of weakness?" He voice echoes in the stairwell.

As I unlock my door, I say, "That's an extreme trivialization of what went down, but… yes. I am."

When I open the door, he shoulders his way in right behind me, before I can slam it. I suddenly picture him on the rugby field, his arms wrapped around the ball, his elbows flying left and right as he bowls through a muddy group of bodies.

"How can you do this?" he demands, his face screwing up into an expression I've never before seen on it. If I had to name it, I'd call it "agony." "I've said I'm sorry. I've… I've…" Suddenly he stops. Every muscle in his face slackens. He raises his hand and drops it, nodding his head. "Right. Well. I refuse to beg you to reconsider."

"Good. I think you should leave." Before I change my mind. Before I cry most unattractively.

He wrenches the door open fully, pauses, and turns around one more time. "I'm sorry. Again. Really. I…" He chokes but clears his throat and says lucidly, "I wish I could have heard more about your mum and dad."

This statement brings on the most gut-wrenching sobs I've produced since their funeral. Somehow I manage to choke out the biggest lie I've ever told him. "I'd rather find a… a… bum on the street and talk to him about it than tell you another word!"

Chuckling mirthlessly at my immature statement, he

replies, "Right," and exits, pulling the door softly closed behind him.

I drop the laundry basket and stand in the middle of my apartment, sobbing, until even heartless Sandberg starts rubbing against my legs.

23

I slept the rest of the weekend away. It was the only way I could keep from crying. But I slept so much that this morning, I was sore from lying in bed all weekend. And not sore in a good way, like I used to be. With him.

Now it's Monday, and I have to be brave. I have to do one of the hardest things I've had to do in a long time. Harder than any exam in college. Harder than giving up my dream of traveling and observing other cultures and societies. Harder than taking care of my little brother when I was hardly more than a child myself. Today I have to get out of bed. I have to go to work. I have to swallow my pride. And apologize.

Because I can't go through with this break-up. Even if it means I take him back just in time for him to say "See ya" on his way to bigger and better things, I can't be the one to end it. Call me weak, call me spineless, call me whatever you will. What it comes down to is this: I love him. Irrevocably, inexorably, inexplicably, inescapably, and inevitably. And I'm too inexperienced at this to have any pride about it.

I'm wearing a short skirt, high heels, and a low-cut shirt I bought right after Jude and I started sleeping together and I was feeling my hottest. It doesn't matter that it's below freezing outside today. That's what coats are for.

My eyes immediately go to Jude's office when I step onto the floor and walk through the doors. He's already in there, sitting at his desk, typing—or what he thinks passes for typing —on his computer. I took my coat off in the elevator, so when he glances up, he gets a good view of me. As soon as I'm sure he's looking, I smile shyly and head for my station.

I go into my cubicle and bend over a lot while I get situated: putting my purse in my desk, leaning over to check my emails rather than sitting down, and unnecessarily adjusting the position of my trash can under my desk. Then I stretch and reach, watering the potted plant on top of my bookshelf, feeling its leaves and the potting soil to make sure it's still healthy, standing on tiptoe and flexing my calf muscles in the process.

Lisa prairie dogs and says, "What the hell are you doing over there, yoga?"

Despite not wanting the whole world to know, I confide, "Jude and I had a huge fight this weekend. And I sort of broke up with him. But I may have overreacted. Is he looking at me?"

Lisa doesn't try to be subtle at all when she turns around to check for me. "Yep. I think I just saw a string of drool drop into his lap."

"Good. I might need a whole lotta lust on my side later when I ask his forgiveness."

"You definitely have his attention," she says, snickering and returning to her desk. "But it may be a while before you guys get a chance to kiss and make up. I have to order lunch for the whole office, and I was told to double the usual budget because they're making a special celebratory announcement. I think they're finally going to tell us what the heck's goin' on."

I twist in my chair and take a longer look at Jude, momentarily satisfied when I see he's still staring at me. But I'm more interested in how he looks at the moment. He's wearing his newest suit. And he got a haircut. Are those cufflinks? I wish I could see his shoes. If he's wearing his wing tips, he's definitely made a more concerted effort than usual with his appearance.

And then he does something that breaks my heart. He waves shyly and smiles nervously. Almost hopefully.

So I do what any insane person would do: I stick my tongue out at him and turn back around to face my computer.

The morning flies by in a flurry of activity. Every time I get a second to catch my breath and decide I'll go into Jude's office to have a quick chat with him, I turn around to see he's not in there.

Then the caterers arrive with the food, which means all the admins have to go help set up the lunch. I forward my phone to my voicemail, feeling a rising sense of panic that I might not get a chance to talk to Jude before this ridiculous announcement. I wish I could step out of the batter's box and hold my hand up to the umpire. "Whoa. All I need is, like, thirty seconds. All I have to say is, 'Jude, I love you. I'm sorry. Let's talk later.' Just a quick time-out. No frills. Please." But I'm helpless to freeze time. This is no game.

The best I can hope for is that he gets to the conference room before everyone else. Then I can just whisper that to him before the meeting starts. With this in mind, I decide to work as quickly as possible on the setup, then wait for him in the hallway.

Since I've loitered at my desk as long as I can to try to

catch Jude, I'm the last admin to arrive to the setup. As soon as I walk in, Leslie says loudly to me, "Hey, I hear your *ex*-boyfriend is about to get a big promotion."

"You hear a lot for someone with tinsel between her ears," I snap, wishing I could hold my tongue and play it cool but feeling better for lashing out at her. I shoot Lisa a dirty look for spilling the beans about the break-up. I thought I told her it was temporary!

Lisa gives me an innocent look and adds, "Didn't your mother ever tell you it's impolite to eavesdrop, Leslie?"

Zoe says, "You're a whore, Leslie."

Said in her little-girl voice and so matter-of-factly, it's the funniest thing I've heard in days. I hold the edge of the table and wheeze.

Zoe proudly sticks out her tiny chest. "Did I say that out loud?" she asks the room. "Plus you're just jealous."

Too casually for it to actually be casual, Leslie replies, "Been there, done that. When it comes to sex, English men are like English food... bland and cold, especially that one." She points out the door and in the general direction of Jude's office, even though it can't be seen from here.

"Don't listen to her, Libby," Lisa urges, as if I ever would. "She's lying. Jude never gave her the time of day, not even when she was practically offering to express her own breast milk into his coffee."

Leslie calmly continues to arrange the napkins, plasticware, and paper plates at the beginning of the buffet line. "Believe what you want to believe. I'm only saying something now because you guys are caput. I don't ever want anyone to accuse me of being a home wrecker. But would someone who's lying know this?" She leans in close to me and says, "What's the deal with his ticklish feet?"

I just stare at her as I feel all the blood drain from the top of my tingling scalp through the tips of my red-painted toenails. Numbly, I reply, "Well, that's a good question."

"It was before you two were an item... I think."

"This conversation is inappropriate," Zoe steps in. "I'm sorry I called you a whore, Leslie."

Leslie grudgingly accepts Zoe's apology.

My diminutive friend taps her chin contemplatively. "Yeah, I think it would have been more appropriate to call you a 'dirty fucking tw—"

Just as it feels like it's about to come to physical blows between Zoe and Leslie, Gary and Jude walk in, followed by Mr. Peal, the company president and CEO and two inter-changeable guys I always confuse for one another, one the CFO, named Walter, and the other the Marketing Director, Rudy.

"Everything just about set here, ladies?" Gary asks cluelessly.

Jude takes one look at me and mouths automatically, "What's wrong?" as if he has the right to even be in the same room with me, much less ask me about my well-being.

I shake my head, however minutely, and quickly look down at my feet.

Lisa answers for all of us that the food's ready whenever they want the meeting to start, so Gary tells her to round everyone up. More to get out of the room than anything else, I go with her. But I walk next to her like a zombie as she makes her rounds through the office.

Marvin passes us in the corridor. "Yo, Libby, wazzup? You and Jude bustin' outta this town? That's the skinny I'm hearin'."

I smile tightly at him. Well, at least one of my fantasies is still alive and well underneath all of Marvin's frizzy hair.

Thankfully, he doesn't wait to hear the answer. There's free food to be had, after all.

When everyone's been informed that the meeting's about to start, Lisa pulls me into a corner. "Listen, no one would think less of you for skipping this lunch. As a matter of fact, I bet you could take the rest of the day off and no one would notice. I'll even cover for you and say you're in the bathroom or at the copier or wherever anytime someone comes by. You don't have to torture yourself hearing this announcement, whatever it is."

My eyes puddle up but don't overflow. "I bet you're a good mom, Lisa," I say emotionally. I blink my eyes rapidly and take a deep breath. "But I can do this. It's not the end of the world. Think how much worse it would have been if I had taken him back and *then* found out."

She looks dubiously at me, like I'm a seriously drunk person who's promised not to puke in the passenger seat of her brand new car if she'll just give me a ride home.

"All right. If you're sure..."

"I never said anything about being sure," I mutter, following her into the conference room. She gets in line for the food, but I hang close to the door, up against the wall.

When everyone who wants food has it and is seated, Mr. Peal stands up behind the long table at the front of the room, where he's been sitting with Gary, Jude, Rudy, and Walter. The room gradually quiets, and he smiles the kind of scary, grimace-like smile that used to be my specialty.

"Many of you already may have gotten wind of some changes coming to the company," he begins, "and I want to assure you, they're all good. Despite the difficulties other firms have been having in this economy, we're doing quite well. And that's thanks, in large part, to all of you. Give yourselves a round of applause."

There's some half-hearted clapping, then Marvin shouts, "Huzzah, people!" which breaks the tension a little bit. For most people. I still feel as taut as a new rubber band on a teenager's braces.

As the chuckles and murmurs die down, Mr. Peal continues, "You all know we're here today to make an important announcement, and for that, I'm going to turn it over to Gary."

Gary steps forward. Jude pushes his plate of untouched food away and unnecessarily wipes his mouth, throws his napkin on top of the full plate, straightens his sleeves, and generally fidgets. A flash of black under the table catches my attention as he squirms. The wingtips are present and particularly shiny.

Looking at his feet, though, reminds me of what Leslie said, so I have to physically clutch at the wall behind me to prevent myself from bolting for the door.

Gary clears his throat. "Hello, everybody. Today is an exciting day for the company, but in particular for the Commercial Division. We're branching out in a big way, and Mr. Jude Weatherington"—he gestures to Jude—"is going to be a huge part of that growth.

"In the year Jude's been with us, he's been instrumental in some of the biggest, most prestigious jobs this company's had to date. And he's handled everything with tenacity, enthusiasm, and an attention to detail that is second-to-none in the industry. I'm confident when I say that."

Before I can stifle it, a huge swell of pride fills my chest. I know how hard he works and how much he generally eschews recognition for it. I hope he's letting these words sink in.

He still looks extremely uncomfortable, though. Reflexively, I shoot him an encouraging smile when he glances my way. It's hard to tell who's more surprised by it, him or me. I didn't think it was possible for my lips to shape themselves into a smile, especially in this moment, especially in his direction. He blinks—hard—and returns his attention to the napkin on his plate.

Gary continues, "But what really sets Jude apart is his vision. Without it, we wouldn't be kicking the competition's butts like we are." He pauses for everyone to laugh at his impertinence. "Anyway, that's why we've chosen him to be in charge when we open our brand new branch shortly after the first of the New Year... in London, England!" At that, he claps and motions for Jude to stand up.

The rest of the room erupts too, so I feel fairly invisible as I stand open-mouthed and frozen, watching Jude smile as he shakes the hands of all the suits at the front of the room and nods to the room at large. Everyone except me, that is. He doesn't give me a second glance.

I, on the other hand, keep my eyes glued to him after I quickly recover. First of all, I don't want to see anyone else looking over at me to gauge my reaction to the news. Secondly, I'm begging him telepathically to look at me. Just for a second. I want him to know I can handle this. I'm still here. I'm not running. And I'm not a puddle on the floor. On the outside, at least.

But he stubbornly ignores me and nervously addresses the rest of the room when it finally quiets again. "Ahem. Well. Right. Thanks. Wow." He rubs his eyebrow and smiles shyly. "Uh... I want to say, first off, that I'm very honored by this opportunity. So, thanks to those of you"—he gestures down the table—"who have the confidence in me to do this. I'll try not to make a fist of things. Huh-huh." He seems to gain confidence as he continues. "The next few weeks are going to be busy as we assemble a team to populate the London office.

I'm told I get my pick, so that's quite exciting. I'll be getting with some of you very soon to discuss that."

After a deep breath, he adds, "And I'm also excited to be embarking on this venture a bit closer to my family. They're very pleased that I'm coming home. So..." He trails off, then says to Gary, "That's really all I have to say, I suppose. Oh! Except..."

I find myself holding my breath, waiting for that Hollywood moment where he says one sweet, simple thing that fixes everything between us, then proposes to me in front of everyone.

"Libby, I have a very good explanation about what Leslie said. Until I can talk to you in private, please believe me. But"—he steps away from the table and walks over to where I'm standing, pulling a velvet box from his pocket and kneeling in front of me—"for now, would you please make me the happiest bloke in the world and say you'll come with me to London? And become my assistant—no, my partner—for the rest of my life?"

He clears his throat. "I do want to say thank you to everyone who's ever worked on a project with me. Vision can only take one so far; I've had a couple of people"—he points to Marvin—"pull my feet out of the fire and translate my rather vague visions into reality. Thanks for that."

"Do I get to go with you to London, Jude-Dude?" Marvin shouts.

Jude laughs. "Absolutely, if you want to. You were tops on my list, actually."

"Suh-weet!" Marvin declares, going back to attacking his roast beef.

I wish I could laugh with everyone else. I wish I could laugh with Jude later about how the climate in London will suit Marvin's sweat problems much better than anywhere in the contiguous U.S. But the biggest wish I have is that I didn't know what I know and could go with them, even if it means working with Marvin.

Suddenly, a horrifying question occurs to me. Is an admin going to be part of the London team? And, if so, who will he pick? Leslie? Oh, gosh, I don't know how I'd bear that.

When it appears that all of the speeches are over, I decide I've fulfilled my promise to myself to be brave. I slink to my desk, thankful for all the empty cubes around me. I'm slumped there with my fingers against my eyes, mentally trying to go to a happy place that doesn't involve Jude. Or anybody else, for that matter. I picture myself sitting in the centerfield bleachers at Wrigley, all alone but not lonely. Just at peace.

"I'd like to take you with me." A voice behind me makes me jump.

I remove my hands from my eyes and sit up straight, but I don't turn around or say anything.

"That is, if you're amenable to going."

A strong person with a voice takes over my otherwise-useless body. "Hmm. Well, I don't think that's meant to be." *Good reply,* I silently approve of myself. *But don't ask who he's going to take instead, whatever you do.* I have to bite down on my lip to follow my own instructions.

After a long pause, he says, "I, uh, guess we're just going to make do without a secretary at first, then. I'm sure we can do most things electronically with the ladies here until we get really busy." I hear him drumming his fingers against the metal on the top of the cubicle wall.

"Administrative assistant," I automatically correct him.

"Come again?"

"We're administrative assistants, not secretaries."

"Right. Sorry."

Conspicuously, I start moving papers on my desk and

getting to work on actual jobs that have piled up this morning while I've been busy preparing for the big announcement. When I haven't heard anything from him for a while, I chance a peek over my shoulder. He's still standing there, leaning against the wall, one hand casually in his pocket, his feet crossed at the ankles.

"Can I help you?" I ask pointedly.

I seem to have startled him out of a daydream. "Huh? Oh. No. I s'pose not. Although..." He hesitates, but when I raise my eyebrows, he decides to go on. "I was only wondering... would you be willing to help me out the next couple of weeks, if I need it? You know, around here?"

Ever the professional, I reply, "Sure."

"You don't think it'll be awkward as arse, do you?"

"Probably," I admit. "But... I don't know. If you need help, you need help. It's kind of my job."

He nods. "Of course. But I can always ask Leslie or..."

At her name, I turn my back to him again. I slam a binder particularly loudly against my desk as I set it aside. "Whatever, Jude. It's your baby." As soon as the sentence leaves my mouth, I regret it. "Project, I mean. Whatever."

"Okay. Ace. I'll simply... er... leave you alone now."

"Wait!" I spin in my chair again.

"Yes?" He comes to such an abrupt stop that he almost trips. He returns to the entrance to my cubicle.

"I just... I forgot to tell you 'congratulations.' You deserve it. And... I'm happy for you."

He flashes the saddest grin I've ever seen. I make a conscious effort not to look at his dimple. "Oh, right. Well, thanks. Ironic, though, isn't it?"

I cock my head questioningly, so he explains, "I took this job to get away from there."

"But you're glad to be going back, right? That's what you said in the meeting."

He shrugs. "Eh. It's better than a poke in the eye with a sharp stick, I suppose, but I merely said that because that's what everyone expects me to say. I'm happy here. Or I was, anyway." He deliberates for a second, then says, "Yeah. I guess it's for the best, after all."

I nod with difficulty. "Well, I should probably get back to work." I hear people making their way back to their desks.

"Yeah. Absolutely. I'll, uh…" He backs away awkwardly.

After he leaves, I finally take a full breath. My heart races as it struggles to get enough oxygen. I can't believe it's only been two days since we broke up. We sound like a couple who's adjusted to a shaky truce after months of separation. It suddenly strikes me as both sad and funny. And completely abnormal.

In other words, typically me.

❦ 24 ❦

I'm totally convinced that Leslie and Jude really did sleep together, although I'll *never* confront Jude about it. It's not really my place anymore to care about who he sleeps with, now or ever, as long as he wasn't doing it while we were together. And I'm sure he wasn't. But my certainty that he did at some time is bolstered by Leslie's latest hobby of casually dropping intimate details about him into conversation when she's near me.

"What's the deal with that scar on the inside of his thigh? You know, right near his junk? I didn't get around to asking him about that."

"Missionary's not really my favorite position, but *some* people really like it, huh, Libby?"

"I don't think I've ever been with a guy who *doesn't* like tattoos... Oh, wait." Pointed look at me. "Just one, but he was kind of a square."

Now that I expect her to say these things, I've gotten pretty good at avoiding and ignoring her, but there were some cat-fight close calls the first few times (particularly when she asked about the scar). The only thing that keeps me from reacting is that I know she wants me to. And I'll be damned if I'll give her the satisfaction.

I can't believe Jude hasn't told her to shut up. Surely, in this place, he's heard from someone what she's saying. Although... now that I think about it, she and I are usually alone when she drops these gems. Or she'll say something that I know is a dig but nobody else probably would. And, like I said before, there's no way in hell I'm going to bring it up to him.

Because when I'm around him, I'm surprisingly good at maintaining a neutral expression and acting like nothing's wrong. The minute we're apart, though, I feel myself unraveling. Most nights, I can barely make it to my car before I start shaking. I haven't eaten dinner—or much of anything—in weeks. I get home, strip down to my underwear, and crawl under the covers, falling into a coma-like sleep until morning, when I get up and do it all again.

The constant reminders of him (and us) don't help, either. All the cafés, bars, movie theaters, and other hangouts we used to frequent in my neighborhood seem to mock me as I drive past them. Doing laundry has been especially painful. I've taken to hauling my baskets of dirty clothes to a nearby Laundromat, just so I can avoid the room in the basement where our last argument took place.

So lately I've been a prisoner in my apartment, which I've been busy making a Jude-Free Zone. I've snapped in half and thrown away my Snow Patrol CDs, deleting the MP3 files from my computer and player. The few pictures I had of us have been buried in the "cat box," my photo collection of Sandberg. I don't want to get rid of them permanently, but it's going to be a long time before I can look at them again. Maybe someday, when I'm digging through Sandberg's pictures, I'll come across them and be able to smile. Or not. I'll burn them then, I guess. For now, I don't want to get rid of the evidence that I was at one time worthy of someone's affection.

And every room at work has some kind of memory attached to it, even the parking garage. But at least I can sometimes fool myself into thinking everything's okay there. He's right there in his office, after all. We exchange pleasantries. We attend meetings together. We pass each other in the halls and occasionally meet up at the vending or pop machines.

He even called me the day I skipped work for The Anniversary, because Wanda had sent out an email that I was taking a sick day, and he wanted to make sure I was okay. In other words, he knew that without him, I could be dead and no one would find me until Sandberg had eaten half my face. Of course, I didn't actually take his call. But after I listened to his stammering message on my voicemail, I texted him the lie, "I'm fine. Thanks." And I didn't tell anyone—not even Dr. Marsh—how his concern was more depressing than comforting.

Hank came up from Florida for Christmas, so at least I wasn't alone on the holiday. But as usual, he spent more time with his friends than me. Not that I blamed him. I mean, who wants to spend time with someone who's either catatonic or on the verge of tears all the time? I tried to be cheerful, but it required more energy than I had. In addition to the present I actually bought specifically for him, I also ended up giving him the limited edition *Psycho* box set that I had bought for Jude. It didn't make any sense, and Hank probably knew that it wasn't originally for him, but it was the easiest way for me to get rid of it.

I hope it all gets easier when Jude's gone. And he will be soon.

Today he's packing up his office. I've been making myself scarce, not wanting any part of that project. It was bad enough when he had me back up all of his files onto external hard drives. I had to turn my brain almost completely off to get that one done. As the status bar would creep from 0% to 100% on each transfer, I'd picture a door closing by those same degrees. By the time all the files were finished transferring, I was emotionally exhausted.

Now I walk past his office at just the right (or wrong) time, and he flags me down. "Libby! Do you mind giving me a hand here?"

Heart, hand, whatever, I muse with a sigh. "Whatcha need?" I ask perkily.

"Literally, two more hands," he says, pointing to a large box in the middle of his office. "If you could hold those flaps closed whilst I tape them…"

I do, affecting the most bored expression I can while I surreptitiously study him. He's wearing his hair shorter now than he ever used to. Today, since he's packing and doing physical work, he's wearing jeans and what he'd call a "jumper," but the rest of us normal folks would call a sweater. His "trainers" (a.k.a., sneakers or tennis shoes) are new-looking. He smells… well, the best word I can come up with is "nostalgic," although I know it's not possible for someone to really smell that way. But it makes me nostalgic. And horny, but that's a totally inappropriate (and purely physical) response that I must stifle.

"Next," he says, pointing to a box in the corner.

This one's so stuffed, it barely closes. Finally, I have to resort to sitting on it to keep it shut. He pulls the tape across one end, then the other, working around me. At one point, as he's leaning over, he presses his face up against my shoulder and grunts with the effort to pull the tape around. I stand and move away so he can't hear my heartbeat. I'm suddenly sure it's externally audible.

"That was a dodgy one," he states. Although he's still hard to read (harder than ever), I'm almost positive he meant that more than one way.

"Yep," I reply casually. "Do you need me to take these to the mailroom for you?" Then without waiting for his answer, I make an executive decision. "Yeah, I'll just take 'em," I say in a no-nonsense tone.

"No! That's not necessary. I'll do it later. They're a bit heavy."

"I can handle it." I'd planned to scoot them along the floor. As long as it meant I could scoot myself out of his presence. To demonstrate, I bend over and push on one end of the biggest box, sliding it toward his office door.

He intercepts me, mirroring my pose on the other side of the box. "Leave it," he insists. "Really. I was going to get Marvin to help me haul all of these boxes to the mailroom when I've finished packing."

I clench my jaw stubbornly. "Why?"

"Because you're more of a help to me with taping; I've already filled the position of pack mule."

Giving up, I say, "Fine. Whatever."

"Whatevuh," he mocks, smirking at me. "You're supposed to just follow orders, remember?"

Damn charmer. I can't help but smile at him when he's looking at me like that. I straighten and turn in a circle, looking for other open boxes while I avoid his eyes. He follows me around the room as we go from box to box, working without talking.

Finally, he says, "What kind of cake did you order for tomorrow? You know I hate lemon."

Matter-of-factly, I answer, "I wasn't put in charge of that." Thank God.

Tomorrow's his last day. I've already scheduled a vacation day. Even I have my limits. I don't trust myself to keep up the tough act if I have to be here and watch him walk through those doors for the last time. Of course, I know logically that there has to be a last time for *me* to see him, and it won't be any less poignant just because it's not the last time for everyone else. And I guess he'll be back periodically, since this is the corporate headquarters for the company, but I won't be able to hold it together when he says his goodbyes tomorrow. That's a memory I have no interest in making. And I plan to leave tonight without saying goodbye.

"But you told them I hate lemon cake, right?"

I shoot him a look through my eyelashes. "My, my. Awfully particular, aren't you? Get the big promotion and suddenly you're a diva."

Laughing, he says, "Hey, I don't think it's too much to ask to have a flavor of cake at my going-away to-do that I'd be willing to eat."

"You think it's going to be a to-do, huh?" I hold the flaps of a smallish box containing a stack of back issues of *Architectural Digest*.

With a straight face, he answers, "I've been all but promised it will be. Gary told me you've planned the whole thing, complete with streamers, confetti, and... and... a piñata."

I crack up. "What are you, six?"

He looks up from the tape gun, an expression of mock-hurt on his face. "I'll have you know that you don't have to be a child to like those things."

"Just have the mentality of one," I clarify.

"Are you trying to break it to me that none of those things are going to be at my party?"

"I think it's doubtful." I put my hand on his arm. "Are you going to be okay?"

He nods solemnly. "I suppose. As long as you're there…"

Swallowing and blushing, I remove my hand and splutter, "Oh… y-yes. Obviously. Where else would I be?" There are no more boxes to tape, no more distractions.

After a narrowing of his eyes, he says, "I don't know… You wouldn't be thinking of bunking off tomorrow, would you?"

I try to laugh him away. "That sounds like something that's none of your business anymore." My joke falls flat, though, seeing that it hits close to a whole bundle of nerves.

"But you know what I mean, right? Pull a sickie?"

"Whatever. I'm not calling in sick tomorrow," I say honestly.

He turns his head and looks skeptically at me from the corner of his eye. "Promise?"

"Cross my heart," I say, doing just that with my finger.

"Because I expect a proper goodbye from you. So no eating at dodgy Indian restaurants tonight."

"Hm," I reply, rearranging some boxes so there's a clear route (getaway path) to the door. "You're getting really used to having your way around here." Suddenly, something occurs to me. "You're not going to make a scene in front of everyone, are you? Embarrass me somehow?" Of course, he's not going to, since I won't be here, but I want to make sure he never even entertained the idea.

He wipes his brow on his sleeve. "Now why ever would I do that?"

"Yes, why would you do that?" I return.

"I won't." This time, he crosses his heart.

"It's just… I'd prefer not to give everyone a show, complete with hugging and mushy stuff. It's going to be uncomfortable enough as it is." It's the first time I've acknowledged out loud that his going away is going to be difficult for me.

Sticking the toe of his shoe in front of the box I'm currently shifting to the side, he says, "Perhaps we should get the 'mushy stuff' out of the way now, whilst we have some privacy."

I'm about to call him crazy, considering we're at work, and his office blinds and door are wide open, but when I glance out there, I notice everyone's cleared out for the day. I hadn't realized how late it was or how long we'd been in here. Even so…

"I don't think so," I hedge. Suddenly all of this is too real. He's really leaving. We're really over. I don't do well with real.

Cajolingly, he says, "Aw, come on. Just a little hug. We owe at least that to each other, don't you think? A proper goodbye."

Perched on the edge of his desk, I shake my head and whisper, "I can't."

"Sure you can." He stands in front of me and opens his arms. "I promise, no funny business. And no one's here to see you being nice to me, so your image is safe."

He walks into me more than I lean forward into his arms. But the result is the same: a hug that starts with me sitting there on his desk with my arms hanging limply at my sides and him wrapping his arms around me and resting his chin on the top of my head.

A hundred images flash through my head in less than two seconds. It seems like I relive every minute with him, like some kind of time-lapsed film in extreme fast-forward. But I manage to see, hear, smell, and taste it all like it's happening in real time.

I bring my arms up and wrap my hands around the back of

his neck, my fingertips sinking into his hair. He sighs. My breath catches in my chest. We fit together like two halves of a raindrop that split when it hit a piece of grime on a dirty window. Two halves that will forever fit perfectly together but will never rejoin.

"God, how is this happening?" I sob, mortified when I realize I've said it out loud.

He pulls away and looks down at me. "Say the word, and it ends differently. I don't want to leave you here." His lips move in. They're a millimeter from mine when he says, "Remember when you trusted me implicitly?" and I imagine them kissing Leslie.

"Stop," I say, pulling away, breaking the spell. I duck around his body and under one of his arms. "I'm sorry, but I can't."

"Why not?" he demands, more than a little impatiently. "It's obvious you're not happy the way things are now."

Instead of answering him, I flee his office, barely stopping at my cubicle for my purse and coat.

"That's right, Libby. Run!" he calls after me. "Run away from the biggest cock-up of your life!"

I'm not sure if he means he was my biggest mistake or if rejecting him was. Either way, he doesn't have to tell me twice to run. I was there before he even suggested it. I don't want to wait for the elevator, so I crash through the stairwell door and begin a twenty-four flight descent into the parking garage.

After ten flights in these heels, though, I'm done. I emerge on the fifth floor, crying and out-of-breath. I limp to the elevators and press the down arrow. The doors immediately open, so I stumble into the empty car, frantically pressing the button for the parking garage level where my car is waiting. It's as if I think the harder and faster I press the button, the faster my life will proceed, until it's just a blur that I don't really have to experience.

When the elevator spits me out in the concrete garage, I hobble as fast as I can to the row where my car is. I'm simultaneously relieved and annoyed when I see that Jude's not already there waiting for me, but that an identical navy blue car is parked next to mine.

"Stalker," I mutter, double-checking the license plate and the presence of Bobblehead Ryne in the car that I get into. It doesn't matter that my keyless entry wouldn't work on Jude's car. I don't want any chance of another accidental switcheroo, especially tonight. I'm almost free of him.

I've just twisted the key in the ignition when my cell phone chimes to alert me to a text message. The masochist in me can't resist reading it. All it says is, *Please don't.*

Scrunching my eyes closed, I toss the phone into the passenger-side floorboard. I suck the cold, stale car air in through my teeth, open

❧ 25 ❧

ONCE AGAIN, I BECOME ONE WITH MY BED, KEEPING TIME IN relation to whatever I imagine Jude is doing at the moment. At four o'clock on Friday, I sit up in bed and mentally follow his progress: *He's eating his cake right now. Locking his office door for the last time. Returning his keys to Wanda. Saying his final goodbyes to Lisa, Zoe... and* her. *Maybe he's even wondering where I am. He's getting into his car, driving through the parking garage for the last time, taking a second to get his bearings before he can pull onto the street (he always gets turned around under there). Driving even more cautiously than usual (if that's possible) to his empty apartment, because it's snowing. Eating Spaghetti-O's straight from the can (don't even get me started listing the ways that's disgusting) in the middle of all the boxes piled around him. Showering, standing under the hot stream until the water goes cold. Setting his cell phone alarm for an early wake-up call to go to the airport. Going to bed on a mattress in the middle of his bedroom floor.*

In actuality, my imaginary Jude reality show only lasts about twenty minutes. He's probably not even finished eating his chocolate cake (would I let Lisa order anything but his favorite?) when I jump from the bed, suddenly compelled to do one last thing before he leaves forever.

I dig my laptop out from under some dirty laundry on my couch, open it, and boot it up. Quickly, I open the letter I wrote to Jude and that I was going to give to him on The Anniversary. But the break-up was still too raw then, and I never found a good time to give it to him. If I hurry, I can run it over to his place before he even gets home to eat his revolting dinner. I'd email it to him if I knew he'd have access to email during his move. But I want him to read it before he leaves Chicago. It's suddenly of utmost importance to me.

Before hitting print, I proofread it (sorry; unbreakable habit).

Dear Jude,

I know you don't understand many things about me (there are things I don't understand, either), and you will have to resign your-self to the fact that you never will (as I have), but I promised you months ago that I would tell you things that would go a long way to shedding some light on my quirks and no matter what's happened between us, I think it's only fair that I make good on that promise.

Six years ago, I was riding in the backseat of a car. My dad was driving. My mom was in the front passenger seat. It was snowing as we drove down the highway, but the road wasn't covered yet. One or two inches stood in the grass of the median and the shoulders. The fall semester of my senior year at Loyola had just ended, and my parents had come to the school to pick me up and bring me home for Christmas break. I was bored with the college experience, in general and with Loyola specifically. I had already registered for my spring classes, but what I really wanted to do was study abroad for that semester, then take an extra semester to finish any requirements that had been pushed aside for my semester abroad. My parents were trying to talk me out of it. I kept telling them that I didn't feel like I was getting the most out of my college years, stuck at a private

Midwestern university that hardly seemed any different, socially, from my high school. The whole point of my discipline of study was to learn about other cultures, yet I had never been further than 200 miles away from my hometown. Everything I knew was from books, not from real-life experience. Over-protective, Mom and Dad told me I could always travel after graduation.

The closer we got to home, the more intensely we argued. I felt like I had to get them to agree before we pulled into the driveway or I'd never get them to agree at all. I unbuckled my seatbelt and sat in the middle of the backseat, leaning forward between the two of them. They both told me to put a seatbelt on, but I ignored them, too focused on the next part of my argument to listen to what they were telling me.

When I kept talking, Dad half-turned, taking his eyes off the road for a second, if that, to see if I was buckled in, like he had asked. The semi next to us fish-tailed. Dad overcorrected, and we skidded off the deceptively slick highway into the median. I remember turning upside down at least twice, but I obviously lost count, because the Highway Patrol report later said the car flipped four or five times, based on eyewitness accounts. Every window in the car shattered. Not wearing a seatbelt, I was thrown through the back window. Then it was black.

I don't know how long it was before I woke up, but when I did, I was lying on my side, face down in the frozen grass, and it was just... silent... all around me. I felt nothing. I couldn't even think clearly enough to process what I was doing or where my parents were. It wasn't until I was being loaded into the back of an ambulance that I saw the white sheets on the ground, almost camouflaged by the snow.

With no adult family members (besides me) to take him in, Hank (who had been at a sleepover at a friend's house), was put in a foster home until I could heal up, graduate, get a job, and support both of *us. I wanted to quit school and get a job right away, but my academic advisor convinced me my parents would want me to finish.*

First, though, I had to undergo several surgeries over the next few months. But as soon as I was healed, physically, I completed my degree. A week after graduation, I got the job that I still currently hold, and Hank and I moved into a two-bedroom walk-up close to our old house, so he wouldn't have to change schools. When Hank graduated from high school and took off for the University of Florida, I moved to a completely different part of the city, where I live now. I'm in charge of my parents' estate, which is probably the only thing that keeps Hank and me in touch with each other. He insists it's not true, but I think he blames me for their deaths. I know I do.

I'm sorry for not telling you this sooner. My therapist, Dr. Marsh, has been urging me to tell you for months. But it's something I never talk about, not even with Hank. I also want you to forgive me for reacting the way I did when you didn't respond to my original revelation the way I imagined you would. It's nothing you did or said, really. I'm hopelessly damaged, and it all happened way before we ever met.

Now I add, my fingers flying over the keyboard:

Soon an ocean will separate us, and maybe then things will get easier.

I wish you the best.

Thank you. For everything. You were a bright spot in an otherwise-bleak life.

Love,

Libby

I print it, fold it, stuff the pages into an envelope, and seal it before I can think better of it. It's going to be close, I realize as I look at the clock on the microwave, but I think I can get to his place, slide it under the door, and get out of there before he gets home from work.

~

When I arrive, I'm relieved to see his parking space is empty. I park on the street around the corner, shove a quarter into the meter, and slip-slide up the slushy sidewalk and the front steps of his building.

I buzz the landlord, Mr. Feingold, who knows me and lets me in, saying, "It's been a while since I seen you around here, pretty lady. Thought maybe you finally wised up and found yourself a nice American guy, maybe even a White Sox fan. I have a grandson, you know." He says all this with a wink, keeping alive our friendly ongoing disagreement about hometown baseball teams.

Smiling easily, playing the part of the young, carefree ex-girlfriend, I say, "Nah, I've been schtupping another Cubby-lover. Just wanted to drop off something for Jude before he leaves for England."

"Yeah, how do you like that?" Mr. Feingold asks. "Now I gotta find a new tenant in the middle of winter. Not an easy thing to do. But whaddya expect from a foreigner? I wish I could legally refuse to rent to 'em."

I pretend to believe he's kidding and edge up the stairs. "I won't be long," I promise him. "I'm just going to slide something under his door."

"Take your time, honey," he says, waving. "He'd be an even bigger idiot than I think he is if he just lets you drop that and run."

I run up the last flight, taking the steps two at a time. My mission is to drop off the letter and get back to my own apartment, preferably before the snow covers the streets and everyone starts acting like they've never seen the white stuff before.

Unfortunately, the letter is a little fatter than the opening under his door. After two false starts, I take the envelope and try to flatten it against my thigh.

The door swings open, revealing a wet-headed Jude in a pair of baggy workout shorts and, fittingly, the Loyola sweatshirt he thought I would appreciate him buying but that I made him promise (without explanation, of course) never to wear around me.

"I thought you were Mr. Feingold... again," he says, while at the same time I say, "I thought you weren't home."

Both of us chuckle nervously. Then he steps aside to invite me in.

"Oh," I say. "No. Thank you. I... uh..." I hold up the envelope. "Was just bringing you this."

"You're a few weeks late for a Dear John letter," he cracks helpfully.

I play along. "Yeah, the U.S. Postal Service isn't what it used to be now that everyone uses email."

Warily, he takes the envelope. He slides his finger under the flap, but before he can tear it open, I say, "Please. Wait until I'm gone."

After a tiny hesitation, he agrees. "Are you sure you won't come in, just for a minute, to warm up?"

I look past him, and I'm surprised to see his furniture and no boxes.

"You don't look like someone who's moving," I comment, not making any moves to go inside.

He runs a hand through his hair. "Yeah. The movers are coming next week. They'll do all the packing."

"Where's your car?" I ask suddenly, then explain when he gives me a puzzled look, "It's just... I thought you weren't home, because it wasn't parked down there."

"Ah. That. I sold it. Can't very well drive it across the pond."

I don't know why, but I take it personally that he sold "our" car.

"Who'd you sell it to?"

He starts to answer, then says, "Really. If we're going to have a conversation, can we do it inside? It's brass monkey cold out here."

My curiosity is strangely stronger than my flight instinct at the moment, so I edge past him and stand just inside the door when he closes it.

"Well?" I prod.

"Well what?"

I sigh. "Who bought your car?"

"What does it matter?"

Realizing it's kind of odd for me to care, I blush. "I don't know. I'm just curious."

"Bloke from my rugby team."

I try to imagine someone else driving his car, and it almost chokes me up. So I change the subject. "What're you doing home so early, anyway?"

He laughs. "You should have been a reporter. Or a copper."

Leaving me in the entryway, he steps into the kitchen. I hear him running water. "Can I get you a cup of tea?"

"No, thanks," I reply. I really just want him to answer my questions, then I can go. "Did you enjoy your going-away party?" I inquire lightly, as if it's completely normal for me to be here, asking all this stuff.

From the other side of the wall, he calls back, "Not really. Although thanks for the chocolate cake. They made me take the leftovers home. Fancy some?"

I *am* kind of hungry. I inch into the kitchen doorway. "I guess. It'd be a shame for it to go to waste."

He cuts two slices and slides the plate with the exponentially larger piece toward me. Without asking, he pours me a glass of milk and sets it next to the plate.

"Thanks," I say shyly as we begin to eat standing up. After a few bites, I proclaim, "This is really good."

He smiles slightly, his piece already gone. "Yep. Too bad you missed the party," he says pointedly.

"Vacation day, not a 'sickie,'" I say, to make the distinction.

"Yeah, Wanda told me. Said you'd had it planned for a while." Pointing to the envelope he's tossed on the counter, he asks, "What's this about?"

I shrug, keeping my eyes on my fork as I collect some crumbs from along the edge of the plate. "Just something I promised you a long time ago."

"But I can't read it now?"

"Nope." This cake sure is interesting to look at.

I can feel him watching me. Eventually, he says, "What if I have questions when I've finished reading it?"

Draining my glass of milk buys me some time. I don't want to sound cold, but this letter is supposed to be the last word on our relationship, my "secret,"... everything. "Sorry. No follow-ups." When he cocks an eyebrow at me, I say, "I'm pretty sure I covered everything. About what happened."

"You think so, eh?"

"Sure." I push the plate away, a quarter of the slice remaining. He takes up the fork and finishes it.

After thinking about it for a few minutes, while he washes our dishes and puts them away, he concedes, "Right. If you say so."

"I do." I wipe the corners of my mouth with my fingers, making sure I don't have any chocolate icing or crumbs loitering there. "Well, thanks for the cake." It sounds so trite and inadequate. I'm glad I wrote a more meaningful thank-you in my letter.

"Leaving already?" he asks, coming around the kitchen island.

I back into the entryway and bump into the wall when I run out of space. "Uh... yeah. I should. Before the weather gets worse. And my meter runs out."

He looks just as determined to keep me here as I say I am to leave. Towering over me, he rests his hands lightly on my upper arms. "Are you sure?"

I nod but don't move. His body's so warm up against mine.

"Because I'm not going to lie. I still want you."

I gulp. "Oh. Okay," I reply stupidly.

He doesn't seem interested in conversation, anyway, thankfully, so my insufficient grasp of the English language isn't a problem. The kiss he plants on my lips sends an immediate signal to my brain to get every intimate part of my body humming. His tongue does more than fill my mouth; it fills a space inside me that's been empty and cold for more than a month.

As he unbuttons my coat and slides it off my shoulders, I stay with the kiss. There's no harm in a little goodbye kiss, right? Nothing more, just a kiss. I press my hands against the wall behind me, reasoning that if I don't get any more engaged than with my mouth, it's still legal. It's not making out if hands aren't involved. It's just a kiss. A really good, intense kiss. But still a kiss.

I'm somewhat aware that we're moving down the hallway by millimeters. My suspicions are confirmed when I open my eyes to see we've arrived in the living room, still attached by the lips. My coat fell off somewhere along the way. I should be concerned that I'm losing articles of clothing. But I'm still in control. Still just kissing. My hands are only on his shoulders for balance now. Honestly.

But the living room doesn't seem to be the ultimate destination for this train. Jude keeps his mouth on mine and his eyes behind me as he walks me backwards toward his bedroom. Kissing in the bedroom is nice, I suppose. More comfortable, anyway. He's just being a good host. A little food, a little drink, a little conversation, a little affection, and a big…

"Oh!" I finally pry my lips away from his, just before he pushes me down onto the bed. I fall backwards with a squeak and immediately scramble back up.

He reaches for me and grasps my wrist. "Please, don't be skittish," he begs, tugging on me.

While I plant my feet on the wooden floor, the tread of my sneakers sticking nicely, I avoid looking him in the eye, but that means my gaze falls on the bulge in his shorts. *That's been inside Leslie,* I remind myself (crassly and unnecessarily, I might add).

"Oh, God!" I say out loud, frenetically tucking my hair behind my ears, straightening my bra, and biting my swollen lips.

"What?" he asks, sitting up. "What's wrong?"

I look disbelievingly at him. "*This!*" I cry, twisting my wrist and yanking my arm away from him. "This is wrong!"

He shakes his head and reaches for me again. "No, it's not. Please don't run away again."

"Can I walk?" I ask pathetically. "This was… You weren't supposed to be home! Chocolate is an aphrodisiac! I have to go!"

I stumble through the bedroom door and the living room, which would be a lot easier to navigate if his furniture was gone, like I'd imagined. I snatch my coat from the floor, but I don't put it on. I don't need it.

"Bloody hell, Libby!" he says, following me. "I don't understand you!"

"You started it!" I defend myself. "It was supposed to be a goodbye kiss, that's all."

"When you showed up, I had no intention of this being 'goodbye,'" he states.

One hand on the door, I say, "It has to be, okay? There are things that we can't fix. I can't change who I am or what I've done. And neither can you."

"Tell me what you think is the biggest problem, and I'll find a way to fix it," he promises. "Please."

When I remain silent, then open the door, he lets loose a frustrated, anguished sound somewhere between a groan and a scream.

"I'm sorry, Jude. I really am. I didn't mean for this to happen today." There's nothing more for me to say. I walk—not run—down the stairs and out to my car. When I get home, I stand in the shower long after I run out of hot water, but I can't seem to wash the smell of him from my skin.

❦ 26 ❦

THE ODDEST THING HAPPENS. MONDAY I GO TO WORK, AND everyone in the world seems to be acting like it's just another day. Two people honk at me and one flips me off during my commute (although I have to admit, I probably deserved all three). The people in the elevator face forward on the ride up to the tenth floor and look like they don't have a care in the world other than that it's another Monday. Some of them even talk about their weekends and who they're going to root for in the Super Bowl next weekend, since the Bears aren't one of the teams involved. In the office, coffee is brewing, the phones are ringing, and I'm pretty sure—yes, there it is—I hear people laughing. And I think, *How can anyone laugh when that office over there is dark and empty?*

As melodramatic and teenage-angsty as it sounds, I can actually feel Jude's absence from the city. He's not here anymore. Not even in the same country. He might as well be on a different planet. And I'm grieving over it.

I remember when I started to forget what my parents looked like. The first time I realized it was happening, I had a panic attack. Never ones for photography, they didn't keep pictures of themselves around the house. We never even had a family portrait made. My mom seemed to be afraid of people pointing cameras at her, even though she was a moderately attractive woman (I think... again, her face has grown fuzzy in my memory over the years). There were pictures of me as a baby, and a few less of Hank, but my parents didn't bother taking out the camera for special occasions. Come to think of it, I don't know that they even owned one. I guess they had to have, but I don't remember seeing one around the house.

Anyway, my parents' faces becoming less and less crisp in my memory has been traumatic. But I might welcome forgetting what Jude looks like. And what he smells like. And tastes like. And feels like. And sounds like. I wish I could forget every sense related to him. But my memory seems to be holding onto every detail as if my life depends on it. I can't erase him.

I get through Monday. And Tuesday. By Wednesday, I'm feeling like I might not have to quit my job. Heath has taken over Jude's position as Lead Architectural Designer, and he's slowly settling into that office, which he's rearranged to suit his preferences. I'm getting used to turning around and seeing a profile that features a beer gut and a big nose. It's actually comforting. I hope he never closes his blinds so I'll always know that Jude's not a few steps away.

I make it all the way to Friday without having a nervous breakdown, without any messy scenes. I come to work, I do my job, I go home, I sleep. Repeat process four times. Somewhere in there, I feed the cat. At least he always seems to have food, so unless he's learned to serve himself, I'm still managing to fulfill some of my responsibilities. But I'm doing it all on autopilot.

Now I'm walking away from the plotter, rolling up a set of

blueprints that I need to take to the mailroom, when I hear his voice. Clearly. *His* voice.

"Things are brilliant here. We're all set up; everything's sweet as a nut. Now we merely need some accounts." He laughs nervously. "Only kidding. That is, it's true we need some accounts, but I've been told our name has already been mentioned in very promising circles, so it's only a matter of time. I think if we focus more on restoration instead of new construction, at least to begin with, we'll really build a reputation for ourselves."

And there he is. He's a little pixilated, and his mouth isn't moving in time with his words, but he's right there on the other side of the glass, on the big screen in the videoconference room.

I lurk out of sight as Gary asks, "What do you need from us? What resources would help you get off to a running start?"

"I have everything I need, actually. I can't think of a single thing I'm lacking. It's early days yet, and I'll let you know as soon as I notice anything, but I really think it's good. Nothing missing at all."

"How about admin support?" Gary presses. "Seeing any gaps in that department yet? I'm not sure it was wise to send you guys off without someone to do all the day-to-day stuff that no one else wants to do, if you know what I mean."

They laugh about that for a second or two, then Jude says, "Nah. I can always ring Leslie if something comes up that I can't handle. Meanwhile, I think I can manage opening my own post and making my own coffee." They laugh again.

Fuck them, I seethe, stomping away.

My blueprint has come unrolled as I've stood there, slack-jawed, listening to their pompous chatter. I walk and roll at the same time, giving myself a giant paper cut in the process. When I get to the mailroom, I grab a shipping tube from the rack, stuff the drawing into it, and rattle off the name of the recipient to Bruce, one of the mailroom technicians.

"It has to get there tomorrow, unfortunately," I gripe. "Once again, someone created an emergency for the rest of us by procrastinating on a job that wasn't that big a deal."

"I hate that," he commiserates. "Those guys are lucky to have you when it comes to shit like this, Libby. If it was up to them, they'd never meet deadlines."

I snort and say sarcastically, "Oh, Bruce, don't you know I just make the coffee?"

"Who said that?" he asks indignantly, printing the label for the tube.

Catching myself just in time, I say, "Never mind. I'm just feeling a little sorry for myself." I touch his shoulder, barely, careful not to get any blood from my paper cut on his shirt. "Thanks for getting that out today. I know Jake won't thank you, so I will." I absently suck on my injured finger.

He laughs. "Oh, I'm not in it for the recognition." The mailing label goes on the tube, which he tosses into a basket of other parcels on their way out the door. "So, uh... don't take this the wrong way, or anything, but I was wondering... I don't know... If you'd like to, sometime, maybe soon... have a drink after work? Or something?"

His question catches me completely off-guard. I blink at him a few times and recover. "Really? Well..."

I've never paid much attention to Bruce or any of my other male co-workers, but I quickly size him up during the pause before my answer. He's always been really nice to me. And he's pretty funny. As far as looks are concerned, he's okay. He shaves his head, I suspect to take a proactive approach to a receding hairline, but it looks good on him. Very smooth, in any case. He wears a style of glasses that make him look smart and trendy, rather than nerdy. Kind of a younger Stanley Tucci, I suddenly realize.

But... I can't go there. Yet.

I bite my lip.

He accurately reads my body language. "Never mind. It was just a suggestion. You know, now that *he's* gone. His loss, by the way."

I swallow loudly. "Oh." Giving him a shaky smile, I back toward the door. "Well, maybe some other time. Just not now."

"Sure!" he says cheerfully, but I can tell he knows it's never going to happen.

Back at my desk, I imagine what Jude would say... and how I'd respond.

"As if! Keep dreaming, Brucie."

"It's not him. I just don't feel like socializing."

"You don't want to snog Bruce!"

"That's none of your business. Maybe I do."

"You don't. You know you don't. He licks envelopes all day. And he looks like Uncle Fester."

"What do you know about Uncle Fester?"

"Nothing. I've never even heard of the bloke until you just thought of him. So you must think he looks like him."

"Well, you're crazy. I happen to think his bald head is sexy."

"Ha! You're a hair-puller. What would you do with your hands?"

"What's it to you? Go open your mail and make yourself a pot of coffee. Wanker."

A little later, Jude sits on the edge of my desk, distracting me while I try to fill out a purchase order.

"I wish you'd stop allowing people to believe you're the victim in all this. 'His loss'? I'm well aware of that! And it wasn't my choice!"

"You had a choice when you slept with that ho-bag Leslie."

"I was new in town. And lonely."

"Don't say that word to me. It's no excuse. She's gross. And

promiscuous. Who knows what you exposed me to by sleeping with me after her!"

"I certainly didn't have unprotected sex with her! Or you, for that matter, so keep your hair on. Or you and Bruce will be quite the couple."

"I'm perfectly calm. I'm just telling you the biggest reason I don't want you back."

"You're threatened by Leslie?"

"No! But I don't want her sloppy seconds. And I don't appreciate that I had to learn from her that you two were intimate before we got together."

"Well, that takes the biscuit."

"English, please."

"That beats all. I can't reclaim my virginity and wipe out all sexual partners who came—no pun intended—before you."

"I never expected you to be a virgin. Just honest."

"Would you have gotten serious with me if you had known about Leslie and me?"

"No. And that's exactly why you never told me. You tricked me."

"Well, that's some interesting rewriting of history."

"What would you call it then?"

"Irrelevant. What happened with Leslie and me was nothing. It wasn't even good."

"As comforting as that is to know..."

"Don't get all snarky. I'd change it if I could—"

"I would hope so."

"—but I can't."

"Exactly! And that's what I told you the night before you left. But you didn't believe me. You can't change what happened; and it's a deal-breaker for me. So drop it."

Sweet silence follows, but just when I think he's gone, he says behind me, "So, are you going to go out with Bruce?"

"You already know I won't, so shut up."

He laughs. "Mmm-hmm."

"Why, because you're such a tough act to follow?"

"Hey, you said it, not me."

"Get over yourself."

"Only kidding! Why won't you give the guy a chance? It's the paste breath, isn't it?"

"I'm not discussing this with you."

"Don't mind me; pretend I'm not here."

"You're not *here. That's one of my biggest problems right now."*

"Aw, do you miss me?"

"You're never going to leave me alone, are you?"

"That's totally up to you."

27

I'VE BROUGHT DR. MARSH A PRESENT.

He opens the envelope and belly laughs. It's one of the few pictures I had of Jude and me. Someone took it at the company Christmas party, the day after Thanksgiving, just a week before we broke up. But I've replaced Jude's head with a picture of Dr. Marsh that I got from the clinic's website.

"Uh, my face doesn't match the rest of my body," he points out.

"Skin condition?" I hypothesize helpfully. "You get gradually whiter the further down your body you go?"

He looks at the picture again and laughs. "This is great. But is that Jude under there?" Carefully, he tries to peel his face away so he can see, but I have it pasted firmly on there.

"Jude who?"

"Ah. Okay. I see. Well, thank you. I'm sure we had a wonderful time that night."

Before he sets the picture aside on his desk, I say, "I'd like you to notice the size of the picture. It's a nice three-by-five and would fit perfectly in there." I point to the frame that currently holds the college graduation picture.

His shoulders slump. "You really hate that picture, don't you?"

"'Hate' is a strong word, Dr. Marsh. But yes. I know it's not right, and you have a right to have pictures of happy memories, but it's psychologically painful for me to look at it. I would think that would be counterproductive to your goal of helping me." I cross my legs and bob my foot up and down. I'm trying to keep it light, but I'm absolutely serious.

After staring at me for a minute, he rolls his eyes, but he rises and removes the picture from the shelf. "Fine. You win." He opens one of his desk drawers and sets the photo gently inside. "Gone."

"Are you going to display the picture I made for you?" I ask, batting my eyelashes at him.

"We'll see. Now, let's talk about you."

"Oh, that tired topic," I mutter, sighing.

"You're particularly sassy today," he declares.

"Jude used to say I was 'saucy.'"

"And did you like that?"

I shrug and make a face. "I didn't hate it." Honestly, I miss it.

"How are you doing?" he asks sincerely, leaning forward with his elbows on his knees. "How long has he been gone now?"

I look up at the ceiling, as if I need to calculate, when really I know that it's been exactly "Forty-six days."

"And no contact with him whatsoever?" He jots down a note in my file.

"Hmm... That's a tricky question."

He studies my face. "Is it? As far as I can tell, it's 'yes' or 'no.'"

I chuckle self-deprecatingly. "Yeah, for a normal person.

But... Let's put it this way: I've been having conversations with Jude, unbeknownst to him."

"Oh. So you've been imagining these exchanges. For how long?"

I swipe a tissue from the box, feeling the tears already. "Since about a week after he left." My face collapses. "I just feel so *alone*. It was bad after we broke up, but I still saw him nearly every day. I still *talked* to him. Now... nothing. So I started making up conversations. And they're... weird."

"How so?" He's writing furiously now, which always makes me feel super-freaky. Like he's thinking, *Oh my gosh, I can't write this down fast enough! Wait until I write my next paper! Move over, Freud!*

But I have to get this off my chest. "Okay, first off, it used to drive me crazy that he used all these strange, slangy words and phrases that mean nothing over here, but I scatter them all over our imaginary conversations."

"So you didn't really hate when he did it; it was one of his endearing quirks."

"I guess. And we rarely agree on anything. It's like he's tormenting me. But I know exactly what he'd say in these situations, so I make him say it. So, in essence, I'm arguing with myself. Like the homeless people under the overpasses."

He ignores my self-diagnosis. "Did you argue often when you were together?"

I think about it. "No, not really. Kiddingly sometimes. I mean, we didn't agree with each other all the time, but we didn't *fight*."

"And you'd describe these imaginary exchanges as 'fights'?"

"Borderline. Sometimes. Most of the time, he's just mercilessly teasing me."

"Tell me some of the subjects of these discussions."

"Sex, mostly." When Dr. Marsh raises his eyebrows, I clarify, "A guy asked me on a date recently. A guy from work. I talked to Jude about why I turned him down, but at the same time, I was trying to make him jealous."

"Did it work?"

"No. He acted like he couldn't care less. He pretty much joked the whole time."

"Is that how he typically reacted to things that made him uncomfortable, though?"

"Actually... yes."

He nods, so I continue, "And I confronted him about Leslie. That's about the only venue where I'm willing to confront him about it. I kind of got his side of the story."

"Which was?"

"He was new in town and lonely, blah, blah, blah." I open and close my hand like a flapping mouth.

"Anything else you guys talk about regularly?"

Wincing, I answer, "Everything?" When he bites his lip, I say, "I mean, I don't have anyone else to talk to, except Sandberg. I don't know which one is more pathetic, talking to a cat or talking to a person who's not really there. At least my conversations with Jude are silent. I'd have to talk out loud to Sandberg."

Dr. Marsh precisely clips his pen to my folder and takes a deep breath. "Do you want to hear my professional opinion about what you're doing?"

"Let me guess: driving myself insane?"

He smiles gently. "Perhaps. That may be the ultimate conclusion to this, but no. You're allowing yourself to be told what you want or *need* to hear. From him. And some of it is combative, because you feel a need to be punished for breaking up with him. You know him well enough to know that he would treat most serious things irreverently, which also serves to relieve the tension and stress for you. And because you left so many questions unanswered—on both sides of things—you're fabricating his side of the story. So you can sort through it and bring yourself some closure. But I have a question."

"Just one? Really?"

"Why didn't you talk to him about it—the real him—when you had a chance? From what you've told me, he was willing. You weren't. Why not?"

Holding the tissue to my mouth, I say, "I'm weak. I would have taken him back."

"And this is a bad thing?"

I nod, trapping my tears as they slide down my cheeks.

"Forgiveness is weakness?"

Coldly, I assert, "Sometimes we do unforgiveable things. There are consequences."

His brow furrowed, he tries to understand. "And Jude did what to you that was so unforgiveable? Slept with someone before you were dating?"

"Didn't tell me! Things happen. Even with *her*. She was convenient; she was crap. Like fast food. But why didn't he tell me?"

"Have you, historically, been an easy person to break difficult news to?" he asks, then defends his question when I give him a dirty look. "I'm not excusing it; I'm just trying to understand the circumstances and his motivations for keeping it a secret. Do you think he's ashamed?"

"He should be!" I'm sobbing and hiccupping and snotting everywhere, like a child throwing a massive temper tantrum.

Dr. Marsh sits next to me on the couch. It's the closest he's ever been to me during a session. "Libby," he says softly, handing me a fresh tissue. "I want you to take a minute to calm down."

I nod and work hard to do just that.

After several minutes, when it seems like I'm breathing normally again, with only the occasional hiccup-sob, he asks, "Now, have you ever done something that you're so ashamed of, so disgusted with yourself about, that you've gone to great lengths to conceal it from everyone, even someone you know you can trust?"

I freeze mid-hiccup. It hurts.

"Have you?" he prods. "What was it?"

"This isn't about me; it's about him. And what *he* did."

"If this were about him, he'd be here, not you. This is *all* about you." He sighs. "You and I, we don't have secrets. I already know the answer to my question."

"Then why are you harassing me about it?" I snap. "You know everything."

"But I want to know what you tell *yourself*; why you can't forgive *yourself*. And I want you to say it out loud."

Now he waits patiently. It's clear after several minutes of silence that he's not going to say another word.

Twisting the soggy tissues in my hands, I take a deep, shuddering breath. "I—" I begin only to choke on the next three words. He hands me the glass of water from the table in front of us, but without taking so much as a sip from it, I blurt it out: "I killed my parents!"

❧ 28 ❧

IT WAS EXTREMELY DIFFICULT TO GO BACK TO WORK AFTER THAT session. I was late, because I had to do a lot of repair work to my makeup. And then I had to find a way to make myself concentrate on work when all I could think about were the things Dr. Marsh had brought to my attention. But I've already burned enough sick and vacation days running away from my feelings. It's a bad habit I've developed recently, and it's time to break it.

So here I am. I sit at my desk. I type and proofread and format. I answer my phone. And when I get hungry, I open my snack drawer to see if I have anything in there to save me a trip to the vending machine and possible interaction with my co-workers. I'm not hopeful, because I haven't stocked it in months and haven't looked in here in at least several weeks. My appetite hasn't been what it used to be. But I seem to remember putting a can of peanuts in here. Peanuts don't go bad, do they?

As the drawer slides out, I see something strange. Sitting on top of the peanuts is a square gift of some sort, wrapped in a piece of old blueprint. When I turn it over, I see there's a yellow sticky note on the back of it.

In case you ever change your mind... J

I look around, feeling like I might be on camera. I stare at the precise block lettering on the sticky note. It's his handwriting, all right. I tear the blueprint away carefully, so that a strip of bright orange peeks out from underneath it. When the rest of the wrapping falls away, the Kit Kat is revealed.

I smile and take a breath when I realize this must have been in my desk for months, waiting for me to find it. Since our fight about my brother. Or maybe he found the candy bar when he was packing up his office, wrapped it, and stuck it in my drawer. Kind of a going-away present from him. After I speculate about it for a while, I bite my lip and stare at my computer.

What would it hurt? I finally decide, opening an instant message window.

WEDNESDAY, MARCH 4, 10:21 A.M.
Libby.Foster:
Thank you

Jude.Weatherington:
??

Libby.Foster:
I just found the present you left me
Kit Kat
My favorite

Jude.Weatherington:
Yre wlcme. Tht was donkeys ages ago, tho

Libby.Foster:
Clever packaging

Jude.Weatherington:
Tht's me... cleevr

Libby.Foster:
Still a great typist, I see

Jude.Weatherington:
V

Libby.Foster:
Not nice

Jude.Weatherington:
How r u?

Libby.Foster:
Okay. You?

Jude.Weatherington:
Busy. TTYL?

Libby.Foster:
Sure
TTYL

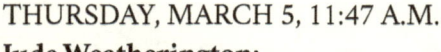

THURSDAY, MARCH 5, 11:47 A.M.
Jude.Weatherington:
What did u hurt?

I stare at my computer screen for several seconds, first making sure my eyes aren't deceiving me, that Jude really is initiating communication with me. Then I try to figure out what he means. Finally, I give up.

Libby.Foster:
??

Jude.Weatherington:
N the accdient

Oh. Hm.

Libby.Foster:
I thought I said no follow-up questions

Jude.Weatherington:
Dont anwer then

I cup my hands over my nose and mouth, my middle fingers stroking my eyebrows as I deliberate.

Jude.Weatherington:
U there?

Libby.Foster:
Shattered tibia, cracked ribs, broken hip, fractured skull. Various other broken bones in hands and feet. Bruises, cuts, and abrasions

Jude.Weatherington says:
Shit
U brke ur head?

I laugh out loud and cover my mouth so I don't draw any attention to myself while I'm slacking off.

Libby.Foster:
Yes. Metal plate up there

Jude.Weatherington:
Tht explians a lot

Libby.Foster:
Doesn't it?

Jude.Weatherington:
I'm still angry with you

Libby.Foster:
Understandable
I'm still a little mad at you, too

Jude.Weatherington:
Did I gve u blu-balls and break ur heart?

The smile dies on my face as my heart starts beating a little harder.

Libby.Foster:
No. Not the first part, anyway

Jude.Weatherington:

I dnt remember doing either
But I've tried to forget a lot
maybe I'm misremembering

It's a lot easier to end an IM conversation that's not going the way I want it to go. I simply don't respond.

My morning chats with Jude are becoming a regular thing. If I don't hear from him by noon, I feel compelled to send him a message, knowing that it's 6 p.m. there, and he's probably getting ready to go home. Or not. Once he IMed me at 4:00, which is 10:00 his time. When I asked him about it, he said, "Oh, is this weird? I hardly ever leave work before 11." Of course, he didn't type that neatly, and it took me a while to translate it, but that was the gist.

Since the day he asked about my accident, we haven't discussed anything important or serious. But I've learned a lot about him and his life there. He still plays rugby, only with a "better group of blokes." He visits his parents nearly every weekend, because "I have fuck-all else to do." And he hates his "flat," because it's not his style at all, but he's hardly ever there, anyway.

It's fascinating stuff. Seriously. I have a hard time imagining him in any setting besides Chicago, even though I know he was a complete fish out of water here. But it sounds like he's not really any more in his element over there, which is befuddling to me. I wish I could rig up a Jude Cam to follow him around and get a better idea of what's going on in his life.

Today I get the next best thing. I get to set up a video-conference call between him and Gary. For the privilege, I have to arrive at work at 7:30, but it's worth it. It was originally Lisa's responsibility, but she had a conflict with her step-daughter's school carpool, so I readily volunteered to step in.

"Are you sure?" she'd asked. "I can ask Zoe. Or Leslie."

"No! I'm all over it!" I'd replied. "Really. As a matter of fact, I'd be glad to always be in charge of early meeting set-ups." Because I know the earliest meetings are scheduled for Jude's benefit.

"O...kay," she said, but I walked off before she could ask any questions.

I've been here this morning since 7:15, awake since 4:30. I couldn't sleep, knowing I was actually going to lay eyes on him for the first time in months. And he's going to see me. But I didn't spend a lot of time getting ready this morning. (Yeah, by this morning, I only had a few things left to do. I'd done all the other stuff last night before I went to bed.) Turns out I could have waited, since I had plenty of time after taking sleep off the to-do list. Oh, well. Better safe than sorry. I think I did a good job of making it look like I didn't try too hard, though. That's what's most important.

At 7:45, I'm still the only person on the floor that I know of. I do one last touch-up of my lip gloss and stride to the videoconference room. In there, I pick up the remote and consult the list to make sure I have the right number to dial in to get Jude. I press the numerical buttons and hit the green "call" button. After a series of beeps, I see a room with a round table and six chairs around it. But I don't see anybody in the room.

"Cheers, Lisa," Jude says dully from somewhere off-camera. "How're things in the good ole U-S of A?"

My heart flutters when I say, "That's twice now you've called me 'Lisa.'"

Suddenly he ducks into the camera's view. "Crikey! Libby!

I didn't even look up at the telly. I thought Lisa was setting this up."

"She couldn't make it," I explain simply. I don't want to waste time talking about her.

"A big sacrifice for you, I take it?" he says, joking about the early hour as he dunks a teabag up and down in the mug in his hand.

I'm too uncool to play it cool convincingly. "No. I, uh, volunteered. I don't mind."

He laughs. "Oh, is 'early riser' a new personality trait?"

I blush and hope it's not visible on camera. "No, I just meant, I was happy to get a chance to see you."

"Ah," he nods. "Right. Well, you look well. All suited and booted, aren't we?" When I stare blankly at the camera, he interprets, "Dressed up."

"Not really," I deny lamely, chagrined at how obvious I am. "Anyway, you look good too. Only six more months of winter there in the U.K., right?"

We joke about the weather some more while I examine him from head to toe. His hair is longer again; probably no time to "faff around" with haircuts. He's wearing a suit with a vest, although it's a gray one I've never seen before. It's slightly shiny and cut a lot slimmer in the legs. European, I'm guessing. It's nothing I would have picked out for him, but he wears it well.

He inquires, "What's the latest gossip there in the Windy City office? Anybody giving someone else a good seeing to? Who's the current office fanny magnet? I always thought that Bruce bloke in the mailroom fancied you."

I laugh nervously. "I don't know. I don't really socialize much. I think there's a guy in IT who's popular, since he's under 25 and has a full head of hair."

"Ah, yes. I seem to remember him. Ginger bloke," Jude

acknowledges. "I feel so out of it over here. I see Lisa once in a while when she sets up these calls, but she's not very chatty with me. Did you tell her something nasty about me, Foster?"

I know he's joking, but his question reminds me of the make-believe conversation I had with him. "I haven't told anyone anything," I say a touch more defensively than I intend to. "I mean, like I said, I pretty much come to work, do my job, and go home."

"Yeah? And how's Sandberg, the pompous bastard? Glad to be shot of me, I'm sure."

Just then, Gary walks into the conference room. "Jude! Sorry I'm late. Bad accident on the highway this morning. Traffic back to BFE... Anyway, how are things there? I got a call from a Geoffrey something-or-other..."

"Haversham," Jude supplies smoothly. "Right. He wants us to submit a proposal on a project in a very up-and-coming part of the city. Plenty of potential for other jobs if developers there see and like what we've done."

"Excellent. That's what I like to hear. Oh, excuse me a minute, Jude." He turns to me as I'm exiting the room. "Libby, you mind grabbing me a cup of coffee? There wasn't any made yet."

"No problem," I reply brightly. "I'll be right back." As soon as I clear the door, I grit my teeth and mumble, "Anything else? A shoe shine, perhaps?"

The office is filling up now, a lot of people talking about the accident that Gary mentioned to Jude. While I make the coffee, I wonder—as I always do—about the people involved. To everyone else, a traffic accident seems to be just a major inconvenience, something that causes them to be late for work. But I always whisper a little prayer to help those involved get through what may be the worst day—or several days, weeks, months, and years—of their lives.

As I'm pouring Gary's coffee and putting two scoops of sugar in it, as he likes (and ruing the fact that I know this), Leslie walks in, giggling with the computer guy I was telling Jude about. When she sees me, she mock-sobers. "Oh, Libby. There you are. Jude was asking for you."

I can't resist perking up at the news, but I immediately regret it when she continues, "Yeah, he asked for me first, but I was busy, so he said you would do in a pinch."

Her barely post-pubescent companion snickers as he buys a pop for breakfast. Leslie smirks and licks her lips to try to keep from laughing out loud.

"Funny. I get it."

She looks concerned. "Are you sure? Because I can explain it to you: he slept with me first, but I found him boring, so he moved onto you. And you seemed to suit him just fine, for a while."

It takes every ounce of my self-control to resist splashing Gary's scalding coffee into her face. But rent's due in a week.

I do say, though: "Leslie, is this ever going to get old for you? Because I have to tell you, it's not very classy for you to be so proud of being a one-night stand."

"Who said anything about one night, honey?"

Her comeback throws me. I'd always assumed…

As I mope off, no witty insult at the ready, every good feeling I've been collecting for the past couple of weeks of cyber-flirting with Jude disintegrates.

But after I quietly deliver Gary's coffee, I decide I'm not finished with Leslie. It's not fair for her to torment me with these details. I don't have to put up with what amounts to harassment. Feeling empowered, I go back to the break room, where I hear her and her new boyfriend murmuring and snickering, no doubt about me.

Just as I'm about to round the corner and confront her, I

hear her say quietly, "I can't believe it still bothers her after all this time. I mean, talk about lame!"

He says something I can't make out and then she laughs. "Whatever. And, no, it's not getting old. It's amazing how entertaining it is. To think that I could get so much material from a couple of emails. What? Well, it serves her right for leaving her computer logged on overnight. That's against the rules, you know. I was actually trying to help her when she called in sick that day. How is it my fault that when I went to turn off her computer, her email was up for anyone to read?"

This time I hear him say, "Yeah, but you had to open several files to find the emails you've been using to fuck with her."

"Hey, she and Lover Boy shouldn't have been using work email on work time to talk about their sex life. I'm just having a little fun with it." I hear her heels clacking against the tile floor, getting closer to me.

Quickly, I duck into the ladies' room, my heart flapping like a deranged bird. The first thing I think when I realize she's not going to find out I was listening is, *That bitch!* The second is, *Oh, shit! What else did Jude and I talk about in those emails?* I'm suddenly thankful he never confided in me about his promotion. She would have spread it all over the office, and he would have been fired for leaking it. I might have been fired, too, for that matter. My third thought is, *I can't believe Leslie knows anything about my sex life! How mortifying!* But the fourth, strongest thought is, *I'm so sorry, Jude,* followed closely by *How do I make this right?*

❧ 29 ❧

MY FIRST INSTINCT—AFTER I RECOVER FROM THE SHOCK—IS TO
go straight to Leslie and punch her in the face. Thanks to her
snooping and her lies, I've been through one of the worst
periods of my life, which is saying a lot, considering my life
so far.

Fortunately for Leslie, though, Lisa walks into the bathroom before I can get up the nerve for physical violence.

"I have to get a passport!" I blurt to her, encouraged by her
bright smile as she passes me on the way into one of the stalls.

She doesn't even pause, but as she locks the stall door, she
asks, "Why? Gonna go abroad and find someone to replace
that man-whore Jude?"

I probably shock her by replying, "Hey! Don't call him
that," but before she can ask what's gotten into me, I say, "He
never, ever, ever, ever, *never* touched her!" My elated statement echoes loudly off the glass tiles. Quickly, I explain to her
what I overheard Leslie and IT-boy talking about, but when
Zoe walks in halfway through the telling, I start over again.
And I don't even care. I could repeat this wonderful story a
hundred times and never get sick of it.

Lisa says to Zoe as she washes her hands, "Did you notice that we were entering a parallel dimension when we stepped off the elevator this morning?"

Zoe smiles at both of us in the mirror and shakes her head. "No. But I think Libby just volunteered something personal, so we must have been."

"What I don't get," Lisa says, "is why you didn't tell Jude right away what Leslie was saying about him. I mean, you could have saved yourself a whole lotta heartache, sweetie."

I'm too happy to dwell on that right now. I wave it away. "Yeah, well, I wasn't about to discuss his and Leslie's supposed sex life. Oh my gosh! I have so much to do, including getting a passport and eating a lot of crow." I've never been so happy to swallow my pride, though. "And talking to Gary about taking some time off!"

Wincing, Lisa informs me, "Ahh, well, that's probably not going to happen today... talking to Gary, that is. He just popped in for his meeting with Jude, but he's out of the office at off-site meetings with clients the rest of the day."

Not letting it discourage me, I say, "Oh, well. I guess I don't have to talk to him right away. I have plenty of other things to do."

Zoe clears her throat. "What if... I mean, don't get mad when I say this, but what if...?"

Lisa finishes for her, "What if Jude's moved on? It's been a while."

My heart sinks at the prospect, but I say bravely, "Well, that's his loss. I have to stop waiting for other people to rescue me. I have to start being proactive and help myself."

"Atta girl!" Zoe cheers.

On cue, Wanda pokes her head into the ladies room, but our boss doesn't have to say anything to get us to scatter. Lisa and Zoe retreat to their own cubicles, where they start typing loudly and frantically to make themselves sound busy.

I really *am* busy. Just not with work. I spend the rest of the morning researching how to get a passport as quickly as possible. Then I look into how many vacation days I have left, how much money I have available to me right away, and how much a flight to London will set me back.

Right before noon, an IM almost makes me jump from my chair when it pops up on my screen.

TUESDAY, MARCH 30, 11:56 A.M.

Jude.Weatherington:
U there?

Libby.Foster:
Hi!

Jude.Weatherington:
It was good to c u this a.m./p.m.
And nice to hear u

Libby.Foster:
Same here

I type, then erase, any mention of my plans. I don't want to say anything until I talk to Gary. Well, I *want* to tell him everything, but I know it's not wise. I have to exercise some uncharacteristic self-restraint.

Jude.Weatherington:
I ws supposed to b n town next week, but...

Libby.Foster:
Now you're not?

Jude.Weatherington:
Nope. Change in plns

Libby.Foster:
Bummer
What happened?

Jude.Weatherington:
Too busy here
Ws jealous of G's coffee service
Haven't had a dcnt cuppa in days

Libby.Foster:
Yeah, I brew a mean pot of joe
And I'm okay at some other more complicated
things, too

Jude.Weatherington:
I know

Libby.Foster:
How busy are you?

Jude.Weatherington:
Soooooooooooooooooo busy
Incredibly
Sleep? Waht's that?

Libby.Foster:
You're not too busy to IM tho

Jude.Weatherington:
I'm gd at prioritizing
And delegating

Libby.Foster:
Oh, so someone else is writing this for you right now?

Jude.Weatherington:
No. Smone else is doing my real work

Libby.Foster:
Get back to work
Slacker

Jude.Weatherington:
Sigh. TTYL

I know if I "talk" to him too much, I won't be able to resist telling him everything. And I have to keep in mind that he may have moved on, like Lisa and Zoe suggested. It would be beyond mortifying to be rejected on instant messaging. Best to just act like nothing's different, even though my life's about to change forever, no matter what happens with Jude.

❦ 30 ❦

AFTER THREE DAYS OF TRACKING DOWN THE ELUSIVE GARY, I set up a formal meeting to talk to him. At the meeting, he was distracted and perfunctory... until I told him I was giving him my notice. That got his full attention. While I had it, I told him I was quitting to "explore other opportunities," but that I wanted my last big assignment to be finding an administrative assistant for the London office.

"Jude and the other guys really need someone to do the day-to-day things that no one else wants to do," I'd said, purposely using the exact words he'd used when I overheard him talking to Jude. I managed to maintain eye contact, keep a straight face, and not blush, too, which was a major accomplishment for me.

Of course, the statement was lost on him. He probably thought I was brilliant for realizing my place and feeling the same way he does. But sure enough, after that, his buzzing cell phone, dinging computer, and the papers scattered on his desk started calling out to him again. He readily agreed that I should work with a placement agency in London to find someone, and he agreed that I'd spend my last week of employment with the company over there, training her.

He dismissed me with, "Just work with Jude and keep him informed. I know he needs someone, but I'm too swamped to deal with it myself."

"That's exactly what I figured," I said cheerfully. "I'll take care of everything."

On my way past Lisa and Zoe later, I gave them the thumbs-up, causing them to squeal like high school cheerleaders. Leslie poked her head out of her cubicle. I flipped her off. It felt good. What are they going to do? Fire me?

I immediately sat down at my computer when I got to my desk and fired off an email to Jude:

Hey,

I've been put in charge of finding someone (a.k.a., an admin) for the London office. I'll be working with a temp agency there to find him/her. Any specific qualifications you want me to list? I'll be writing up the "advert" today, so shoot your ideas to me in an email.

Libby

An hour later, I got this response:

Woo-hoo! Just make sure she (or he) knows how demanding I am. And how to make a decent cup of coffee.

J

My fingers twitched with the urge to type a response telling him everything else, but I didn't. I didn't have time, anyway.

∾

THURSDAY, APRIL 8, 9:22 A.M.

Jude.Weatherington:
Any lck w/ the admin search?

Libby.Foster:
You want to lick an admin?

Jude.Weatherington:
U know wht I mean
And yes, sort of, by teh way

Libby.Foster:
Inappropriate

Jude.Weatherington:
My apolgoies
Stress will do that

Libby.Foster:
I have three candidates lined up
I'll email you their CVs
Do you want to sit in on the phone interviews? I can
conference you in

Jude.Weatherington:
No, too busy
I trust you

Libby.Foster:
Bad idea
Just kidding

Jude.Weatherington:
Who's training the new hre?

Libby.Foster:
Me
Is that OK?

Jude.Weatherington:
There?

Libby.Foster:
No, there

Jude.Weatherington:
In Lodnon? seriously?

Libby.Foster:
Y. In London

Jude.Weatherington:
when?

Libby.Foster:
2 weeks

Jude.Weatherington:
Ah. V. good
Must run

Jude.Weatherington has logged off

I hold the phone to my ear as I file my fingernails. "Yes, I'd like a passport please. And can you get my attorney on the phone when we're finished here? I need to talk to her about distributing my parents' estate. Also, if you could, please put me in touch with a pet relocation service for when I move overseas. Oh! And I need to sell my car. And my furniture. Ha, ha! Yes, everything must go. That's right. I guess I can have all my clothes shipped later. Who would I talk to about that? Never mind. I'll give them away to charity and start over across the pond. Yeah, England. I know, right? Totally exciting. If only I could get all these logistics out of the way..."

Everything is in order, although it was a lot more complicated than in my dreams. After a few weeks of non-stop preparations, all I have to do is wait for the departure date to arrive. Which is easier said than done. It's driving me insane.

During the day, I stay pretty busy, but at night, it's hard to sit still. TV's no help; everything's so boring. I go walking around the neighborhood a lot. It occupies my mind, as I attempt to memorize everything about it. I've lived here for almost five years, but I never really appreciated it. My two requirements when I moved here were 1) close to Wrigley field and 2) a warm, dry place to sleep each night. Now I see it as something a little more. A lot more. It's where Jude and I fell in love. We spent a lot of time here, and I don't want to forget it.

But we're experiencing a very rainy spring, so sometimes I have no choice but to be cooped up in the apartment with Sandberg. In those cases, I take the time to study. I've purchased at a local bookstore several books about British English. I'm sick of not understanding what Jude says. I took French in high school and as part of my Bachelor of Arts degree at Loyola, so I think I could probably keep up better in a conversation with a Frenchman than I can with the guy I love. Not acceptable. So I've been cramming. And laughing at some of the things I *thought* I understood but really didn't.

Speaking of Jude, he's been relentlessly emailing, IM'ing, and videoconferencing me, under the guise of us discussing the new admin. Today we're on a videoconference call, just the two of us, going over the plans for my visit to the London office. We've just gone through my entire itinerary, from the time I land until the new girl's final training day, when I say breezily, "And then that's it. I'm outta here."

He closes the notebook on the table in front of him and leans back, putting his hands behind his head. "You know, this would all be so much easier if *you* would just take the admin position here."

"Sorry, I'm already busy."

"Indeed. Your minions in Chicago need you."

I've almost forgotten I haven't told him I'm quitting. And I'm actually kind of shocked that the news hasn't gotten to him yet. Lightly, in order not to disturb the sleeping butterflies in my belly, I joke, "You weren't kidding when you said you guys over there have no idea what's going on in the rest of the company."

"What? What'd I miss?"

"That's going to be my last day," I state. "For good. I'm not coming back to Chicago."

He processes the news for a few seconds, then ventures, "Not going back... at all?" He sits up straighter and folds his hands on the table in front of him. "Where are you going? What about Sandberg?"

I laugh at his concern for the cat, of all things. "Sandberg will be there with me. I plan to take a year or so off, travel around the U.K. Do some research for a non-fiction book I'd like to write."

He stares at the screen. Finally, he grins and says, "Cor

blimey... For a second there, you had me going! I totally believed you!"

"I'm serious!"

"Don't make me call Gary in there to bubble you up."

Thanks to my studies, I now know this means "rat me out" and not "wash me," as I had previously believed.

I stand and gather all my papers in a pile, clutching them against my chest. "I'm not kidding. In less than a week, I'm leaving Chicago. Probably forever. And London's the first stop on my tour."

He eventually believes me, after he drags a few more details out of me, such as how I'm going to support myself (my inheritance, as uncomfortable as that makes me) and, more importantly, how I'm going to watch my Cubs games this summer (thank God for the Internet).

When he asks what made me decide to do it, I answer truthfully, "I'm sick of wasting my life. I don't have anything or anyone tying me to this job or this town anymore. It's time to move on."

He seems speechless, so I laugh and say, "I'm really excited."

Distractedly, with his eyes on his hands, he says, "Yes. Right. Well. That's quite excellent for you. I suppose you're very busy there, with all your preparations."

The group who has the room reserved after me arrives noisily. "Anyway, that's our cue. I'll talk to you later. Let me know if you think of anything else I need to know before I leave here Tuesday."

He waves limply, then I hit the button to disconnect the call.

Leslie, one of the participants for the next meeting, says, "Ooh... a little high-tech reunion there?" To the rest of the group, she jokes, "We should check the TV screen for kiss-prints... or worse."

A few of them smile faintly, but for the most part her comment falls flat.

"Grow up, Leslie," I say wearily.

"And turn into a dried-up prune like you? No, thanks." She chomps her gum obnoxiously.

The rest of the people in the room go back to their own conversations, so as I edge past her, I lean in and say just loudly enough for her to hear, "You know better than that." When she wrinkles her nose and gives me a questioning glare, I tell her, "I know what you did, okay? So you can end your pathetic little fantasy of having slept with Jude."

"I don't know what you're talking about."

I level the most sarcastically pitying look at her and shake my head slightly. "Oh, Leslie. So sad." With that, I condescendingly pat her arm and walk out.

❧ 31 ❧

AT THE END OF MY LAST SESSION WITH DR. MARSH, HE CLAPS his hands together. "So... this is it, huh?"

"This is it!" I agree, shrugging my shoulders up near my ears and standing.

"When does your plane leave?"

"Tomorrow, first thing in the morning. I have to be at O'Hare at 5:45."

"Are you going to sleep tonight?"

"Probably not," I admit with a grin.

He smiles, then says quietly, "Well. You seem like you're prepared for what you need to do."

"I am," I reply confidently. "Very. And, like I said, I know it may not turn out the way I've dreamed it will. But no matter what happens, it'll be forward progress."

He nods.

"And I'll have all of Europe to explore and get lost in if I have any sorrows to drown. At least I won't be confined to my bed. And I won't have to deal with any nosy co-workers gawking at me."

He stands and holds out his hand for me to shake. "Good attitude."

I shuffle my feet a little and almost chicken out, but then I just do it. Stepping forward, I put my arms around him. He readily returns the hug, to my surprise. Just as quickly, I step back.

"Thanks for helping me be a little more normal. Don't read anything into this—psychologically, I mean—but you're the closest thing to a Dad that I've had, and it's been important to me." I haven't reached for the tissues once during this session, but now I feel like I might need them.

He nods professionally. "You're welcome. It's always rewarding to see a client make as much progress as you have."

"Aw, shucks."

"Now, get on that plane and don't ever look back," he advises.

TUESDAY, APRIL 20, 2:19 P.M.
Jude.Weatherington:
Pick you up at Heathrow tmrrw nite?

Libby.Foster:
I'll just take a cab

Jude.Weatherington:
Sure?

Libby.Foster:
Yes. I'll be tired. And it'll be late-ish

Jude.Weatherington:

It's no bother, really

Libby.Foster:
I'll be fine. Thanks, though. I'll call you Thursday

Jude.Weatherington:
OK
Safe travels

Several minutes pass. The status line keeps saying, *Jude.Weath-erington is writing...* but nothing else pops up until finally:

Jude.Weatherington:
Itll b good to c u

I sit there wondering what he really wrote and decided against until Lisa knocks on the wall and pops her head over the partition. I quickly close the IM window, but not before she sees it was up.

She smiles slyly. "Mm-hmm. Somebody a little excited for your arrival?"

I duck my head as we walk to the break room for our afternoon pops. "I think we both are."

"I don't blame you. But Zoe and I expect a full report as soon as you have access to a computer." She pauses, then says, "Well, maybe not a *full* report. We just want to know the basics. You know, how the trip went, how the talk went, and if you got laid."

"Thanks for respecting my privacy." I smile.

"It doesn't have to be a long email," she allows.

We're still laughing when we get to the break room, but I stop as I realize this will be our last trip like this.

"What?" she asks, alarmed by my sudden seriousness.

Feeling foolish and maudlin, I answer, "Nothing. Aww... we're outta Kit Kats!" hoping to pass off my sentimentality as disappointment.

"You're hopeless. And I hate you. You eat, what, one of those a day? And look at you! Tiny waist and big boobs. No wonder Jude's all over you."

"No, he's not!" Only in my dreams.

"Well," she smirks, "he will be. You'll only have to lick your lips, and he'll take that as invitation enough."

"Lisa!" I blush while I try and fail several times to get the pop machine to take my dollar.

"Come off it. You're not the innocent little virgin anymore." She takes the dollar from me and gets it to go into the machine on the first try while I gape at her.

"What?" she asks when she turns around and sees my face. "It was easy."

"You knew?"

"Knew what? How to put a dollar into a vending machine? Yeah. Mommy 101."

I narrow my eyes at her, trying to figure out if she's being intentionally obtuse. I decide she is. "How'd you know I was"—I look around to make sure we're really alone, and whisper—"intact?"

She throws her head back and gives one of her familiar barking laughs.

I hit the button for a Dr. Pepper and wait for her to respond.

Finally, she says, "'Intact'? What is this, 1928?"

"Just keep your voice down," I mutter from behind my can. "Or does everyone already know?"

More soberly but still grinning, she answers, "No. Don't get all purse-lipped and uptight. I just knew. I *inferred*, let's say."

"You haven't been reading my emails too, have you?"

"I know you're kidding. Or else we're not friends anymore." She buys her own Diet Coke and confides, "Some people have gay-dar. I have the virginity equivalent. Zoe was, too, when she first started working here, if it makes you feel any better. But she's made up a lot of ground since then."

"Well, Zoe," I respond. "That seems a lot more obvious. I was never mousey or shy."

"But you had a 'fight or flight' argument with yourself every time someone with a penis walked into the same room as you. I could see it in your eyes." She nudges me toward the break room doorway, as if herding me back to packing up my desk.

"Well, screw me!" I say in astonishment.

Drily, she replies, "I think I'll leave that up to Jude. From what I gather, he's pretty darn good at it."

"Hot towel?"

"Why, yes, thank you. Oh, and thanks for the refill on my drink, too."

"My pleasure. What else can I get you? Blanket, pillow? Since you're the only one on this flight, I'm at your beck and call."

"A blanket would be great, thanks. What's the in-flight movie?"

"The Natural. A classic."

"Oooh, my favorite! I love when Robert Redford and Glen Close meet up in the café, and you can tell they love each other, but they're so awkward because they haven't seen each other in such a long time. But the spark... it's still there."

"And we should be landing right after the movie ends."

"But I thought the flight was eight hours?"

"Not today. We have some good tail winds, and the pilot's in a *hurry. Plus we're flying a brand new plane that can go three times faster than the old models."*

"Awesome."

"You're also staying at the same hotel as the flight crew, so we'll drive you there. That is, if you don't mind sharing a car with us."

"No, I don't think that'll be a problem. It'll be nice to not have to figure out where I'm going or how to get a cab. I've been awake for more than 24 hours. So excited for my trip."

"You just relax, then, and enjoy your movie. We'll take care of everything."

~

Anyone who's traveled at all—much less internationally—knows that my old dreams of being invited to stay at George Clooney's Italian villa and be his sex slave were more realistic than my fantasy about what my trip would be like when I traveled to the U.K.

No, I don't recommend solo international travel for someone who's never even been on a plane before. I was so focused on the destination that I didn't think of the mode. It was just a given: need to get to London? Take a plane. But air travel is very complicated. And stressful. And crowded.

I spent a lot of time asking questions of anyone who looked remotely like they worked for an airport or airline. "How do I get from here to there?" "Where do I go after that?" "What do I do next?" "Yes, I'm wearing an underwire bra. Is that okay?" "What do you mean I can't take my dry shampoo on the plane with me?"

By the time I got on the plane, I was already exhausted. And it was only 7 a.m. I was glad the company had splurged for the direct flight. I don't know if I could have handled a layover in another airport.

The flight itself was another adventure. I was sandwiched between two businessmen, one of whom spoke exclusively in Italian but judging by his tone was sexually harassing me every time he addressed me. The other was the stereotypical workaholic who kept getting in trouble for operating his electronic devices when he wasn't supposed to be. I was relieved when both of them reclined their seats about halfway through the flight and dozed.

I was too keyed up to sleep, however. Or read. Or do anything but monitor every little sound and bump the plane made. And whoever decided that *Snakes on a Plane* was a good choice for the in-flight movie had a sick sense of humor.

I never thought I'd be a nervous flyer. The concept of flying, in general, has never bothered me. But I was surprised to find that I kind of had to stifle a non-stop, eight-hour scream. I kept worrying my first flight might be my last, and wishing I could just drive to London. When are they going to build that bridge, anyway? Surely we have the technology.

It goes without saying that I'm mentally exhausted, nervous, stressed, and feeling not-so-fresh when the plane finally touches down at Heathrow. And I know I still have to get my baggage, find a cab, and make it to my hotel before I can truly breathe again. I estimate I'll have to ask at least three dozen questions before I'm in a bed.

However, the terminal where I land is surprisingly easy to navigate and well marked. I thank God I'm still in an English-speaking country, even if it's a sort of English that I frequently don't comprehend. Thanks to my evening studies, though, I'm delighted to find out that I understand more of what everyone around me is saying than I would have six months ago.

After I have my bags, I wander over to one of the free-standing airport maps so I can figure out where to go to find a cab. Someone touches me from behind, but I ignore them, thinking it's an incidental brush-up in the crowded terminal. I step a little closer to the map, in case I'm in someone's way, but I stay focused on what I'm doing. Now a hand wraps around my upper arm. Reflexively, I bring my elbow down and back, looking sharply at whoever's trying to put their hand in my messenger bag.

Jude grabs his lower abdomen and steps back. "Oi! It's only me!" he protests.

I gasp and apologize in one breath, reaching for his arm. He quickly straightens, assuring me he's fine, and as soon as he's fully upright, I fling myself at him. Surprised, he takes a second to recover and hug me back.

"Blimey, I didn't realize I needed to wear protective gear to come fetch you from the airport," he grouses good-naturedly, stiffly patting my back.

Without thinking, I bury my face in his neck and take a deep breath of him. Then I muffle, "You weren't supposed to be here. I thought you were mugging me!"

He pushes away first. "Right. Well, I couldn't in good conscience allow you navigate all this alone. Strange city, stranger people, after a long flight... That wouldn't be very hospitable, now, would it be? How was your flight?"

"Long," I confirm. I'm suddenly self-conscious, tucking my hair behind my ears and fidgeting with my necklace. "I wasn't expecting it to be such a big deal."

We stand there looking at each other for a beat, then he smiles and asks, "Do you need to exchange any cash?"

When I answer, "yes," and look around for the nearest kiosk or exchange counter, he shakes his head at me and says, "Not here. The exchange rate is bollocks. I'll lend you some bees and honey— er, money, until we can locate a bank ATM close to your hotel."

I merely nod, grateful almost to the point of tears that he's here to help me out.

"What else do you need?" he asks.

If only I knew. This is unbelievable. This morning, I woke up in Chicago, and now I'm in a completely different country. After eagerly anticipating it for weeks, it's hard to convince myself this isn't just another one of my fantasies.

I laugh. "You tell me. I'm so lost it's not even funny. I can't believe I'm here!"

"It's more than a little surreal seeing you here," he agrees, moving me aside with a gentle hand as someone behind me tries to get past us. "Do you want to grab a bite to eat?"

I'm too nervous to eat, so I merely say, "Not really. Honestly, I'm looking forward to a hot bath and a soft bed. And then about seventeen hours of sleep."

He nods curtly, as if my request is completely reasonable. "Absolutely. That can be arranged. Would you like to wait here whilst I get the car?"

I shake my head. "I'll just go with you."

"It's a bit of a walk."

"It feels good to stretch my legs. Let's go."

He wasn't kidding about the hike. But I don't utter so much as a sigh, since he warned me. And he's carrying my heaviest bag. Outside, I squint against the cold drizzle and ask him, "So how're Marvin and some of the other guys adjusting to life over here?"

"Really well, for the most part," he answers. "Marvin's quite the ladies' man, believe it or not."

"Not," I say.

"Not kidding! The birds like his American accent."

I laugh at the reversal. "That's crazy. What about all of his other, um, traits? None of those are a turn-off?"

"Guess not." He switches my suitcase to his other hand.

We fall into an easy silence. I'm too psychologically weary to be tense or wonder what he's thinking and what I should say next. My brain is slowly shutting down. Without warning, though, the mist turns into a downpour, huge drops bombing us from the night sky.

"Feck, that figures!" he gripes, speeding up to a jog. "I'm parked straight ahead."

I keep pace with him until the last fifty feet or so, which he does at a sprint, pulling ahead of me as he pops the trunk of the car and tosses my bag in. I arrive seconds after him and follow suit, then I rush to the right side of the car.

He's on the other side, holding the door open. "Over here! Wrong side!"

I laugh at myself. "Shit! Sorry!" I run around the back of the car and slide in. He slams the door after me and runs around the front of the car to get to the driver's side. We look like two kids doing a Chinese fire drill at a stop light.

When he's behind the wheel, he starts the car and lets loose a giggle that ends in an extended "Aaaaah" that makes me laugh. I've missed that so much!

"Welcome to London," he says sarcastically.

"Lovely weather you have here."

"Yes, we really highlight it in our tourism literature. Brings in loads of revenue." He wipes his face on his wet shirt and puts the car in reverse.

It's disconcerting and downright scary to be sitting on the driver's side of a car but not have a steering wheel to hold onto. I assume a position with one hand on the dashboard and the other clenched next to my leg on the seat. I angle my body towards him and bring my right foot up to prevent me from constantly trying to stomp on the brake or the gas.

Without looking directly at me, he navigates the roads away from the airport, smiles, and says, "Everything okay over there?"

"I'll let you know after I can breathe again," I reply. "Was it really this scary when I drove you around?"

He laughs. "Oh, so much scarier. I'm not even driving fast. Or weaving in and out of traffic. Or shouting at other drivers."

I gulp. "It feels like you're driving pretty fast."

"Well, I'm not. Let's talk about something else to distract you."

All I can think about is the car, so I comment on it. "I see you got around to buying a car. What's this thing called?"

"A necessary evil. I drive it as little as possible, but I had to get something to take to client meetings, lunches, site walks, and that sort of thing. It's come in useful." Suspiciously, he asks, "Why?"

I squirm. "Nothing. It's just… I don't know." I look around at all the leather and lacquered wood-grain. I want to say it's a grandpa car, but I don't want to be rude, so I settle on, "Not your style."

"That's because it's not mine. It's the company's. I didn't pick out this pretentious piece of rubbish." He merges onto a very busy highway. "Speaking of cars, what'd you do with yours?"

"Sold it to a bloke on my rugby team," I joke.

He grins and looks at me. "Seriously."

I frown, hoping I can tell him without crying. "Actually, it was kind of emotional," I admit. "I took it to a dealer and they paid me peanuts for it, since I wasn't trading it in or anything.

I would have gotten more money for it if I'd sold it myself, but I ran out of time."

It was the first thing I did that made this whole life change real. Everything else was pretty superficial. You can get a passport without going anywhere; you can transfer your adult brother's inheritance into his own name anytime you want. But when I walked away from that dealership and got on a bus to go home, Ryno nestled in my hoodie pocket, I realized I was really leaving the only home I'd ever known.

"I'm sure it'll find a good home," Jude says sincerely, as if we're talking about a beloved pet. "And you won't need one here; you can take a train just about anywhere." As the rain slows to a drizzle again, he turns down the setting on the wipers. "That reminds me: let me see your passport." He sticks a hand toward me.

"Just keep both hands on the wheel," I implore. "You don't need to see my passport."

"I want to see how squeaky-clean it is!" he urges. "Give over!"

"No!"

He waves dismissively at me. "Ah, well. I'll see it later, I s'pose."

"I guess yours is all stamped up, since you're such a sophisticated world traveler. And I'm just a hick."

"What's a hick?"

"A yokel. A bumpkin," I translate.

He smiles. "Oh. Then yes." He reaches over and pushes playfully against my shoulder. "Only kidding. You've proven before that just because you're inexperienced doesn't mean you're ignorant. You're a fast learner."

I blush in the dark car.

He clears his throat.

Neither of us speaks for a while, the windshield wipers the

only sound for several minutes. Then he says, "We're almost to your hotel. What're your plans for the next couple of days?"

Focusing my eyes from my staring out the window at all the unfamiliar things around, I answer, "Oh, I don't know." I took two days of my leftover vacation time so I could let my body adjust to the time change. "I'll probably explore the area around the hotel and try not to get lost. Sandberg's supposed to be delivered to the hotel tomorrow, too."

"So soon?"

"Yeah. I thought it was going to be a huge deal, but the thought of re-homing him was a deal-breaker. Found out that the U.S. has some sort of agreement with the UK, so I worked with a pet relocation service that knows all the ins and outs with that. And since he's chipped, my Yankee Doodle cat is being welcomed with open arms."

He nods as I give my long-winded, rambling explanation, but as soon as I stop talking, he blurts, "Can I have you over for dinner tomorrow night?"

"At your place?"

"Yeah. Unless you don't want to. I can take you somewhere else. I'm an embarrassing regular at several places close to work. But they're noisy sorts of places. Pubs, mostly. We wouldn't be able to talk as easily. You know, people playing snooker and arrows and such. Loud music."

His nervous prattle is adorable.

"I'm not picky. Whatever's easiest for you."

He pulls beneath the hotel awning and hits a button to open the trunk. "I'll pop round at about seven, then, and we'll see what we're in the mood for."

Shyly, I reply, "Okay."

The moment I've been planning for more than a month is nearly here. It's almost show time. But who would blame me for wanting to delay it just one more night?

❧ 32 ❧

I THOUGHT ALL I WANTED WAS A BATH AND A BED, BUT WHEN I get the second half of my wish, I realize that my mind is unable to shut off. It must have gotten its second wind while I was checking in. So I stare at the punched tin ceiling of my room, my thoughts scattering in a hundred different directions.

I wonder what time Sandberg will be here tomorrow.

Is it going to be weird to be alone with Jude in his apartment after all these months?

How is he going to react to what I tell him? How am I even going to broach the subject?

I hope the London office has all the office supplies I'll need to get Talia set up on Monday.

I'm not in the United States right now. I'm on a completely different continent.

This room smells funny.

I wonder where I can get a newspaper in the morning to look for a place to "live" here when I'm not traveling. Maybe I should wait until after I tell Jude everything. Maybe I'll decide to set up my home base in another town, if it doesn't go well. Or another country. Scotland? Ireland?

Maybe Snow Patrol needs another roadie. Or an administrative assistant.

These sheets are itchy. Bedbugs?

That idea has me on my feet, pulling back the covers and inspecting the linens at close range. Nothing.

Back in bed, I quickly return to my runaway thoughts.

What if I can't figure out how to use the coffee maker here? I wonder if it's very different than the ones back home.

This is home now. Doesn't feel like it. I miss my bed. I hope Lisa's stepdaughter's enjoying it. Is she sleeping in it right now? I do the math on my fingers. *Probably.*

Is Sandberg okay? What's he doing right now?

Jude's going to hate me after I tell him.

No, he's understanding. He'll forgive me.

Nobody's that understanding.

It's not my fault. Really. Can't we just skip the distasteful revelation and go straight to the making-up part?

What if there's no making up?

Ohohohohoh... Breathe. If that's the case, I hear there are lots of pubs in this region and no shortage of alcohol.

What if he's still mad at me about the Leslie thing on Monday, then he falls in love at first sight with Talia?

What if he's over me? He was pretty cool at the airport.

He came to pick me up, though, even after I told him it wasn't necessary. And he was babbling in the car a little, like he was nervous.

So? He could be nervous because he thinks I might still have feelings for him, but he doesn't feel the same way anymore.

Maybe he's thinking right now about how to best tell me that he's met someone new.

Maybe he'll be introducing me to her at dinner...

Gaaaaaaaa!!!

By 6 a.m., I give up trying to sleep and turn on the TV in my room. The early morning news is on, but I can't keep up with the speed at which the presenters speak. I was afraid of this. I knew I'd be lost here. I knew I'd stick out like a sore thumb, the obvious foreigner, clueless and ignorant, bumbling around, not knowing what she's doing. And trying to operate on no sleep, to boot.

To be fair, it's only midnight in my mind. But that means when Jude stops by this evening to get me, it'll be 1 p.m. to me, and I won't have had any sleep.

Well, don't panic. I decide to try to sleep again in a couple of hours. I still have plenty of time to get in some rest. This is exactly why I took today and tomorrow off. As soon as the excitement wears off, I'll crash. My circadian rhythms will kick in. It'll be fine.

I was just dozing off when the pet relocation service came by to deliver Sandberg, who then spent the entire afternoon ignoring me. And when I finally decided to stop trying to get back in his good graces and take a nap, he decided he wanted to play. Now it's 6:30, Jude will be here within the hour, and I can hardly keep my eyes open.

I've tried jogging in place, sticking my face in the mini-fridge, and drinking several cups of coffee. But I've hit the wall. For good.

Or not.

I was worried about not being able to adjust to such a big time change, so I bought and packed some mild over-the-counter uppers, the kind popular with cramming college students. Digging them out of my suitcase, I read the instructions and take the recommended dose. Then I go into the bathroom and try to use makeup to hide the outward signs that I haven't slept in thirty-three hours.

I'm just lamenting the dark circles under my eyes when I hear the knock on the door.

"Frack," I mutter, quickly blotting the green concealer. "Coming!"

When I open the door, Jude smiles charmingly at me. "Cheers. I'm a bit early. I hope that's not a problem."

"Not at all," I reassure him. "Sandberg and I were just resting."

"Jet lagged?" he asks, wincing.

"Me? Nah!" I lie. "Adjusting just fine."

He peers past me into my room and eyes Sandberg. "And how about His Nibs? Not giving you too hard a time, I hope."

I laugh. "At first, yeah. But he got over it faster than I thought he would. Of course, now I'm going to leave him again, so I can probably expect a present waiting for me when I get back later, but oh, well." I grab my messenger bag from the chair next to the tiny table that's supposed to serve as a desk and dining table in one. "Where are you taking me?"

He looks from me to the cat and back again. "Well, if you don't mind ordering in at my place, you can bring Sandberg."

After going back and forth for a while about the logistics of such a thing (and my obsessively making sure it's really okay), we load the cat into his carrier and set off on foot, at Jude's insistence that he lives minutes away. In a surprisingly short amount of time, we're standing outside his apartment door.

"You have to promise not to laugh when you see this place," he says, turning the key in the locks. "It's quite posh. I rather hate it, actually."

"It doesn't look very fancy from out here," I declare in the politest way possible. The hallway we're standing in is actually kind of dim and dank and smells like mothballs.

But as soon as he opens the door, it's like we're stepping into an entirely different building. I noticed the huge windows when we were on the street, but they're on the second floor, and since he led me to a ground-floor door, I didn't think they were part of his place. But they are.

I stare open-mouthed at them. "Holy shit," I breathe, taking in the industrial-chic kitchen, white furniture, and metal stairs leading up to a loft with a giant bed in its center. It's not his style at all, but I would know blindfolded that he lives here. It smells like him: cinnamon Altoids, shaving cream, and laundry detergent.

"I know. Please don't think less of me for being the kind of prat who lives in a place like this. It seemed like a good idea four months ago, but…" He sets the carrier down and releases the catch on the door. Sandberg immediately jumps onto the pure-white couch and makes himself comfortable.

"No, no, buddy," I tell him, picking him up.

Jude takes him from my arms and sets him down where he was. "He's fine." Obviously unconcerned, he steps away and goes into the kitchen, where he opens a drawer and pulls out a stack of paper menus. "Let's see… Chinese, Indian, Thai, kebabs, pizza, fish and chips… what's your fancy?"

"I think it's only right that I have fish and chips, don't you?"

He shrugs. "Sounds fine. I'll just go upstairs, call them, and change my clothes."

He presses a button next to the stairs, sending blinds down from a slot in the ceiling to cover the windows. Then he bounds lightly up the stairs, leaving me alone to look around.

This place is eerily similar to the London maisonette of my fantasies, complete with one entire wall of crammed bookshelves reaching to the ceiling. A catwalk connected to the loft and a ladder allows access to the higher shelves. I wander over, perusing the titles at eye level. I've never seen these books before in Jude's possession. They're all British classics. Heavy on Dickens and the romantic poets.

I stifle a grin and move on to his music collection, an old-school assortment of vinyl, CDs, and even a few tapes thrown in. When I'd questioned why he'd dragged all of this stuff across the Atlantic when it could have fit on a tiny device in his pocket, he'd shrugged. "I like having physical copies of stuff. Same with books and blueprints. Digital files are convenient, but you can't touch them. You can't smell them."

I'd teased him about sniffing CDs, and he'd distracted me by sniffing my neck and murmuring that he'd never replace me with a digital Libby, so why should his music be any different?

I shiver at the memory and snap back to the present.

Everything seems to be mostly the same as it was in Chicago, with a few oddballs thrown in (Neil Young? Johnny Cash?). Unable to resist, I pluck an old Snow Patrol CD from the rack and turn it over to read the song titles. Not a bad song on the entire album. By design, it's been forever since I've listened to anything by them.

"Put on whatever you'd like," he calls over the railing above, startling me so much that I drop the CD with a clatter, and the front of the case pops off and skitters under the coffee table. I drop to all fours and fish it out, suddenly feeling nervous and jittery.

Even though I suspect it's dangerous, I nonetheless insert the disc into an ancient CD player that was probably state-of-the-art and extremely expensive when it was originally sold. The notes to the first song blast at me from surround-sound speakers in every corner of the room.

"Aaaghh!" I groan, frantically searching the front panel with shaking fingers for anything that could be the volume control. But without my having touched anything, the music softens.

Sandberg gripes at me from the couch, where he's crouched into a defensive position.

"Sorry!" Jude says from the loft, where he's adjusting the volume with a remote. "I tend to keep it a bit loud. Food's on the way!"

I want to reacquaint myself with the lyrics to the first song, but I'm distracted by my racing heart. My eyeballs feel like they're jiggling in their sockets.

Jude trots barefoot down the stairs in shorts and a t-shirt. "What can I get you to drink?"

"Water?" I suggest unsurely, blinking rapidly. Sweat breaks out at my hairline.

"Really?" he asks, surprised, standing in front of the open refrigerator. "I have all manner of beverages in here. Just no food."

"Really," I reply, trying to take a deep breath and slow my heartbeat.

"Okay," he says, pulling out a bottle of beer and a bottle of water, prying off the top of his beer bottle on the edge of the counter.

I meet him halfway between the kitchen and the living room and take the water from him. He sits in a chair at a right angle to the sofa. I take the loveseat cushion not already occupied by Sandberg, who's dozing.

For lack of anything better to say, I point out, "He's getting dark gray fur all over your couch." My leg starts bouncing. I stare at it, wondering why it's doing that and why I can't stop it.

Jude finishes a long pull on his beer with a *thwong*. "Would you stop worrying about the bloody furniture? If anything, he's making it more interesting." Looking completely relaxed, lounged back in the low-slung chair with his hands resting on each arm, his legs spread wide, he smiles at me.

"You must have taken your sofa selection duties too lightly when you bought this furniture. Sounds like you needed my help. Huh-huh!" The nervous laugh that jumps from my mouth startles both of us.

He looks suspiciously at me and says, "Yes... That would have been nice... if I had wanted to search and search and never decide on anything. Are you okay?"

Even though I'm pretty sure I'm not, I lie and say, "Yeah, yeah. Fine!" I put both hands on my leg to try to still it, but it's no use, so I fold them in my lap and smile tightly. "Just fine! Why?"

"You're acting like you're on one," he states bluntly.

"No, I'm not!" I hastily object. "I wouldn't know the first thing about taking drugs; you know that!"

Laughing, he imitates my blinky, twitchy, jumpy behavior. "What's all this, then? Tweaker."

I blush, making the sweat come harder and faster. Then I start hysterically laughing. Gasping for air, I manage to say, "I'm not a tweaker!"

He sets his empty beer bottle on the floor by his feet and leans forward. "Then what the hell's going on with you?" It's said with a smile.

I can't bear to sit anymore. Jumping up, I cross the room and turn to face him. "Uh, nothing! Well, I mean... That is..." I scratch at a spot on my arm that doesn't get less itchy, no matter how hard I scratch. It's worse to have him think I'm on drugs than to just admit, "I took some, um, pep pills before you picked me up."

"Pep pills." It comes out more like a statement than a

question.

"Yeah. Caffeine. Concentrated."

He laughs, standing and walking over to me. "Oh. I wouldn't have done that if I were you. Why the bloody hell did you do that?" He grasps my shoulders, which makes me giggle like Leslie, which reminds me about what I need to tell him.

"Oh, shit!" I blurt, ducking away from him. I practically run into the kitchen, keeping the island between us when he follows me. We circle it a few times before the level-headed one of the two of us stops in front of the refrigerator and opens it for another beer.

"You're going to be up for days now, you know," he informs me calmly. "You should have just let your body get naturally used to the time shift.

"I was!" I defend myself. "But I couldn't sleep last night, and Sandberg wouldn't let me sleep this afternoon, so by 6:00, I had been up 32 hours, and you were about to show up, and I was falling asleep on the toilet!"

Beer sprays from his mouth onto the floor and island in front of him. He scoots back and bends at the waist, cupping his hand under his dripping chin. After he mops up the worst of it with the front of his shirt, he grabs a dish towel and says, "Well. That was unexpected."

"Sorry. I'm just telling you, it was necessary. I had to do something if I was going to hang out with you tonight."

He mops up the beer and tosses the towel into a machine in the kitchen that looks like an old-timey dishwasher but upon closer inspection is a combined washer and dryer for clothes.

"Whoa! That's weird! A laundry machine in your kitchen?"

"Focus, Foster!" he demands, taking advantage of my being distracted and catching me by the hand. "Why didn't you just call me at the office and tell me you were too cream crackered to do anything tonight? I would have understood."

His sympathetic tone hits another chord with me. I look up into his face and catch myself puddling up. "I know. You're so understanding." I sniffle and push on. "But I *wanted* to be with you tonight. I mean, hang out. Talk. You know."

"Yeah…" he says, trailing off and leaning closer to me, gazing into my blinky eyes. "Libby?"

"Uh huh?"

A buzzing noise gets our attention. Whereas I don't know what the source of the noise is, Jude curses under his breath and moves away from me. He digs his wallet out of his pocket and goes to the door, where he presses a button and says into the speaker, "Yes?"

"Food delivery!"

"Right. It's open." He turns to me. "Sorry."

After he pays for the food, he sets the bags on a tiny table tucked under the metal stairs. He gets a fresh beer for himself and a fresh bottle of water for me. I search through the cupboards for some plates. But he comes up behind me and puts his hands on my hips, murmuring near my ear, "Why don't you have a seat and let me handle the breakables?"

What would have normally been a tiny shiver manifests itself in my current state as a convulsion. My shoulder comes up and bangs against my ear. "Ow!" I hiss, spinning around to face him. I'm trapped between him and the counter, my head against the top cupboards.

After what feels like forever, he backs away and frees me to go to the table. I do and furiously begin to unpack the bags, as if we're in a hurry.

Shaking his head, he joins me with the plates and cutlery. "I really wish you had asked my advice before taking those pills. You're going to regret it."

Irritably, I answer, "Well, I didn't think I needed a second opinion. I needed to stay awake; I took the pills. End of story. They'll wear off; I'll crash. It'll be fine." When he continues to smile and shake his head, I say, "What? Have you taken these before, or something?"

He nods as he distributes the food. "I'm not sure if you took the same kind, but yes. I have. Once. That's all it took. Never again."

Great. I try to pretend I'm not concerned, though, repeating, "It'll be fine."

"In the meantime," he says, "what're you gonna do with all this energy?"

I cut into my fish. "First, I'm going to eat. Then... I dunno." My leg jounces under the table. "We're gonna talk, right?"

"If you insist," he mutters, then looks up at me and smiles, saying more loudly, "Absolutely. But talking's not going to tire you out."

He has no idea what kind of monster conversation awaits him. My nervous giggle is back. To my dismay, I flirt. "What do you suggest, then?"

His fork stops midway to his mouth. He places it on the edge of his plate and sits back. "We could, uh, go for a walk. I don't know... maybe drop into a pub? Maybe alcohol would counteract the effects of the pills."

I wrinkle my nose. "I don't want to start some kind of chemical warfare in my body. One substance is enough, thanks."

He shrugs. "You might change your mind in about twenty-four hours when your eyelids feel like they're glued open and all you want to do is sleep." At my horrified expression, he laughs. "Try not to think about it, though. Let's talk about something else. Such as... Who at work are you going to miss the most?" he asks, a twinkle in his eyes.

Without hesitating, I answer, "Lisa," eliciting a comically indignant response from him.

"Uh!"

I set aside my water. "No offense."

"Some taken, sorry. I can't believe you're going to miss Lisa more than me!"

I don't tell him I hope there'll be no need for me to miss him. Instead, I defend my answer. "She made me laugh. And stood up for me."

He starts ticking things off on his fingers. "Well, *I* bought you sweets and made you laugh and made you... well, I guess we can't count that, because I never did that at work, but still..."

I roll my eyes at him. "Here we go. It always comes back to that, doesn't it?"

"For me, yes. It's important." Clearing his throat and the table, he takes our dirty dishes into the kitchen and places them in the sink. Then he turns around and braces his weight against his hands on the edge of the counter. "So, who are you going to miss the least? I guess I shouldn't assume it's not me."

I'm not ready to utter her name yet. Twirling a piece of my hair to the point of pain, I say coyly, "It's not you."

"Marvin?" he guesses. When I shake my head and look down at the table, he tries again. "Gary? No? Ah, Leslie!"

My head snaps up, giving me away. He laughs. "Ah, yes. Lezzzzzlie. You and she were a bit like oil and water, weren't you?"

"She's a horrible person, Jude," I insist, adding, "Really!" when he waves dismissively at me and chuckles.

"She's harmless. Just an insecure little girl with daddy issues," he claims.

This is it! Say it! I scream at myself. Get it over with, so you can relax... or relax as much as it's physically and mentally possible to do on these stupid pills. But I can't. I can't bring myself to tell him that the past six months have been a waste. That our break-up wouldn't have stuck if I hadn't been so gullible.

So, I chicken out. I let him keep talking.

"Plus, the only reason she was like that to you was because she was jealous. You're lovely. Inside and out."

It's such a simple statement, but it almost brings me to tears. I think it's the nicest thing anyone's ever said to me. "That's the nicest thing anyone's ever said to me," I let slip as soon as I think it.

He shrugs and smiles shyly. "It's true. It's a shame no one's ever told you that." The next minute would be filled with awkward silence if not for the sound of my foot tapping against the table leg.

Then we both speak at the same time:

"Would you a fancy a walk?"

"I still love you."

My declaration definitely takes precedence over his question.

He blinks at me. Blushing, sweating, shaking me. When he doesn't respond right away, I say, "I mean, it's probably obvious, so I thought I'd toss it out there. Just, uh, for your information. But, yeah. A walk sounds fine. If it's not raining. Is it always this rainy here?"

I stand up, wiping my sweaty palms on my jeans, straightening my tunic top, and trying to wet my lips with my dry tongue. I grab my bottle of water and take a long drink, closing my eyes and wishing I could magically transport myself and Sandberg back to the hotel, back in time, to before I took those stupid pills. I picture myself picking up the phone and calling Jude, telling him I'm too tired to do anything tonight. Then falling into the itchy bed and sleeping for a day or two.

There's a tugging on the bottle in my hand. I open my eyes to see Jude pulling gently on it. I let go of it with both my mouth and my hand. As soon as he sets it on the table next to us, he takes my face in his hands and kisses me. I can feel the condensation from the bottle on his fingers, leaving tiny drops on my cheek as he moves his hands into the back of my hair.

My heart feels like it's literally about to explode. It can't handle all this stimulation.

"Oh!" I breathe into his mouth, doing something resembling the pee-pee dance.

He pulls away to avoid injury as our faces bump against each other. "What?" he asks, looking concerned.

"I can't stand still!" I whine. "It's like someone's sending tiny electric shocks to my muscles."

He sighs. "Come on. I think I have something upstairs that can help." He leads me by the hand up the metal staircase. As long as I stay in motion, I don't feel like I'm going to fly apart.

In the loft, he goes into the bathroom. I hear water running, and when he comes out, he offers me the glass. "Drink this," he orders. I do. "And you need to drink another one in thirty minutes." Taking the glass from me, he sets it on the bedside table. "Until then..." He takes one step and pulls me against him, kissing me so deeply and firmly, I have to hold onto him to keep from falling backwards.

But he keeps pushing, until I realize that's his intent: to make me fall backwards, onto the bed. Okay.

"Nice bed," I approve. "Is it new?"

Breathlessly, he replies, "Yes. It's a virgin bed." Then he kisses my neck and yanks on my shirt.

Soon, we're naked on top of the snow white duvet. And

now my emotions are running away from me. "I'm so sorry!" I whisper forcefully, choking back tears.

"Shhh." He pulls back and brushes my hair away from my face. "No worries. Just... this." He enters me slowly, keeping his eyes on mine. "I love you."

"Okay," I reply dumbly, still trying not to bawl. The incessant, involuntary blinking is actually helping in that department.

"And I've missed you. So much."

I wrap my legs around his waist. "Me too. You, I mean. I've missed you."

He smiles and presses his lips against mine as he moves above me. "Is this active enough for you?"

Honestly, I answer, "I'd rather be on top right now. I'm feeling a little claustrophobic."

"Oh-ho! Be my guest."

We quickly re-arrange ourselves, and after we're together again, it hits me: I'm making love to Jude in England. On a white bed. In a maisonette. Surrounded by books. Listening to Snow Patrol. It's so identical to one of my fantasies that it makes me dizzy. "God!" I moan, grabbing fistfuls of his hair.

"Aggghhh!" he utters below me. I take it as encouragement and move faster. But as soon as I've climaxed, he sits up halfway, propping himself on his elbows, and says, "Ah, Libby? I'm rather... uncomfortable. Could you? That is, maybe you can... let go of my head?"

"Oh!" I dismount and collapse onto my back. "Sorry. I, uh... wow."

He rubs his head. "No worries. It'll grow back, perhaps."

We laugh at my crazed behavior. Then he goes back to kissing me, placing one every inch or so on my body. "Saucy minx," he mutters against my breast.

We're back!

❧ 33 ❧

GOOD NEWS: I'M NO LONGER MANIC. BAD NEWS: I'M STILL awake. Worse news: I still haven't told Jude what brought me back to him. Or what started the whole nightmare.

But he's sleeping so peacefully. I don't want to wake him up only to have such a horrible discussion. I can see, however, how this could become just like telling him about my parents and the accident. I can put it off and put it off and put it off until it becomes a huge problem in our relationship. And I'm not willing to do that. My deadline for telling all is before I sleep again. Which could be a while, granted, but hopefully it will happen before the weekend is over.

I'm sitting up in bed, taking stock of my body. My eyesight has returned to normal—no more jittering eyeballs; my heart has stopped racing—at least it only races when I'm doing something to warrant it; I can keep my limbs still for relatively long periods of time, which I'm sure is a big relief to Jude who's been trying to sleep next to a spaz (of course, I offered to go away, but he wouldn't hear it); and I'm no longer swinging between euphoria and despair, giggles and sobs.

Good thing, too. I need to be in total control of myself when I tell him what I need to tell him. And I need to be prepared for it to go badly.

He stirs behind me, but he's only been asleep a few hours, so I'm not expecting it when he sits up and presses his chest against my back, kissing my shoulder. "How're you feeling? When was the last time you drank some water?"

I glance over my shoulder at him. He's tousled and scruffy and warm. *No sex for you, Elizabeth Lynn Foster, until you tell him,* I order myself firmly.

"I'm fine," I say in response to his query. "I think the worst is over."

"Do you have the headache yet?" he asks.

I wince. "No. Is that yet to come?"

"Maybe you won't get it," he says unconvincingly.

That settles it. The conversation has to happen before the dreaded headache hits. I can't handle both at once.

Turning, I sit cross-legged and face him. "I have to tell you something," I say solemnly, fashioning the sheet into a strapless toga.

"Blimey. That sounds scary," he says half-kiddingly. "But this time I'll let you finish before jumping to any conclusions that could get me into trouble."

I smile weakly at his attempt at levity. Taking a deep breath, I say, "For five of the past six months, I've believed something really terrible about you." When he simply tilts his head and wrinkles his brow, I continue, but I have to look away from him. I focus my attention on the bedspread. "But before I tell you, please try to understand where I was coming from. We'd had that horrible fight about... well, you know. And you wouldn't tell me what the big secret at work was, so I was pretty tender when it came to trust issues and you."

I glance up to see his reaction to this. He merely nods, as if encouraging me to go on. I can't tell at all what he's thinking. Typical.

I sigh. "So... when Leslie told me that you and she had been intimate..." He flinches, and his mouth drops open, but he doesn't say anything, so I go on. "And she had details that only someone who had seen you naked or had had sex with you would know, I believed her."

"Leslie?" he cries. "Me and Leslie?"

"Yeah."

"She told you that I slept with her? When?"

"The day of the announcement."

"No, I mean, when did she say this happened? Did she say I'd cheated on you?" He looks as sick as I feel.

"Oh." I blink. "No. She said it was when you first came to town. Before we started dating."

"And you said she told you things... That is, however would *Leslie* know what I look like naked?"

Quickly, hardly breathing, I tell him about the "proof" she gave me and how I eventually found out she got the details from our emails. Closing my eyes again, I say, "I know. It's so stupid and improbable now that I know it's a lie, but at the time... She couldn't have timed her little joke any better—or worse, depending on how you look at it."

"This is no joke!" he comes close to shouting, startling my eyes open. "This is... is... something that could have had dire consequences. *Did* have dire consequences. For months!"

"I know, but look: we're together again. I found out the truth—"

"And how is that? By coming to me straight away and asking me if it was true? No. You chose to believe I would..." he shivers rather than says it. "With Leslie?" He scoots and rests his back against the headboard. "I wouldn't touch her with a bargepole!"

He pulls the sheet higher up his body and crosses his arms over his chest. Sullenly, he says, "I can't believe you chose to believe her rather than say, 'Jude, did you ever get a leg over on that walking STD Leslie?' I mean, I think I deserved at least that much from you, a chance to defend myself!"

While I'm trying to think of a good reason why I didn't just ask him, he's still thinking out loud about the timeline of events. "And when I tried to convince you to take me back, before I left to come here, you wouldn't, because of her lies?"

"Yes." It's barely a whisper.

"What a fucking waste," he mutters, staring into space.

"But," I point out, remembering why I didn't ask him about it, "if I had asked you, and you had denied it, it would have just confirmed my suspicions that you were a bastard. Her proof was so overwhelming and incontrovertible that I would only have been asking you in order to hear a confession. And when you denied it—as you rightly would have—I would have written you off as a lying man-whore! Her plan was simple but genius."

"You would have taken her word over mine?"

"It wasn't just her word, Jude. It was details. A *lot* of details. Your rugby scar, your favorite positions, your ticklish feet… Again, I'm so sorry! But, honestly, I don't know how I would have done anything differently. You and I were broken up. I didn't feel comfortable asking you about something that supposedly happened before we ever got together."

His response is to put his hands over his eyes and say in a voice so cold it gives me goosebumps, "That fucking bitch. You have no idea the *misery* I've endured every. Fucking. Day. There hasn't been a single day that I didn't think I couldn't get out of bed. Because I thought I had lost you, and I couldn't figure out why. I just knew it was probably permanent. And now I find it wasn't my fault at all. Not a bit of it."

He removes his hands, revealing red eyes.

"I should have told you sooner," I suddenly realize. "I've been sitting on this information for a month, dreading how angry you'd be at me, trying to come up with the perfect way to break it to you, making all these extravagant plans. It was selfish. I should have just told you!"

"Yeah," he says huskily, blinking at me. "Maybe. Although…" He brushes his foot against my leg under the covers. "I could tell recently that something had changed. I almost had… hope. I suppose I didn't really need to know why you seemed to care again, since I never knew why you stopped."

Now I join him at the head of the bed. He puts his arm around me as I burrow next to him. "I never stopped caring. Never. But I thought I knew the truth. And it was devastating."

"I have every right to be furious with you," he declares bullishly, as if I've been saying otherwise. But he grabs my hand and rubs the back of it with his thumb.

"I agree. I'd be livid, if the roles were switched."

"If you had asked me about Leslie, I would have at least known to confront her about her lies. And make her tell you the truth." He barely skims his fingers against my upper arm.

I shiver. "You're right. That would have saved us both a lot of heartache. I was just too proud to bring it up to you. Please don't be mad at me. For long. I understand if you are right now."

"I'm not angry with you," he replies, seeming surprised by the statement. "But I'd like to hop on a flight and murder Leslie."

"Then you'd go to prison. We can't have that."

"Then you'd better find a way to restrain me here."

"Don't make me pull your hair again."

Laughing, groping, and murmuring, we disappear under the covers.

❧ 34 ❧

Lisa,

I seem to remember promising you an update (it must have been one of my weaker moments). You said it didn't have to be long, so here goes: flight was fine; talk was fine; yes I did. Several times. Tell Zoe I said hi. I'll send you guys some postcards from my travels.

Libby

❈ 35 ❈

SOME STRAY PIECES OF FOIL-WRAPPED HARD CANDIES ELUDE ME under the table in the middle of the conference/break room. Finally, I give up trying to be graceful about it and crawl under there to retrieve them. I guess I could leave all this for Talia to clean up on Monday, her first solo day as the office's admin, but it would seriously piss me off if someone did that to me. Plus, I have nothing better to do while I wait for Jude to finish up his latest phone call with Gary (I swear the man has a crush on my boyfriend). And the candy's under here— along with a few scattered scraps of confetti—because of my going away party, so it's only fair that I clean it up.

"Now that's an enticing sight," Jude says, his voice danger- ously close to my raised rear end.

"Get away!" I screech laughingly after bumping my head and trying to pull my skirt further over my butt.

Instead of honoring my request, he moves in closer, laughing and poking his finger past my hand. "I see London, I see France…"

I kick back with one foot, almost catching him in the face with one of my stilettos.

"Oi! Oi!" he cries, but he crawls out backwards and sits on his heels.

I scramble through to the other side of the table, candy and confetti in hand, and pop to my feet. "You're a pervert," I accuse playfully, pitching one of the candies at his head.

He ducks, and it misses him by a long shot. "And you're abusive! *Elizabeth.*"

"No hanky-panky in the office," I remind him sternly, ignoring his pointed use of my real name, which he's been obsessed with since seeing it on my passport when he finally snuck it out of my purse to get a peek at it. Hearing him call me the name no one has called me since my parents were killed actually bothers me a lot less than I'd thought it would. It almost sounds… right.

"But it's your last day. And everyone else is long gone." He stands and walks around the table, grabbing me around the waist before I can move out of his reach. "What would it hurt? Just a little slap and tickle. So we could say that we did."

As he kisses my neck, I close my eyes, but I say weakly, "No… especially not in here. All it would take is for someone to dial into the videoconference, and it'd be instant porn in the Chicago office." But I don't push him away.

He freezes but keeps his lips pressed against my neck. "Hmm. Right." Loosening his grip, he straightens and pats my butt. "Well, I s'pose I enjoy receiving a paycheck, so that won't do."

"Exactly." I turn to face him, tapping the tip of his nose with my finger. "Thanks for my party. The piñata was a nice touch. Until Marvin crushed it to smithereens."

"Yes, well, we encourage his youthful exuberance. Keeps us all on our toes." Surreptitiously, he glances at the clock on the wall over my shoulder. "Speaking of your last day, I have a leaving present for you."

My heart skips. "Oh? How fun!" I turn to lead the way to his office, where I assume the present is waiting, but he grabs my hand.

"Actually, it's in here." He reaches for and snatches the videoconference remote, punching in the numbers for the system in Chicago.

"Aw!" I groan. "I thought we were done with work!"

Before hitting the green button to connect the call, he raises an eyebrow at me. "You'll like this; trust me." He perches on the edge of the table and presses the button. After a few beeps, the videoconference room in Chicago appears before us, revealing Zoe and Lisa, sitting at the end of the conference table closest to the camera.

Lisa shouts, "Hey! There they are. Finally! We've been waiting for you for ten minutes!"

"Apologies," Jude says, sounding completely unapologetic. "Lost track of time here."

"I'll bet," Lisa replies knowingly. "I wonder what we would have seen or heard if we had called you instead of waiting here patiently."

Zoe waves her hand frantically. "Hi! Happy last day!"

"Hey, guys!" I bounce a little with excitement. "Oh, my gosh! It's so good to see you!"

"I told you," Jude mutters under his breath, then grins at me.

Lisa and I both try to talk at the same time, then stop and simultaneously say, "Oh, go ahead," and laugh.

"This delay is the pits," Lisa gripes. "Anyway, what I was going to say was, we didn't want to miss your real last day. How'd it go? Talia sounds nice so far. But she has a big bra—I mean, big *shoes* to fill."

This is high praise from Lisa, but I try not to get too serious or I know I'll get choked up. "Yeah, yeah. I'm awesome. But she'll do. My last day was a lot of fun. We had a big party."

Zoe pipes up, "When do you start touring the rest of the U.K.?"

"Monday, bright and early." I glance at Jude, who's looking down at his leg, which is swinging casually from his perch on the edge of the table. "But we're not talking about that in front of Jude."

"You'll be fine, you big baby," Lisa cajoles. "Honestly. Men!"

"What about your cat?" Zoe asks, getting back to business. It feels like she has a mental list of questions she needs me to answer. I'm surprised she doesn't have a notebook in front of her.

Amused, I answer, "Sandberg and Jude are going to be swinging bachelors for two weeks while I'm gone."

Lisa gapes at the camera. "You trust him with your beloved cat?"

"Absolutely!"

"I'm more than capable, thank you," he defends himself.

"I think I have to worry more about what Sandberg might do to Jude than the other way around. Lying on his face in the middle of the night, tripping him on the stairs... there are all kinds of ways Sandberg could get his revenge. He's still pouting about his kinked tail, I think."

"Now I'm a bit worried," Jude says.

"You should be," Lisa warns. "Cats are diabolical. So... have you introduced Libby to your parents yet? It'd probably be best if she met them *before* her cat does you in. Less awkward at the funeral."

I rescue him from the hot seat. "We haven't had time yet for that. I'll, uh, meet them when I get back."

The last thing I need is for that topic to be resurrected. I've already told Jude I don't want to spend the two days before I leave in some tense meet-the-parents scene in an unfamiliar house. I want him all to myself before I get on that train Monday morning.

"Anyway, ladies," Jude cuts in, "sorry we have to cut it short, but I actually have some business to attend to with one more person. Favor for Gary, really. You wouldn't mind fetching Leslie, would you?"

The two of them push away from the table. "We'd be glad to, as long as you're firing her," Lisa says ultra-sweetly. To me, she says, "Don't be a stranger, sweetie. Kiss an Irishman for me. And stop by the office next time you're in town. There or here. We wanna see proof that you're happy and healthy."

"Yes, Mom," I tease.

Zoe blows me a kiss. "Send me some postcards so I can hang them in my cubicle and pretend I'm there with you."

"You got it. See you guys."

After they leave, I walk to one of the windows, where I look down the two stories to the busy street below. It's a typical Friday night, groups of friends in their "going out" clothes, walking in clusters down the sidewalk, laughing at each other, sharing cigarettes; couples walking hand-in-hand or arm-in-arm on their way to dinner or to the nearest pub; and everyone generally enjoying the fact that they're free to do whatever they want until Monday morning.

And while I'm watching them and already missing Lisa and Zoe, it hits me that I can do whatever I want until... *whenever*. I'm free. No responsibilities, no obligations (unless you count Sandberg, which *he* doesn't, so I don't), no constraints. I suddenly remember how it felt to wake up on the first day of summer vacation. My belly jumps thrillingly.

Jude interrupts my reverie with a subtle clearing of his throat and, "I need to talk to Leslie about something for Gary."

"Oh!" I shake my head to clear it. "Sorry. I'll wait for you in your office."

As I move toward the door, he stops me. "No. I want you to stay."

I cock my head doubtfully. "I don't know. I feel weird. I really don't want to see her."

"This is part of your leaving present," he insists. "But you need to sit over there"—he points to a chair in the corner —"where you're not on screen. I could get in a fair bit of trouble if anyone finds out you were here during this."

Intrigued, I do as he says, and he zooms the camera further in on himself to make sure there's no chance of my being seen by anyone on the other end. "Here she comes," he whispers. He nervously flaps the end of his tie and turns his body further away from me so I'm not in his line of sight.

"Jude," I hear her say tepidly, uncertainty making her voice wobble a little.

"Lezlie," he returns even more coldly.

Suddenly, I don't feel very good. I mean, he looks terrifying and intimidating right now. I have no idea what he's going to say to her, but it doesn't look like it's going to be anything good. Is he going to confront her about the emails? My mind is racing, mostly screaming at me to get out of the room. I don't know if I want to watch this. But it's too late. There's no way for me to exit the room without walking in front of the camera.

"You wanted to see me?" she prods.

He stares her down, making her squirm. Finally, he says, "Yes. Right. Gary wanted to be the one to tell you this, but he was unavoidably detained in client meetings this afternoon, so I told him I'd—what do you call it?—'pinch hit' for him."

"Nothing bad, I hope?" She gives him one of her flirty girl

giggles, and I change my mind, hoping this *is* what I think it is. Or even worse.

Fire her, I silently urge him.

"No, no. On the contrary, actually," he surprises me by saying. His voice remains devoid of any warmth, though. He pulls a piece of paper from the inside pocket of his suit jacket, unfolds it, and glances at what's written on it. "The company has acquired a small firm in Bismarck, North Dakota." My eyes widen at this news, but I remain focused on what Jude's saying. "Jake will be transferring there temporarily to help the staff transition into our corporate culture. And Gary's chosen you to take the only administrative assistant position at that location."

"Temporarily, right?" she says after a slight hesitation.

"No, permanently, as it were," he says cheerfully, as if this is the greatest news he could be giving her. "Jake will be instrumental in helping everyone there get used to our ways of doing things, but everyone knows the secretaries are the ones who really know what's what."

I snicker behind my hand.

She laughs. "Well, this is flattering. Really. But, Jude," she says a little too familiarly for my taste, "come on. Bismarck? I mean, what the hell's in Bismarck?"

"Our new branch," he says seriously. "Of which you'd be a vital member."

"Hmm." Smirking, she says, "Well, as tempting an offer as this is, I'm going to have to turn it down."

Jude shakes his head and winces. "Yeah, I don't think that'd be wise."

She taps her acrylic nails on the polished conference table. "Thanks for the career advice, but I'll take my chances for advancement here in Chicago." Standing, she pushes her chair under the table.

"There are no chances left for you in Chicago, Lezlie," he says firmly but quietly. She becomes so still, it looks as if the picture has frozen. "I'm sorry if I wasn't quite clear. This isn't really a request; this is an assignment."

Her mouth drops open, and her gum almost falls out. I'm so close to laughing that I have to press both hands over my mouth and bite on the fleshy part of the inside of my middle finger.

"Uh… wait. What? I mean, what are you talking about?" she sputters. "Th… this isn't the military. It's a privately owned company. I mean… I d…don't understand."

Suddenly, Jude pours on the charm. "Now, Lezlie. You're a clever girl. Surely, you understand what's happening here."

She narrows her eyes and sniffs, crossing her arms over her chest. "Maybe you should help me understand a little better, Jude."

He shrugs, tossing the paper he's holding onto the table in front of him. "Well, obviously we could hire someone local there to do the administrative work, but your transfer would solve two problems at once: your sagging workload in Chicago and our need for an administrative assistant at the new branch, where your workload would increase threefold. Either way, your job in Chicago is about to become—how shall I say this?—redundant. We thought you'd be glad to have a soft place to land."

"In *Bismarck?*"

"It's better than no job at all, wouldn't you say?"

"No! I wouldn't!"

Jude frowns and rubs his eyebrow. "Right." He stands, placing his hands in his pockets. "Very well. I'll, uh, let Gary know your decision. Wanda'll have some leaving paperwork for you to sign—"

"How soon are we talking about here?"

"Pardon? Oh, immediately, I'm afraid. But no worries. You'll qualify for unemployment benefits, I'm sure." He leans forward and smiles encouragingly, but I can see there's no smile in his eyes. He looks absolutely ruthless.

"You're an idiot if you think I don't know what's going on," she spits.

His smile fades, his eyes widening innocently. "I'm certain I have no idea."

"I'm certain you do," she says, mocking his accent.

"Reorganization is sometimes not very pretty," he continues benignly. "We were trying to make it as painless as possible, but you're right; we can't force you to stay with the company."

Ignoring him, she persists, "I know this is about you and your crazy little girlfriend. This is your way of getting back at me for reading those stupid emails."

I stiffen at the word "crazy," but I resist the urge to defend myself.

Jude's face hardens. "You really shouldn't talk about that, Lezlie. Someone—like Gary or Wanda—could hear you. Then you'd be looking for a new job with a black mark on your CV. Let's try to remain professional, shall we?"

"Professional, my ass. This is all your plan to get rid of me. I'm sure you jumped at the chance, knowing that Gary would go along with anything you said, because he's pathetic and has some kind of man-crush on you. It's disgusting."

"Leslie?"

All three of us flinch at the sound of Gary's voice. Irrationally, I pull my knees up and rest my forehead against them, closing my eyes.

Nobody says anything for what seems like forever, then Gary asks, "Jude, mind catching me up on what's going on?"

Jude clears his throat. "Ah. Yes. Right. Well, I've, uh,

explained the, er, situation regarding the acquisition in Bismarck, and Lezlie there has turned down our transfer offer."

"I see."

I chance a peek in time to see Gary move closer to Leslie and mirror her crossed-arm pose. "I'm sorry to hear that, Leslie," he says sincerely. "I hope there are no hard feelings. When I walked in, it sounded like maybe there were?"

Her bright red lips slice through the air in the middle of her pale face as she shakes her head. Her voice falters when she tries to talk, but she clears her throat and says, "N-not at all. I was just telling Jude that Bismarck's not really my kind of town. Plus I have family here, and I'd hate to move so far away."

Gary nods. "Understandable. Yes. Well, we wanted to try to be fair and give you the first swing at the job there. I trust that Jude's explained to you that we'll be eliminating your position here as part of the reorganization?"

A pleading note enters her voice. "But Gary, what about Libby's position? It's open now, right? Why can't I just slide into that?"

Gary scratches his head. "Oh. That. Well, we're not replacing Libby. Her resignation came at a pretty fortuitous time and saved us some tough decisions. We're only keeping two admins in the Commercial Division. And we went strictly by productivity numbers to come to our decision about who to keep here and who to send to Bismarck. But if you don't want the position, I'll let HR know to advertise locally for someone. It's not ideal, but what can we do?"

The resolution on the picture makes it difficult to read exact expressions, but I can see in her face that she's about to reverse her decision. She bites her lower lip and glances from Jude to Gary. But then the opportunity passes when Jude says hurriedly, "Right, then. Well. It's getting rather late here, so if we're finished…"

Gary turns completely away from Leslie. "Oh, yeah. Sorry about that, Jude. Thanks for staying late on a Friday to help me out with this."

"Not at all," Jude replies graciously. "Have a good week-end." He reaches for the remote.

"Got any big plans this weekend?" Gary asks genially. He never was one for taking a hint.

Jude sighs and smiles. "Nah. Pipe and slippers, I suppose. You?"

Leslie stalks out of the conference room. Gary glances over his shoulder at her retreating form, then returns his attention to Jude. "God, I thought she'd never leave," he mutters. "Coupla buddies and me, we're going to hit the links tomorrow. But we'll probably spend more time at the nine-teenth hole, if you get my drift."

Jude grins. "Absolutely. Well, have fun. I have a patient girlfriend waiting for me, so…"

"Oh!" Gary startles, making me fear for a second that he can see me. "I'm sorry! Geez, Jude, you shoulda said some-thing. Here I am, just talking your ear off, like an idiotic old coot. I'll talk to you Monday."

They finally disconnect, and I almost sag off the chair and onto the floor when I'm finally able to relax my muscles. "Holy shit," I breathe.

Jude turns around. "Sorry. I couldn't get rid of the bloke."

"No, not that!" I put my hand up against the side of my face. "Leslie! And you…You were a bad ass!"

He chuckles self-consciously and looks down at his feet. "Right. Well, uh, that. She never should have fucked with me. Maybe."

I walk over to him and grab his arm. "Important lesson

learned. Wow. You were, like, 'This isn't a request, Lezzlie,' and she was like, 'Huh? What?' and then when she accused you of getting rid of her, you were so calm!"

Shyly looking at me through his lashes, he admits, "I was bricking myself on the inside."

"Well, you looked cool as a cucumber. It was a total turn-on!"

"Really?"

"Yeah! But can we leave now?" I tug on his hand, pulling him toward the door. "I really wasn't expecting my last day to be nearly thirteen hours long."

Again he apologizes, but I put a finger to his lips as he hands me my jacket and purse. "Save it. The last thirty minutes made the other twelve and a half hours well worth it."

He snickers. "I thought you'd like that."

As he locks the office door, I whisper next to his ear, "You were right. Know what else I'd like?" He raises an eyebrow at me and turns his head to kiss me, but before our lips meet, I say, "How about showing the new girl in town the best place to get something to eat?"

The look he shoots me is priceless. But he laughs with me as we step onto the sidewalk, joining the throng of other people just like us.

THE END